back to life

Rachel Riley (sort of) seizes the day

D1439972

21/2/24

WITHDRAWN

Other books by Joanna Nadin

My So-Called Life
The Life of Riley
The Meaning of Life
My (Not So) Simple Life

WITHDRAWN

back to life

Rachel Riley (sort of) seizes the day

Joanna Nadin

OXFORD
UNIVERSITY PRESS

OXFORD

UNIVERSITY PRESS

Great Clarendon Street, Oxford OX2 6DP

Oxford University Press is a department of the University of Oxford.
It furthers the University's objective of excellence in research, scholarship,
and education by publishing worldwide in

Oxford   New York

Auckland   Cape Town   Dar es Salaam   Hong Kong   Karachi
Kuala Lumpur   Madrid   Melbourne   Mexico City   Nairobi
New Delhi   Shanghai   Taipei   Toronto

With offices in

Argentina   Austria   Brazil   Chile   Czech Republic   France   Greece
Guatemala   Hungary   Italy   Japan   Poland   Portugal   Singapore
South Korea   Switzerland   Thailand   Turkey   Ukraine   Vietnam

Oxford is a registered trade mark of Oxford University Press
in the UK and in certain other countries

© Joanna Nadin 2009

The moral rights of the author have been asserted

Database right Oxford University Press (maker)

First published 2009

All rights reserved. No part of this publication may be reproduced,
stored in a retrieval system, or transmitted, in any form or by any means,
without the prior permission in writing of Oxford University Press,
or as expressly permitted by law, or under terms agreed with the appropriate
reprographics rights organization. Enquiries concerning reproduction
outside the scope of the above should be sent to the Rights Department,
Oxford University Press, at the address above

You must not circulate this book in any other binding or cover
and you must impose this same condition on any acquirer

British Library Cataloguing in Publication Data

Data available

ISBN: 978-0-19-272922-4

1 3 5 7 9 10 8 6 4 2

Printed in Great Britain by CPI Cox and Wyman, Reading, Berkshire

Paper used in the production of this book is a natural, recyclable product made
from wood grown in sustainable forests. The manufacturing process conforms
to the environmental regulations of the country of origin

Tuesday 1

New Year's Day

1 p.m.

This is utterly the worst start to a New Year ever.

How things change. This time, last January, I was nestled in warm cocoon of love with Braintree College rock god and potential ONE Justin Statham. Whereas today am alone in non-cocoon-like John-Lewis-decorated bedroom, with borderline hangover. Is not even warm as dog has eaten radiator knob and heating is stuck in off position. It is utter metaphor for life. Am wretched outcast like Joan of Arc. Or Amy Winehouse.

It is all so-called best friend Scarlet's fault. As usual. She has, yet again, snogged the object of my desire. This time it is potential future first-ever black Prime Minister Hilary Nuamah. It is an utter betrayal, not just of me, but of our anti-snogging sisterhood pact of abstinence thing. Which would have said last night only was so in shock immediately downed several glasses of punch. Then, fuelled by experimental vodka and eggnog mix, had brilliant idea of going to Justin's house for midnight kiss. But, when I got to the mock-tudor mansion, I could clearly see him grappling Sophie Microwave Muffins Jacobs against the mock mahogany DVD shelving unit, underneath the mock mistletoe, so had utterly missed boat again. So, drowned sorrow immediately in five Marks & Spencer cherry liqueur chocolates, which had brought along for energy-giving purposes (no Kendal

3

mint cake to be found), then had next brilliant idea to go back to party to snog Jack, Scarlet's brother, who have kissed previously to some effect (admittedly onstage in questionable production of *Bugsy Malone*, and in dare during mind-slippage episode at Glastonbury, but there was definite frisson, and even thought was possibly the ONE for a while). But when I threw arms around him and said, 'You may kiss me now, Jack Stone,' he did not seem too excited at all. In fact, his exact words were, 'You've been at bloody Justin's, haven't you. I am sick to death of being your sloppy seconds, Riley.' Or words to that effect, as memory may be slightly impaired by alcohol intake. Anyway, outcome is same, i.e. the sisterhood, and my love life, are in tatters. Plus had to watch Scarlet entwined with Hilary in the seventies wicker loveswing thing until Sad Ed offered to walk me home out of pity.

On plus side, am not the only one livid about Scarlet and Hilary. Mum is equally incensed. It is not because she favours him as potential lover for me, it is because he was supposed to repatriate her moronic parents to St Slaughter this morning but, as yet, he has failed to reappear from Scarlet's house. She has just been in to demand that *a*) I stop malingering in bed; *b*) I call Scarlet and tell her to send Hilary home as Grandpa Clegg and Dad are locked in a no-win situation over something to do with Andy Murray's hair; and *c*) I take dog for walk as he and Bruce (offspring of dog, now owned by Cleggs) have combined to form one giant

idiotic canine force and are taking it in turns to disgrace themselves on the dining room table. It is official. My life is pants.

2 p.m.
Have called Scarlet to demand *a*) repatriation of Hilary to 24 Summerdale Road, and *b*) to know why she was snogging him last night when she was: *subclause i*) signed up to anti-snogging pact; and *subclause ii*) fully aware that I was, in fact, in love with him.

She said, *a*) no, he is spending the day in bed being nursed by her and Suzy following potential concussion due to the loveswing falling off the ceiling hook; *b*) *i*) whatever, and *ii*) I had told her I was not interested in him one bit so it is my fault for not being honest about my feelings, in fact.

I said, *a*) that will not go down well with Janet Riley i.e. my mum; and *b*) that's such a lie, you boyfriend-stealing, pact-breaking vampire.

So Scarlet said, *a*) tell Janet to take a chill pill; *b*) *i*) check your diary, you moron, and *ii*) I am not a Goth any more, I am semi-emo, how many times?

So hung up as there is no way can tell Mum to take pills of any kind, let alone chill ones (she is still reeling from the day I experimented with calling her 'Janet'). Plus all the subclauses and degrees of emo-ness were getting confusing. But have checked diary and Scarlet is totally right. I did say I was utterly not into him. Which is very annoying as now cannot officially hate her. Even though she is traitor. Am going round Sad Ed's. He will cheer me up. Or will at least be more depressed than me, which is always heartening. Will take dog. Its absence will appease Mum for the non-return of Hilary.

4 p.m.
Am back earlier than intended due to dog not fully appreciating Sad Ed's mum's many and varied Aled Jones icons. It is now being comforted on sofa by James and a box of Elizabeth Shaw mints. Mrs Thomas is on her own sofa being comforted by Mr Thomas and a CD of 'Walking in the Air'.

On plus side, at least I still have Sad Ed for company in my tortured solitude. He had also broken pact and snogged Melody Bean (apprentice witch, owner of tarantula called Arthur, obsessed with Sad Ed) but is now utterly regretting it. Not only will he have annoying Melody stalking him around John Major High for months, but he says his mojo appears to have been lost somewhere between Hallowe'en and Christmas. Apparently the snog failed to cause any trouser-area stirrings.

He is blaming the sisterhood for depleting his masculinity and says we need to burn all Wicca-related paraphernalia in a ritual sacrifice. Have agreed. It is utterly the way forward. Am going to make it one of my New Year resolutions. Along with following progessive, pro-snogging promises:

1. Tell the truth at all times. If had not lied about Hilary it might well be my lips he was glued to now instead of Scarlet's treacherous ones.

2. *Carpe diem*, i.e. seize the day! Which means utter experimenting as far as snogging is concerned. Am never going to find the ONE if just keep having accidental liaisons with Jack or ill-advised flirtations with Justin. The ONE is out there somewhere. Maybe even right under my nose. I just need to be open-minded. And open-armed. And possibly open-mouthed.

3. Find someone to return Sad Ed's mojo to its rightful state. His depression is off the scale when he is not getting some. Plus now he does not even have the option of untimely death, having spectacularly failed to drown himself in the shopping-trolley-clogged 'River' Slade last year.

4. Pass all AS level levels. Especially Philosophy as it is completely the subject of generally day-seizing experimental types. In fact might even have started new philosophical theory without knowing it!

5. Get new diary. Charlie and Lola may be ironic but have had to staple several sheets of A4 paper to page already in order to fit more than three words in the allotted space. Plus it was purchased by Scarlet and is therefore contaminated with betrayal.

Life, as they say, is what you make it. And am definitely,

no doubt about it, going to make mine fabulous. Starting now.

. . . .

Wednesday 2

9 a.m.

Hurrah, it is Day One of my new, forward-thinking, truth-telling, love-embracing life. Will start by being honest with all family members.

9.30 a.m.

Am back in room. And not through choice. It is for telling Grandpa Clegg that he is deluded, prejudiced, and smells of athlete's foot powder. It is good job they are going home today as it is quite hard to be honest with Cleggs without referring to them as smelly, racist, or mad. Also Dad not amused as named and shamed him for bringing Cadbury's Roses into house (substandard chocolates, and not to be purchased under any circumstances) when he had blamed Clive and Marjory. Am now political prisoner, like Nelson Mandela, incarcerated for speaking the truth. Hurrah! Am going to phone Scarlet immediately to highlight my philosophical left-wing credentials. And also invite her to the ritual burning of all sisterhood paraphernalia tomorrow.

10 a.m.

Scarlet says I am not like Nelson Mandela and there is

8

nothing philosophical or edgy about telling Mum that Dad prefers Praline Moments to Quality Street Green Triangles (superior in every way, for reasons known only to Mum). Nor have I started a new philosophy by seizing the day or experimenting snog-wise etc. Apparently liberals are always doing that. Plus she has declined the invitation to the ritual burning of Wicca/sisterhood paraphernalia. She says Suzy is using the cauldron (i.e. the Nigella soup pot) to make parsnip soup, plus burning is environmentally unfriendly and the excess CO_2 could melt too much polar ice cap and drown half of Alaska. This is a lie. It is nothing to do with meltwater, it is because she is ashamed of being the one who ended the dream. That is why she is not coming to wave the Cleggs off on their return to St Slaughter in the environmentally friendly Nissan Micra either. I said she had no need to be embarrassed about her relationship with Hilary, even if it is based on lies and deceit. She said *au contraire*, she is proud of her relationship, but does not want Granny Clegg attacking her with her loaded Spar bags. She has a point.

11 a.m.
The Cleggs have finally left the environs of Saffron Walden taking Hilary and the perpetual smell of Fray Bentos with them. Mum has opened all windows and turned the Glade plug-ins on to full. Even the dog is relieved. It was being upstaged by Bruce in the hairy,

moronic stakes and has now been restored to its rightful position. It is currently licking the carpet in celebration.

The departure did not go completely smoothly though. Scarlet was right about the Spar bags because, when Hilary finally arrived, unshaven and with telltale scratch marks on upper chest, Granny Clegg smacked him round the leg with a particularly heavy one. I pointed out that it was potential racial harassment and/or employee abuse but she says it is not that he is black, it is that he has betrayed me, and her, for a commie. (She means Scarlet, who is not a commie. She is a social Marxist. Apparently they are entirely different.) I was worried she might decide to sack Hilary but she says she is going to keep him on so she can wheedle sordid details out of him and pass them on to me. I said if I wanted sordid details, which I do not, I could just ask Scarlet, but Granny Clegg says she cannot be trusted not to put a New Labour spin on everything. This is true. She has learned from the best, i.e. Suzy, who worships at the altar of Alastair Campbell. Anyway Granny Clegg cannot afford to sack him, as her new non-fortune-telling hip is still settling in and Grandpa Clegg is still weakened from his appendix operation and cannot bend down to restock the freezer with Viennetta on his own.

Before he went, Hilary asked if he could speak to me in private (i.e. the garage, the only room not infested by Cleggs or Mum and her all-seeing eye (aka James)) to say he was sorry if there was any misunderstanding about his intentions, which were entirely honourable, that I was in no way a lesser person than Scarlet, just that their hearts both beat to the same tune (i.e. the 'Red Flag' and/or 'A New England') and that, if it was any consolation, he would always think of me as a sister. Annoyingly was duty-bound (or resolution-bound) to tell truth so said his Facebook poking was entirely misleading, that I knew as many Billy Bragg songs as Scarlet, and that no, it was no consolation at all, as it was bad enough being a sister to James, who makes the mathletes look edgy. Luckily at that point Dad came in to find Bruce (consuming bottle of ant powder) and Hilary escaped before I could maim him with a Swingball racket. I pity him now though. He has seven hours confined in a small space with the Cleggs who will witter non-stop on their preferred topics—is Stonehenge 'real' (no idea); is Bruce better than the dog (no, equally mental); and aren't the Exeter services amazing (no, unless you come from Cornwall). Whereas I am in 24 Summerdale Road, which is Clegg-free and peaceful at last. Just the 'click click' of James Googling frenetically, the 'psshhht' of Mum Cillit Banging the suspicious ring off the bath, and the 'tap, clonk, "bugger"' of Dad trying to putt practice balls into an Ovaltine jar and hitting the DVD player instead. The sweet sound of normality.

Also have new diary. James agreed to swap as he got three: This Day in History, Cats and Kittens, and bog standard WHSmith desk. I went for the WHSmith one as do not like whimsical kittens (have inherited fear of

11

them from Mum) nor do I want such gems as *Today in 1872 Brigham Young was arrested for having 25 wives* clogging up my philosophical thoughts. James is pleased with the transaction as says he can sell the Charlie and Lola one to an impressionable Year 2 for £3 or a term's supply of first break biscuits. (He is becoming well-versed in the ways of a playground gangster. Mum is right, the sooner he is away from St Regina's menace Keanu O'Grady and lackadaisical headteacher 'Nige' the better. She is counting down the days until his secondary place offer comes through and she can purchase his St Gregory's Girls uniform.) Anyway, point is, am only two days into the New Year and it is one resolution down already. Maybe will find love of life tomorrow and will seize day and embrace him with immediate snog. Hurrah!

. . . .

Thursday 3

Did not find love of life. In fact only saw two men who are not related to me. Sad Ed for ritual sisterhood burning, and former Criminal and Retard Mark Lambert (now of BTEC bricklaying fame) going in to Thin Kylie's house for a booty call, and there is no way he is my ONE. He has a Nike tick shaved into his head.

Sad Ed says I need to be patient and that love will manifest itself when I am ready. I said I am ready and, if waiting patiently was the answer, why was he so desperate to find his missing mojo that he would resort to

asking to borrow James's talking Nicola doll (fortunately deceased following extended stay in dog's intestines)? He said he did not want it for pornographic purposes, he wanted to burn it as part of the ritual as she symbolizes all that is wrong with sisterhoods (synchronized outfits, questionable hairdos, backstabbing friends). This is a lie. I clicked his internet history and he has been on the official Girls Aloud website seven times today trying to arouse himself. Obviously to no avail as he is still utterly miserable. He says he will not find inner peace until he can 'stand to attention'.

5 p.m.
Oh God. Have just had thought. What if Sad Ed is ONE after all? Should I have embraced him over the dying embers of our melted Wicca wands (broken light sabre and electric fly swat)? Maybe it is not plastic Nicola he needs. Maybe I am the one to stir his mojo. We have snogged before, after all. And even though earth did definitely not move, did not vomit either. Plus would kill two resolutions with one stone. Ooh, maybe will try it tomorrow. Yes. Will seize day and experiment with Sad Ed. Hurrah!

. . . .

Friday 4
9 a.m.
Today is crucial day as may well discover I have been

living several doors away from potential ONE all along, and also that I am the answer to Sad Ed's missing mojo. Am wearing carefully calculated Sad Ed arousal outfit. It is combination of Tuesday's psycho/emo look and border-line homoerotica, i.e. excess lipstick, fishnet tights, and a Morrissey T-shirt that he left behind at Scarlet's once. One of them is bound to turn him on.

9.30 a.m.
Mum has sent me back upstairs to change. She says there is no way any daughter of hers is going out dressed like Scarlet. It is not the lipstick. It is the Morrissey T-shirt. Which says 'Meat is Murder'. She does not want Marjory next door thinking she condones militant vegetarianism in any way. On plus side have already done another res-olution, i.e. was totally honest, i.e. when she said 'Where do you think you are going looking like that?' I said, 'To seduce Sad Ed.' Clearly she thinks this is either sarcasm or an impossibility as she has not batted an eyelid at my Mickey Mouse T-shirt which is age eight so very tight and bust-revealing. Anyway, have Morrissey T-shirt in bag to put on when am out of her jurisdiction and am off to seize day and fulfil several of my resolutions and Sad Ed's desires!

1 p.m.
Or not. Apparently I am in no way the answer to Sad Ed's mojo issues. Sight of Morrissey T-shirt just made

him all wistful about Tuesday because apparently she wore it the first time they did 'It'. I offered to talk in American accent and show him my bra (now 34B, official measurement) but he said he was dead, heart-wise and penis-wise, and nothing would revive him. He says he is thinking about becoming a famous celibate instead like the Pope or Stephen Fry and channel his energies into his artistic leanings instead. I said that was an excellent idea, even though he has no discernable creative talent unless you count being able to draw the Powerpuff Girls.

Anyway, left him to it and am back home, having fulfilled no resolutions or desires whatsoever. Am somewhat relieved though as finding out Sad Ed is your ONE is total double-edged sword, i.e. like discovering you are related to someone famous and it turns out to be Anthea Turner. Maybe will focus on Resolution Number 4 and read some Nietzsche instead. He is totally pro-tragedy and will no doubt find inspiration in his wise thoughts.

4 p.m.
Cannot understand a word of it. Am going to watch *Mary Poppins* with dog instead. It is strangely fond of Dick Van Dyke and licks telly whenever he comes onscreen and does unfathomable accent (Dick Van Dyke, not dog. Dog cannot speak. Obviously).

15

Saturday 5

8 a.m.

Was looking forward to day of forward thinking but sadly the coalface (or tofu-face, i.e. Nuts In May healthfood outlet i.e. my Saturday job) beckons. It is a shame did not make resolution to give up work but sadly still have shackles of third-world-scale debt around legs, i.e. owe Mum £78. Am going to make New Year resolutions amendment i.e.:

6. Do not fritter away money I do not have by breaking fake babies, using Dad's mobile to phone two-timing rock gods from overseas, or going to waterlogged music festivals where end up snogging best friend's brother and weeing in a Pringles tube.

6 p.m.

Work was as awful as anticipated. Not only has Mr Goldstein (proprietor of Nuts In May, beard, hunchback) made a resolution to change in-store music from CDs of our choice (eclectic mixes of ambient sound, as created by Sad Ed) to CDs of his choice (not-at-all ambient Beverley Sisters), but ailment-ridden Rosamund has made resolution to visit her equally ailment-riddled parents in Wales more often, which meant that Jack was in today. Normally this would be a positive thing, because Jack does not flinch from the till of death, plus he is much better at playing Who'd You Rather? than Rosamund (who has no TV and does not read magazines so is limited to 'celebrities' like Hugo Thorndyke MP (Con) or Prince Charles). But today he was clearly still sulking at being last in line in my ill-thought-out New Year's Eve snog list. I said I had turned over a new leaf and this year I am being honest with myself and others and am not going to not snog someone if I feel like it (I think that is right). But he said I would not know the truth if it smacked me in the face with a wet kipper and that I am emotionally illiterate. I said that was ridiculous as I got nine GCSEs and am well-known for my literacy skills (enforced by Mum). He said case proven and went off to unbox the ayurvedic toothpaste. Am more determined than ever to snog random people now. And as soon as one of them stirs my mojo, I will tell them immediately. I will hide from true love no longer. That will show him how emotionally literate I am.

. . . .

Sunday 6

Hurrah, have been dealt a last minute reprieve from Mum's Sunday-morning conversational French lessons (imposed following my illicit switching from French (real subject) to Politics (made-up subject) A level). It is all thanks to the *Sunday Times* pasting news of the Norovirus vomiting bug stalking hospital wards and classrooms on today's front cover. It has sent Mum into a frenzy of anti-bug precautions in the run up to school tomorrow. She is at Waitrose with James bulk purchasing anti-bacterial wipes and probiotic yoghurt drinks—hygiene takes precedence over a rounded language education any day.

Am quite looking forward to school, vomit-strewn corridors or not. At least it will be replete with people to potentially seize day with. Am running short on options in environs of Summerdale Road. The only passing males are Clive, Thin Kylie's stepdad Terry, and Rory De'Ath (aka 'the grim reaper') at Number 12, who is in Year Eight and called Rory, both of which are grounds for avoidance.

. . . .

Monday 7
Back to school.

This is typical. I finally get to be in Sixth Form, i.e. with all its accompanying kudos of ditching regulation kilt and blazer in favour of own wardrobe of utterly vintage outfits, when school is overtaken with *St Trinian's* madness, and uniform, albeit a slutty, miniature version, is suddenly de rigueur. Even the goths are hitching up their voluminous black skirts and revealing pasty legs and suspenders. As is Scarlet. I said was outraged as *a*) I did not know she had kept her kilt, and *b*) this kind of fashion-following would never have happened in the days of Trevor and if she is trying to please Hilary she is mistaken as he is not interested in *Grazia*, he is more of an *Economist* man. She said, *a*) Suzy kept it in case she ever has another baby (she is getting broody—it is the threat of

Jack leaving home); *b*) it is not fashion following, it is fashion-forward, do I not watch Gok? And *c*) *au contraire*, *Grazia* is compulsory Labour Party reading to know what the masses are thinking and she is just trying to connect with the potential electorate at an early age so she cannot be accused of bandwagon jumping later in life when she is Education Secretary. She is mental. Hilary is obviously brainwashing her. Or she is blinded by love. I don't know which is worse. Anyway, told her about my truth-telling, day-seizing, love-embracing new lifestyle. She said, 'It will end in tears. And Levonelle.' Which thought sounded nice until got James to Google it and it turns out it is the morning after pill. Anyway, she is wrong, being experimental does not mean doing 'It' with everyone. That is province of Fat Kylie and she is far from philosophical. In contrast, will just do kissing and possibly read poetry to each other. It is utterly French.

Asked Mum if she had kept my kilt when I got home. She said James had borrowed it. Asked James why he had borrowed it and where it was now. He said he had worn it during Ghost Hustlers' hunt for the Hounds of Hell down Battleditch Lane and it is in a recycling plant somewhere as it got soiled when a hound (Fat Kylie's poodle Tupac, so quite hellish) jumped on him and knocked him into a pile of poo. Will just have to improvise. There is bound to be enough uniform in the house. Mum thinks it is the answer to all of society's ills and would be happy if everyone had to wear it throughout life. She would do well as headmistress. Or prison guard. Or fascist dictator.

. . . .

Tuesday 8

8.30 a.m.

Am totally *St Trinian's*-ed up. Am wearing very short skirt (aka Thin Kylie's old boob tube), one of James's school shirts (i.e. too small so buttons cannot feasibly be done up at all), Dad's knee-length fishing socks and golf club tie. Look definitely borderline slutty, though possibly with a hint of insane bag lady. Outfit did not go down too well at Shreddies table, i.e. James said, 'Good God, is that what teenagers are wearing these days?' And Dad said, 'Don't get anything sticky on that tie, I've got a crunch four-ball with Wainwright coming up.' But luckily the gatekeeper, i.e. Mum, was otherwise engaged untangling dog from the banisters so managed to escape without a thorough vetting. Will be utterly star of saggy sofa, beating Scarlet and her run-of-mill regulation kilt version. Am totally Alexa Chung uber-fashion forward model type, and she is Coleen Rooney, i.e. mere follower.

4 p.m.

Am not Alexa Chung. Or even Coleen Rooney. Cannot keep up with this fashion-forward thing. Already the look has progressed to involve ironic straw boaters and

prefect badges. Saggy sofa was awash with 'Head Girls' and 'Team Captains'. Scarlet even had Suzy's old 'Milk Monitor' lapel pin. I pointed out that all this trend-following was compromising her semi-emo ideals and what had happened to the old, stand-out-from-the-crowd, bat-embracing Scarlet but she said gothness is totally passé now that entire lower school thinks they are being clever and interesting by dressing like corpses. She cited the fact that Goth Corner Mark II in the upper school canteen has swollen to three tables, forcing the mathletes to move to the 'lurgy' table (with Nigel Moore who has impetigo (not potato blight as widely rumoured)). She is right, there are minigoths every-where. Trevor Pledger (head goth, owner of vegetarian leather coat, ex-boyfriend of Scarlet) is like Pied Piper, i.e. swarms of becaped wannabes follow him wherever he goes and guard him outside the toilet like gargoyles. Scarlet says the adoration is not healthy and is giving him 'bad batitude'. She is right. He actually thinks he has vampiric powers now. I have seen him trying to fly off the top of the bike shed roof.

. . . .

Wednesday 9

Have given up on *St Trinian's* look and am going to go back to vintage. Will say it is fashion fast-forward, i.e. at some point is bound to be back in vogue and will be leader of pack.

4 p.m.
Vintage look definite improvement. That tie was hazard in canteen, i.e. it kept hovering dangerously near vats of baked beans (vegetable of the day). Jack agrees. At least I think he does. He said, 'Thank God someone has the courage not to follow the herd.' Did not say it was because could not keep up.

4.15 p.m.
Ooh. Though probably should have under terms of being honest resolution. Yes. Will definitely have to try harder tomorrow. Especially as stance totally backed by brainy philosopher Immanuel Kant who said we have categorical duty to tell truth regardless of consequences. And he was from Enlightenment, so must be right.

. . . .

Thursday 10
Truth telling not as easy as it sounds. In theory, honesty should be refreshing and empowering. In reality just annoys people and is potentially disaster-causing, e.g. was quietly minding own business at fruit and nut dispensing machine, purchasing yoghurt-dusted blueberries with Scarlet, when Melody Bean appeared from behind machine in disturbing manner and asked me whether Sad Ed had said anything about her since their liaison on New Year's Eve. I said yes, in fact he had: he said the snog was a colossal mistake and that he didn't fancy her at

22

all and his lack of penis movement only confirmed this sorry fact. At which point she burst into tears and had to be taken to school secretary Mrs Leech (bad hair, too much face powder, biscuit habit) for reviving Peak Freans, and Scarlet thwacked me round head with a packet of Bombay mix, causing me to choke on blueberry. Plus, then Scarlet told Sad Ed and he rushed to comfort Melody and is now officially going out with her out of guilt even though she is utterly non-mojo-arousing. I bet God didn't envisage this sort of trouble when he wrote the commandments. He should have thought ahead and added some subclauses. And Kant should have known better as well. No wonder he was celibate.

. . . .

Friday 11

Ha. Have had truth revelation in philosophy. It turns out that Kant is possibly wrong and not at all enlightened and that honesty is NOT always the best policy. Apparently there is opposing opinion that ends justify means, i.e. only tell the truth if it is in the interests of all concerned. DO NOT tell the truth if it is going to annoy someone and get you thwacked for your efforts. It is called consequentialism and am definitely following doctrine from now on. Why did they not teach us about this on Wednesday? May well write to Gordon Brown to demand radical rethink of AS level syllabus to ensure mix-ups like this cannot occur.

Anyway, have had resolution rethink and will limit truth-telling imperative to matters of the heart, i.e. when have found ONE and have to tell them before Scarlet pounces. Or when have not found ONE and want them to go away before do purple sick on them (to avoid future Kyle O'Grady incidents).

. . . .

Saturday 12
6 p.m.

Oh my God. 24 Summerdale Road is awash with honesty issues. It is not James, who is the usual perpetrator of cover-ups, mostly to do with the dog. It is habitually truth-telling Colin Riley, i.e. Dad. He has been caught speeding on the B1383 Saffron Walden to Stansted Mountfitchet road. Mum is livid. It is not the law-breaking (though she is a stickler for limits, and only does ten miles an hour in heavily populated areas), it is fact that he tried to disguise it with web of deceit, i.e. when a suspicious envelope from Essex police arrived this morning he claimed it was a letter warning them about potential burglars operating in the area. But Mum, whose motto is 'trust no one', and is au fait with all burgling habits (they are concentrating on Seven Devils Lane at moment, home of pint-sized eighties pop star Nik Kershaw and someone who once played for Leyton Orient), dug it out from under his tax returns and found the evidence in black and white, i.e. a blurry photo of the Passat going past the Elsenham turn-off, not just at speed, but slightly over the white line, thus breaking several rules at once. She is jubilant about one part though. The police have given Dad the option of a fine and three points on his licence or going on a refresher driving course, which is with none other than Mike Wandering Hands Majors, former instructor and admirer of Janet Riley, and sworn enemy of Dad. Dad begged to get the points but Mum has filled in the driving course request and has sent James to post it before Dad can interfere.

Also there is a new 'member of staff' at Nuts In May. It is not replacement for Rosamund, she is back from Wales, complete with new ailment, i.e. glue ear. It is a new non-death-inducing till. Mr Goldstein has finally bowed to demands and invested in fully digital twenty-first-century version. Apparently Mrs Goldstein got little finger trapped in till of death on Wednesday and had to be rescued by fire brigade, which was straw that broke camel's back (or hunchback) and no one argues with Mrs Goldstein, she makes Mum look ineffectual. Anyway, new till is lovely and shiny. But no one knows how to use it and we keep getting random numbers on display so have resorted to improvising with calculator and emergency drawer release button for moment until Rosamund goes on training course. On that point, till of death actually improvement as, though it was life-threatening, at least it was self-explanatory.

6 p.m.
Have called Sad Ed to see if he wants to come over but Mrs Thomas says he went straight to Melody's after trolley-herding duty. He is mad. He is wasting perfectly good moping time with someone who, even if she did stir his mojo, could not actually do anything with it as she is only fifteen and therefore illegal. He should be honest with his feelings like me. It is the route to happiness and fulfilment.

8 p.m.
Or possibly to being in on own on Saturday night watching *Casualty* with dog. Scarlet is too busy superpoking Hilary across the internet ether and even James has an engagement—he is going round Mad Harry's to blow stuff up. Life post-sisterhood is somewhat less edgy than I imagined.

· ·

Sunday 13
10 a.m.
Something odd is afoot at 24 Summerdale Road. It started at breakfast when Mum announced that Conversational French would be cancelled for the foreseeable future as she had a timetable clash with another more pressing engagement. But what could be more pressing in her eyes than conjugating *nettoyer* now that vomiting bug seems to have been successfully avoided? (Am on four Yakults a

day to build up defences. Have so many good bacteria in stomach think can actually feel them crawling.) And now, have just seen her go into dining room, aka Dad's office, wearing rubber gloves and cycle helmet. Hope it is not weird sexual role-play activity with Dad aimed at reviving love life. Had enough of that when Grandpa Riley and Treena were living here. Only Baby Jesus has to suffer that hoo-ha now. And he is easily distracted with Wotsits and Nickelodeon.

10.10 a.m.
It is not sexual. Have just seen James enter dining room armed with a notebook, several felt pens, and a USB cable.

1 p.m.
Aha! Have discovered secret activity. Not by cunning deduction, admittedly, but by more traditional method of bursting into dining room demanding to know what is going on. It is computer lessons with James! Mum is overcoming her greatest fear (bar terrorists, all-you-can-eat salad bars, and Austrian blinds) and learning to surf the web. It is one of her New Year resolutions. (The others are: eat more fish and find a new hobby to do with Dad in bid to rekindle recently strained relationship (due to stresses caused by constant presence over festive period of non-festive Cleggs). Apparently Dad has complained that any new activity would cut into his precious golf time but she said that is the point and got all

thin-lipped so Dad agreed.) I said this did not explain the helmet and gloves, unless their new hobby is bike maintenance. But she says it is protective wear to stop her skull and fingers getting permeated by the WiFi signal during her lesson and frying her nervous system. I pointed out that we did not, in fact, have broadband, we had chuggingly slow dial-up, which actually made cranking noises, but she said, not any more, she gave James the go-ahead last week to sign up to the twenty-first century (following strict criteria set by the *Which Guide to the Internet*) and we are now 'cooking on gas'. I am not sure I like this wise-talking technology-embracing version of my mother. It is disturbing the natural order of things. What if she gets hooked on online gambling and neglects her cleaning schedule? Although it is more likely she will only use it to log into Mumsnet and swap tips on stain removing and fussy eaters (she has conquered James's fruit/meat aversion by cunning use of pork and apple sausages). Said what about online perverts and hackers trying to steal her identity/millions but Mum says she has made James put up seven firewalls. Then before could question further, Dad came in and suggested she take a break from her lesson to prepare a nutritious family meal. Mum agreed. Not because she is subservient non-feminist type who cannot allow man to do cooking, but because if she does allow man, i.e. Dad, to do cooking it will involve beans on toast and the smoke alarm going off several times. James was glad of the

diversion. It is because Mum is not a model pupil. Apparently she says 'Why' more than Baby Jesus, and yelps with fear every time he minimizes a page in case it is lost in the ether. But James says this is a normal reaction for an old person and it will improve with time. Asked him what he was getting out of this arrangement. He said quality time with a parent. He is idiot. Or, more probably, liar.

. . . .

Monday 14
8 a.m.
It is two weeks since New Year and demise of anti-sex sisterhood and I have still not snogged anyone in experimental fashion or otherwise seized day, so am going to rectify immediately and seize Monday by embracing first male I can lure onto saggy sofa, regardless of musical preferences, fashion choice, or GCSE qualifications. (Though am sticking to common room as then I can at least rule out anyone underage as only fully-fledged A level students allowed into vicinity.)

4 p.m.
Oh God. And BTECers. Have done something awful. Have snogged Davey MacDonald, former: ballerina, Criminal and Retard, and ex-boyfriend of Thin Kylie. It is all fault of Mark Lambert who had partially exploded a Pot Noodle in the microwave so the BTECers were out

29

of their designated area and colonizing the saggy sofa. And basically it was him or Fat Kylie. Was going to back out but Sad Ed was invigilating and said seizing day did not include humming and ha-ing because someone is wearing fake Kappa tracksuit. Anyway, did utterly French batting of eyelids but he just said, 'Got something in your eye, Riley?' So upped the ante with some bosom heaving (learned from Suzy, though her bosoms substantially more heavable) but that just made him back away and fall off arm of saggy sofa onto sticky carpet so just straddled him on ground and kissed him before he could crawl to safety under the 'coffee' table. And before Jack hauled me off and asked what the hell was I doing sexually harassing someone with catalogued 'special needs' in that area (he has habit of getting thing out in lessons). Jack pointed out I could be imprisoned, or at least given detention and made to wash up the communal mugs for a week. I said obviously I was seizing the day, which, as a devotee of all things literary and rock star-ish, he should be all in favour of. And also breaking down the barriers between academia and proletariat, which, as devotee of all things left-wing and pro-masses, he should be all in favour of. He rolled eyes and said, 'Jesus, Riley. At least pick on someone you actually fancy. Or who fancies you.' I said, 'Like who?' He said, 'Beats me.' Am undeterred though. Will try again tomorrow. Maybe.

· ·

Tuesday 15

Have had seventeen offers of sofa snogging including four Year Sevens and, surprisingly, Davey MacDonald (clearly Jack was wrong and he was not unwilling victim in proceedings). My snogging skills are more potent than I thought. Have declined all though. Not sure that reputation as school slut was what had in mind when drawing up this resolution. Am going to have rethink and possibly restrict seizing day to situations that have definite potential ONE possibilities to them. Have told Sad Ed to put rumour out that yesterday was momentary lapse of reason brought about by overdose of non-drowsy Benylin, so all actions were under influence of drugs. That will sort things out.

On plus side, Mum has found Dad a new hobby to sway him away from golf. It is morris dancing. Clive does it. Dad has been sent next door to be fitted for leg bells. He is not pleased. I said it was hardly an activity they could share but Mum said *au contraire*, she and Marjory will be able to laugh from the sidelines quite effectively. I said didn't she mean 'cheer'? She said she knew exactly what she meant. She is still sulking about the speeding cover-up. James is trying to get in on the morris action too. He has demanded to be the mascot. It is because he is also looking for a new hobby now that ghostbusting has been added to Mum's ever-increasing list of banned activities. (She says she is sick of having to remove 'ectoplasm' (variously soup, dog vomit, and Badedas bubble bath) from the Hoover bag.) But Mum says he will have to look elsewhere as the job has gone to a sheep called Donald. James is not best pleased. It is the first time he has been out-nerded by a ruminant.

· ·

Wednesday 16
8.30 a.m.
Have got strange text from someone called Mac offering to 'do me' for 'an eighth'. Must have wrong number. Probably for Fat Kylie who has similar number. Am frequently getting calls for her from her many brothers, several of whom seem to be called Liam.

4 p.m.
Was not wrong number. Was result of Sad Ed's rubbish attempt at quashing slut rumours. Apparently now entire school is labouring under misapprehension that am drug addict who will do anything for a hit. Four Year Nines have tried to sell me Nurofen Plus, common room dealer Reuben Tull (enormous hair, staring eyes, entire Pink Floyd back catalogue) said I could have some 'herb' on a try-before-you-buy basis (and do not think he means marjoram), and cannot go down D Corridor (i.e. Criminals and Retards) without hearing muted strains of 'Pusher Man'—which is quite witty for class whose activity is usually limited to raffia and Biff and Chip. Even Jack is joining in. He deliberately put 'Love is the Drug' on

stereo when walked into common room after double philosophy. He claims he is going through a Roxy Music
phase but it is lie. I know for fact he thinks Bryan Ferry is
an effete Tory.

5 p.m.
It gets worse. One of the Liams has just been round to
offer me Ritalin. Luckily Mum was busy on Which.com in
her helmet and rubber gloves and James answered door.
As soon as he saw it was an O'Grady he got Mum's
weapon of choice from windowsill, i.e. Raid Fly Spray,
and temporarily blinded him. He says he is thinking of
becoming a young super-hero as his new hobby. I said,
what, 'Hobbit Man'? He gave me withering look and said,
no, 'Brains Boy'. Then he accused me of being ungrateful
and said I could deal with my own drug-pushing door-
stepping menaces next time. Said sorry as do not think
can deal with entire O'Grady horde on own. Some of
them are deadly. Especially the girls.

. . . .

Thursday 17
Sad Ed asked me if it was true that I was in the market for
a speedball. I said, who told him that? He said Melody
Bean. I said *a*) I don't even know what a speedball is; *b*)
no, you idiot, can you not even recognize your own
shoddy rumour?; and *c*) why are you still with Melody
Bean when you don't even like her? He said, *a*) it is a

combination of heroin and cocaine and is what led to untimely deaths of both John Belushi and River Phoenix (he has been trying to procure one for several years); *b*) sorry; and *c*) every time he tries to break up with her she starts crying and it panics him so he snogs her to shut her up. We are both victims of our twisted ideals. It is utterly Chekhovian. Possibly. Have not actually read Chekhov but is bound to be complicated.

Friday 18

A strange thing has occurred. Grandpa Clegg and Dad have found something in common. It is road impediments. Grandpa Clegg rang to moan about potential tolls on the A30 during tourist season. He says the government is trying to price him out of his car and on to a rusty old bicycle. Mum pointed out that he hates tourists and does not own a car, let alone a bicycle, so he is utterly unaffected. But Grandpa was not swayed and demanded to speak to the man of the house. Mum gave the phone to James but apparently he meant Dad, i.e. someone who is not on Mum's side in all matters, particularly those concerning cleaning and laws. Then they spent forty minutes bonding over speed cameras and road humps and their mutual love of right-wing motoring 'journalist' Jeremy Clarkson. Mum is outraged. She is very much anti Jeremy Clarkson, due to his flagrant disregard for the highway code, women, and rules pertaining to tucking your shirt

in when you have paunch. Plus he ruins her potential holy trinity of BBC-based Jeremys, also involving Vine and Paxman. I predict a chorus of disapproval at tomorrow's morris dancing debut (two o'clock outside the town hall, in honour of ancient East Anglian festival 'Plough Monday', now moved to Saturday for myriads of reasons mostly to do with annual leave and parking).

Saturday 19
8 a.m.
Thank God have got day in confines of Nuts In May selling fungal paté and fake bacon so that do not have to be linked in any way with abomination that is Dad in his morris dancing outfit. He looks like a madman and jingles wherever he goes, which is distressing the dog no end. It is cowering behind the sofa, and am minded to join it. Have begged Dad not to appear in public but he says he is proud to be upholding Essex tradition. He will be pargetting next. Or roof thatching. It is utterly appalling.

6 p.m.
Dad's morris dancing did not go completely to plan. Apparently there was some sort of choreography issue and Dad waved his hanky when he should have been crossing sticks and got jabbed in the eye by Clive. So he jabbed Clive back which initiated some sort of mini morris men riot and the end result was seven black eyes (two

of them Dad's), three broken sticks, and an arrest (Mark Lambert, who is not morris man, but general hooligan who was passing by and joined in for fun). To make matters worse, Mum made James bring Dad to Nuts In May for a sit down while she got the Fiesta from Waitrose car park so now all and sundry (well, hippies and vegetarians anyway) know that am related to village idiot.

On plus side, Dad is giving up the dancing. Even Mum agrees it was possibly a bad idea. She says the all-male atmosphere only breeds violence, and that he needs to do something transgender, i.e. mixed sex, not changing sex, as pointed out to Dad when he had panic that she wanted him to have bits removed à la dog, to curb his fighting spirit. James is disappointed. He is quite taken with the whole morris experience. It is the bells and mysterious and ancient manoeuvres. He is doubly determined to be the mascot now and pointed out that at least he is unlikely to poo outside Halifax, unlike Donald. But Mum still said no. She says he is too easily led and fears he will be caught up in the mania.

- -

Sunday 20

I miss sisterhood. Even though it was utterly restrictive snog-wise, at least it meant there was always someone to hang out with at weekends. Now Sad Ed is busy fending off Melody Bean and Scarlet is busy un-fending long-distance left-wing love Hilary. She says it utterly does not affect her friendship with me and that their phone conversations are entirely political not pants-based. But this is lie. Have witnessed her in 'political' conversation and all that ranting about David Cameron has weird and worrying effect on her. Anyway, instead am spending Sunday on godmother duty, i.e. counselling Baby Jesus in ways of righteousness. Am not actually going to church as it is too fraught with potential danger (requirement to be quiet and generally not draw on hymn books or drink font water). So am going to take advantage of his love of television and use it to subliminally send pro-God/good behaviour message. Have lined up *Sound of Music*, *Jesus Christ Superstar*, and *The Jazz Singer* (do not want to limit him, religion-wise). James (the godfather, though not in horse-head-in-bed insane Italian way) is in agreement with method. He says it is well-practised propaganda tool and am following in footsteps of evil geniuses like Hitler, Peter Mandelson, and Pringles crisps (it is true, once you pop you can't stop). Not sure this is good thing. But is nice being political genius, even evil one, and will possibly win me marks with Mr Slatter (beard, Fair Isle jumper, history of failing miserably in council elections) who, so far, has been utterly disappointed with my A level potential (it is not my fault that my political education up to this point has been Scarlet's rantings and Grandpa Clegg's biography of Thatcher (he has not read it, he just likes everyone to know where his loyalties lie)).

4 p.m.
Mum has ended evil genius subliminal pro-God screening session prematurely. It is not Baby Jesus. He loved the dancing nuns. As did James, who, worryingly, knows all the words to every song and gave simultaneous performance dressed in blue bed sheet. It is dog. It cannot cope with surround sound yodelling and had 'episode', i.e. insane barking fit, ending with consumption of furniture. Dad was disappointed though. It is because he thinks he is Captain Von Trapp, i.e. distant and brooding but potential musical genius. He says he could have been John Barrowman (assume he means leading man, not gay with scary hair and rictus grin) if he had not met Mum at accountancy college. Asked Mum if this was true. She said he can do a passable 'Edelweiss' but that any pretensions to West End possibilities are ill-founded and that in fact she is one with musical talent. James has suggested a sing-off at 7 p.m. but both have declined. They claim they have no need to prove their abilities. But I fear this is not the end of it. Mum is planning something, I can tell. Clearly she will not be outdone hygienically or musically.

. . . .

Monday 21

Reputation as vintage version of Fat Kylie (i.e. snogs anyone, but in better clothes) is still hovering over me like giant bat. Breaktimes are fraught with hordes of lower school boys begging me to kiss them. In stark contrast to Jack who has taken to falling on knees and begging me not to kiss him whenever he sees me, in what he thinks is hilarious ironic manner. It is not. Anyway I said 'as if' then pointed out that being experimental was, in fact, utterly tragic and poetical and am like Byron and Pete Doherty rolled into one. He said, 'Whatever. It's tragic, that's for sure.' Which is excellent as tragedy is utter plus in life.

At least philosophy rises above the tabloid obsessions of the masses to deal with more important questions. Like who is God. Majority conclusion is that God is all knowing, all powerful, and all good. Minority opinions include Sad Ed (God is dead); Scarlet (we should place faith in politics and not a fictitious creation designed to lull working classes into compliance, whose powers appear to be mostly limited to party tricks like making the face of his son appear in a slice of Nimble toast. Whereas Gordon Brown has the ability to change the entire tax system, if he wants); and Reuben Tull (the supreme being is a dog-headed lizard with lasers for eyes).

I said party tricks were just God's way of proving he exists (have no idea why took God's side, maybe it is responsibility of moral education of Baby Jesus). But Scarlet said if an all-powerful God did exist he wouldn't waste his time on being an invisible Derren Brown, he would banish all evil from world and the fact that he hasn't proves he is made up. So I pointed out that *a*) without evil there would be no saints or miracles, and a world without tragedy would be like 24 Summerdale Road everywhere and that *b*) she had fallen prey to patriarchal stereotypes and several times assumed God was a he. At which point Scarlet had panic attack and had to breathe into paper bag (former home of Reuben's 'stash', resulting in her passing out and being carried to Mrs Leech for Tango and bourbons).

Tuesday 22
4 p.m.
Do not need God anyway, as have Mum and James who are all-knowing and all-powerful, i.e. there is nothing that escapes their watchful gaze, and eventual punishment. Got home from school and Mum demanded to know if I was addicted to sex and 'injecting Ecstasy'. Apparently my reputation has seeped down to St Regina's and several Year Sixes are begging their parents to change their secondary choices so they can be tutored in the ways of love by me. Keanu has already offered James £10 and a fake driving licence for lessons, and he is only seven. Told Mum that it is all a colossal mix-up and that was just trying to have positive outlook on life and seize day etc., etc. She said if I seize the day again I will be home schooled before I can say crack marijuana.

Weirdly for someone so puritanical Mum absolutely does not believe in God. She just embraces the restrictive

and guilt-inducing elements of organized religion. James on other hand has eyes firmly on prize. He says believing is the only option because, if God does exist, at least he will go to heaven. Said this was hedging his bets and not at all pious or religious. James then had panic that God will see through his cunning ruse so he said he is going to be good anyway, not for payback, and then he will be in for sure. So pointed out that this was even more cunning and duplicitous so James now in religious meltdown in room trying to find a way to guarantee everlasting life.

6 p.m.
James says he has got it. He is going to embrace all religions, then one of the gods will take pity on him. Said this was hedging bets on Las Vegas scale and there was no way God was going to fall for that one. He is back in room.

7 p.m.
James is out of room. He is going for Seventh Day Adventism because they are glad to take anybody and will overlook his reasons. Said this was as bad as the time he turned to Islam because he thought their God was scarier plus they had prayer mats. He is back in room.

8 p.m.
James has decided any god worth hanging out with for

eternity should be glad of his supreme brain in heaven and so he is just going to wait for one of them to come to him. And in the meantime he is going to carry on following the ways of the Ninja. And the Jedi. And the Hobbit. He is idiot.

. . . .

Wednesday 23

Mum is combining her two New Year resolutions in one forward-thinking activity, i.e. she is surfing web (in regulation cycling helmet and rubber gloves) to find a new hobby for her and Dad (with James's assistance, of course; she is still trying to master shift key and scroll function). Is shame she did not think to consume fishfingers at same time so could have had resolution hat trick. Anyway, so far she has bookmarked pages for the Saffron Walden Historical Society and Friends of the Saffron Walden Museum. She will have hard job persuading Dad to take up either of these. He is rubbish at history (although not on scale of Cleggs who think that the Roundheads were some genetically mutated 'little people') and does not like museum due to 'funny smell'. Pointed out she could just take up golf and be done with it but she says that's what he wants her to do and she is not going to give him the satisfaction. She is wrong. Dad does not want Mum anywhere near the golf club. He says it is sacred time—free from all rules pertaining to spillage and saying 'bugger'. Though it is riddled with

ones pertaining to footwear and trouser length so do not
see the gain frankly.

. . . .

Thursday 24

James says he has found his new hobby. And possibly
his new religion too. It is crap TV game show *Gladiators*.
He and Mad Harry are going to apply. He says it is like
getting paid to be a superhero. They have already chosen
their names: Gazelle (James, no idea) and Sabre (Mad
Harry, as in light, not toothed-tiger, apparently). Pointed
out that it was a battle of bodies not brains and that
neither he nor Mad Harry had the physique of Adonis
(Greek God, not Education Minister, who is more
Andrew than Adonis i.e. bald and weedy). Plus, as usual,
they are several years under age. James is undeterred.
He says spending the next seven and a bit years cultivat-
ing the body of a steroid-obsessed pinhead is a small
price to pay. He is starting with push-ups and all-protein
diet. It is good job he did not put down John Major
High as his secondary school of choice. He would not
last five minutes with all his many nerdisms and obsessions.

6 p.m.

All-protein diet abandoned due to enforced vegetable eating, as dictated by Mum. She says there is no way she is
just cooking him eight sausages for tea, it will bung him

up and cost a fortune. Plus she is sick of him trying to copy whatever Keanu does (he has not told her the precise reasons for his new diet, he is simply allowing her to assume it is the devilment of an O'Grady). They compromised on two and a half sausages, peas (for brain power), and mash (for gladiatorial energy). Push-ups not going too well either. He managed one. Think allowing dog to sit on his back for extra challenge was mistake.

. . . .

Friday 25

Granny Clegg rang after school to update me on all things Hilary. I said I was utterly not interested in his life as was moving on, love-wise. Granny said good, as he is definitely in love with Scarlet, and she is backing him. I said she was a turncoat but she said, 'You can't argue with the spirits.' Apparently Maureen Penrice from the Spar is 'blessed with a fifth sense' and has declared that they are a match made in heaven. Plus Russell Grant (Granny Clegg's favourite fat gay astrologer) says their star signs are totally aligned at the moment. I asked how come she and Maureen knew so much about Scarlet. She says Hilary has told her everything and he is like the grandson she never had. Pointed out *a*) she was supposed to be boycotting Hilary for betraying me, and *b*) she did in fact have two grandsons—James and Boaz (God-bothering offspring of Aunty Joyless). She said, *a*) she did, for half an hour, but he has such nice teeth it is hard to be cross with him, and *b*) they do not count. It is because James baffles her with his encyclopaedic knowledge and Boaz just baffles her.

Am now feeling utterly despondent again. I know am being modern and progressive etc., (in non-sluttish way and only in circumstances where Mum cannot find out) but part of me wishes was in Maureen-blessed relationship with utter soulmate person, like Hilary and Scarlet. Especially as he was in fact my utter soulmate person until Scarlet showed up and out-left-winged me on all fronts. Is not that cannot be complete person without boyfriend to justify existence (illegal in Scarlet's eyes). Just that snogging is nice and weekends are boring.

* *

Saturday 26

Dean 'the dwarf' Denley is back at work. To be fair had not noticed he was missing from his meat-mincing position. But apparently he has been off with measles for three weeks (victim of hippy-perpetrated MMR 'scandal', according to Mum, who thinks we should be vaccinated on yearly basis for all diseases including bird flu) and under strict quarantine. Although not that strict, as clearly the saggy-sofa snogging/drugs episode had slipped past security. He said, 'I heard you were going through a bad time. It happens to all of us in the music business.' (He is not actually in music business now that the Back Doors have disbanded, and nor am I since got sacked as Justin's groupie, but he is right that we are creative etc.) I said, 'It wasn't drugs, it's an experimental thing. Like Jim Morrison, you know.' He said, 'I do. And any time you want to experiment, you know where to find me.' Then Mr Goddard shouted at him to get back to the sausages so he had to climb on his box and ram several pounds of pork down the chute. Which sort of ruined the moment.

6 p.m.
Not that there was a moment. Although am glad that at least he understands my quest for snogging freedom. Even so, will not take him up on invitation. Am not that desperate.

7 p.m.
Yet.

. . . .

Sunday 27
8 a.m.
Scarlet has just rung. Which is unprecedented as usually she does not emerge from her bat cave until after T4. Thought it must be her new emo-ish tendencies allowing her to embrace daylight a bit more but apparently it is because she has not been to bed yet. She has been up all night watching the South Carolina caucus on CNN. I said I thought caucus was something out of *Alice in Wonderland* involving a dodo and liquorice comfits. But she rolled her

eyes (I can sense this even over the airwaves) and said, 'It is in fact a state-wide poll in America to decide who is going to be the candidate for the actual Presidential election.' (Which is possibly another reason why Hilary is going out with Scarlet not me as she does not suffer these habitual mix-ups between fact and fiction.) Anyway, she says we are at the dawn of a new non-racist age because gangly black democrat Barack Obama has finally won one. I said it must have been a hard decision for her, between Hillary (Clinton, with two lls, as opposed to Nuamah, with one l and a penis), i.e. a woman, and a black man (Scarlet is so pro-positive sex discrimination she believes you should always vote for the woman, even if they have no qualifications, or are mental or dead). She said it was a tug of love for feminists everywhere, but that Barack understands our plight, and is an honorary woman. Plus she thinks Hillary (two lls) might in fact be in possession of penis as she has very deep voice and fondness for trouser suits. And Bill is scared of her. Anyway, am invited round for celebratory hummus and olives later with Bob and Suzy.

9 a.m.
Have ingenious plan to fulfil resolution number 3, i.e. locate Sad Ed's missing mojo. Will take him to hummus and olives Obama caucus victory party and casually let slip to Suzy that he is having penis problems. (Obviously will not mention this to Sad Ed. He will not come if he

thinks Scarlet's sexpert mum is going to interfere with him with her plethora of manuals and technical terms for genitals.) Hurrah. Am brilliant friend.

4 p.m.
Sad Ed not entirely in agreement with 'brilliant friend' title. He says he feels utterly raped by Suzy and her demands to see the evidence. I said I had suffered indignities of my own, i.e. Jack giving me bag of liquorice comfits for the 'caucus party'. (I said it was an easy mistake to make, and at least it showed I had wide knowledge of literature. He said, 'And I suppose thinking the Dalai Lama is a sacred camel makes you a genius then.' How was I to know that it is actually old man, not woolly animal?) Plus Suzy said she was proud of me and my completely Marianne Faithfull approach to love, i.e. not very faithful at all. Sad Ed said I should be grateful for the compliment and at least I have not been sent home with 'Get Sweaty With Suzy' DVD. But do not think compliment from woman who has discussed Jeffrey Archer's willy on prime-time telly is really very poetic.

. . . .

Monday 28
Scarlet is jubilant again. This time it is Hilary (one l, penis). He has been accepted by Cambridge University. All he has to do is get three Ds. I said if that is the grade requirement, then I may well apply. She said don't be

ridiculous, they only give low offers to geniuses with outstanding extra-curricular records. Again I said I should apply. She said if you even get past the interview, which given your recent llama/lama mix-up is unlikely, then they will offer you at least four As. Said she was being rather harsh for a best friend. She says it is utterly kind to tell the truth now so I am not disappointed next year. Plus I am the one who kept banging on about honesty. She is right. I think. It is in interest of all parties so conforms to Kantian and consequentialist doctrine. Anyway, asked her if Jack had heard as well but she said she didn't know as Jack is spending day looking around his back-up university (Hull, i.e. only need three Ds even if non-genius) and she would have intercepted post except that, when she left, postman (and notorious gossip) Beefy Clarke was too busy embroiled in a conversation with Edna the non-Filipina Labour-friendly cleaner about Mr Costain at Number 13 and his red gas bill to hand over the post. I said it was risky leaving Edna alone with the post as she has been known to store it for several months in random places according to her crap and frequently changing household management regimes (as witnessed by my own confession to Jack two years ago, when mistakenly thought was in love with him, which got 'lost' on top of the fridge). But Scarlet said Suzy has imposed a new rule, i.e. 'Immediately on receiving post place it on kitchen table in full visibility, and away from any water or incendiary objects'.

49

Anyway, Scarlet is utterly jubilant about Hilary defying his background education-wise. Pointed out that Mrs Nuamah had studied law at Oxford and Mr Nuamah had got a double first in politics and dentistry from Cambridge. She said she meant being born in Wales and raised in Cornwall.

. . . .

Tuesday 29

Hurrah, Hilary is not the only victor in defying his humble roots to enter the playground of the upper classes (i.e. Cambridge). Jack got in as well. Although he is not that humble as Bob drives Volvo and they have never eaten anything with Findus on the label. Anyway, clearly Edna is abiding by Suzy's post diktat because Scarlet brought the letter in to show us. He has to get four As. I said that was unfair as Hilary only had to get Ds and was possibly reversely racist. She said that reversely was a made-up word and anyway it is nothing to do with colour, it is more that Hilary touched on gene splicing, patient confidentiality, and the ethics of circumcision in his interview, whereas Jack spent all of it wittering about whether Billy Bragg deserved a Nobel Peace Prize for contributions to 'agitpop'.

Anyway it is utterly brilliant and wanted to congratulate him but he is still on his way back from Hull, which is hundreds of miles away, possibly in different time zone, so had to text him instead. Said DON'T

WORRY ABT HILARY GETTING BETTER OFFER. U STILL
V BRAINY. X

7 p.m.
Just got text back. Clearly he has entered earth's atmosphere from the galaxy of the north-east. It said THXX.
He is clearly a man of few words. And too many Xs.
Which does not bode well for someone who wants to
be simultaneous Foreign Secretary and Mercury Prize
winner as he is going to have to spend entire life on
Newsnight getting grilling from Paxo, or on *Never Mind
the Buzzcocks* making jokes about knobs with Phil Jupitus
and that goblin one that looks like our road sweeper
Mollo.

. . . .

Wednesday 30

A university-related bombshell has been dropped on the
Stone household. It is that Jack thinks he might actually
prefer Hull to Cambridge. He says the politics course is
second to none, halls are cheaper, and it is the seat of
anti-slavery, i.e. William Wilberforce is from there. Plus
there are fewer rugby shirts and pashminas by volume.
Bob is delighted with his pro-Northern/pro-working-
class/pro-fish stance (he is related to a crabber from
Grimsby). Suzy on other hand is going mental with
premature empty nest syndrome. She says at least if
he was at Cambridge she could pop in whenever she

fancied with a lentil bake and free condoms. Scarlet says Suzy is more adamant than ever that she wants another baby. She has bought ten ovulation kits and Bob is on twenty-four-hour call for insemination duty the minute her eggs are released. Asked Scarlet if she minded having a baby brother or sister, as it would make her the disadvantaged and syndrome-ridden 'middle child'. She said *au contraire*, middle children are in fact utterly brilliant, look at Madonna and John F. Kennedy, and she is all for it. Did not mention other notorious middle children Bill Gates, Princess Diana, or Mark Lambert as do not want to worry her unduly. Suzy will never get pregnant—she is away filming half the week, plus all the drugs in the eighties must have messed with her ovaries.

Mum is in agreement with Suzy as well. It is not middle children, or the empty nest thing. It is that only bad things come out of Hull in her eyes, i.e. Fat Boy Slim and John Prescott (just Fat Boy). Mentioned William Wilberforce but she said even he opted for Cambridge University.

. . . .

Thursday 31

12 noon

Have just seen Sad Ed coming out of the lower school toilets looking ecstatic. Think Suzy's DVD must have done the trick and his mojo is found, and possibly in overdrive.

12.30 noon

Was not mojo-related. Was that Mark Lambert had managed to utilize his BTEC skills and brick in one of the Year Sevens while they were having a pre-lunch poo (speed not quality of wall being aim of game—he actually has certificate for being fastest cementer in North Essex). Mr Wilmott has ordered him to knock the wall down immediately but Mark Lambert pointed out that the wall would thus collapse inwards, possibly injuring Bryce West (pooing Year Seven) and that in fact it would be better if Bryce knocked wall down from his side (which is quite brainy for someone who only got one GCSE). Except that Bryce did not have sledgehammer on his side of door so had to knock wall down with Power Rangers pencil tin. Sad Ed had gone in to cheer him on.

Friday 1

9 a.m.

Dad is in vile mood. It is because he got his letter confirming his date with destiny, aka Mike Wandering Hands and his refresher driving course. Mum has already warned him not to even think about feigning illness. She is investing in a tamperproof digital thermometer to catch out any fakery.

6 p.m.

Hurrah. The sisterhood is back on. Temporarily. Admittedly it is only due to fact that Suzy is ovulating so Scarlet is avoiding the house at all costs, and Melody keeps trying to touch Sad Ed 'down there' so he is avoiding her at all costs. And there will be no Wicca spells or anti-snogging pacts of any kind. But nevertheless, it is utterly excellent as cannot spend another Friday night watching *A Question of Sport* with dog or watching Mum negotiate the interwebnet in her helmet outfit.

10 p.m.

Sisterhood evening a partial success. On plus side, we have solved Sad Ed's Melody sex dilemma. I said the trouser groping was usually a cause for celebration. He said *au contraire*, the lack of response is embarrassing. So I said he should tell her about the celibacy thing. He says he has but she just sees it as a challenge. So Scarlet (in controversial pro-God/anti-honesty move) said he should

57

say he has seen the light and is going to wait until he is married before having sex. I said in fact he had already had sex (i.e. with Tuesday) but Scarlet said he can be revirginized, she saw it on Channel 5. Sad Ed has agreed it is the only way forward. He is going to get a Jonas Brothers-style chastity ring for full effect.

On downside, Thin Kylie also came over. It was not to partake in general discussion on Sad Ed's penis. It was to invite me to her birthday party tomorrow. Declined on grounds that cannot desert friends in hour of need, and Scarlet refuses to cross threshold of anyone who wears fur (Cherie has coat made of rabbits, or possibly guinea pigs). And Sad Ed is barred from Thin Kylie's for various misdemeanours, e.g. being fat, possibly gay, and once wearing tea cosy on head in Badly Drawn Boy phase. But Scarlet said Suzy is away filming tomorrow so she will be back home discussing the religious right with Hilary. And Sad Ed said he will be at Melody's discussing the religious wrong, i.e. not having sex until married. So ended up agreeing to go, as long as no one tried to sell me drugs or make me snog anyone under the age of sixteen. She said most of the O'Gradys are on electric tag curfew, so I should be fine. Asked if there was a theme. She said, 'Like, duh, get drunk.' Scarlet said, 'How imaginative.' Kylie said, 'Why, what do you do at your parties? Talk about the news?' Scarlet said, 'Yes.' Kylie said, 'Bloody lezzer.'

At least the theme is honest. Though am not entirely

sure why she wants me to go. Maybe her and Fat Kylie have fallen out again. Though saw them on wall sucking Chupa Chups earlier (i.e. nicotine replacement therapy). Or maybe she is trying to matchmake me. Oooh. Perhaps she has a cousin who is overcoming his chav roots with poetic or literary talent. Like The Streets. Or maybe actually is The Streets! Hurrah. Maybe will meet my ONE tomorrow after all and marry controversial musical genius!

11 p.m.
As long as it is not Donkey Dawson with the saveloy-resembling penis. I don't care if he is a legend. I am utterly vegetarian when it comes to those things.

Saturday 2
11.30 p.m.
I was right about Thin Kylie. But it was not potentially poetic cousin The Streets (her cousins were there, but they are called Dane and Casey and spent most of evening setting light to stuff, including selves at one point. Which is not at all poetic) or Donkey Dawson and his frankfurter-shaped appendage. It was Davey MacDonald, my saggy sofa snogging victim! Apparently he is completely smitten and gave Kylie a six-pack of Smirnoff Ice to invite me. So had to spend three hours hiding behind Fat Kylie as protection (Davey is scared of her

after she decked 'Big' Jim behind the bins, aka Rat Corner). Which was fine when Fat Kylie was just main-lining Bacardi Breezer, but not so good when Mr Whippy was exploring her Nobbly Bobblys. Plus then I had to compromise my own security due to fact that had been drinking Diet Coke as contraceptive measure (i.e. there is no way would snog a chav when sober) and bladder finally threatened to give way and had to let go of Fat Kylie in order to go to loo (she refused to come with me on 'lezzer' grounds). But Davey MacDonald saw me and cornered me on landing. He said 'I'm, like, glad you came, Rachel.' So I knew he was desperate as *a*) he called me Rachel and *b*) he used the correct tense. So he is obviously trying really hard to better himself. And then had revelation and realized it was all utterly Lady Chatterley. And he is underprivileged but gorgeous proletariat gamekeeper Mellors. But then a bit of wee actually started to come out so had to run to loo before moment ruined by me peeing all over the peach shagpile. Which is not at all Ladylike. (Not even Lady Chatterley. Who did all sorts of kinky stuff, according to Scarlet.)

But once safely on toilet and relieved of gallon of Diet Coke wee, remembered that Mellors was master of love, i.e. schooled in the sexual arts. Not rat boy who gets thing out in language lab. Luckily when opened bathroom door Mr Whippy had got in way of Casey and his trigger-happy lighter and he was claiming that his 99 had been singed, and Davey too distracted by potential penis-related chav fighting to see me escape.

Got home to find Dad was still up watching *Top Gear* repeats on BBC3. I said if Mum caught him he would be for it, given her aversion to Jeremy Clarkson (now grouped with Kyle, in her 'evil Jeremys' subsection). But he said Mum had taken a herbal Nytol to counteract her computer-related jittering and staring eyes and was out for the count. And anyway he was getting tips for his refresher course. Which is great as long as Mike Wandering Hands wants him to drive a Sherman tank over a caravan, beat Ewan McGregor around Silverstone in a Robin Reliant, or fly a Harrier Jump Jet.

. . . .

Sunday 3
11.30 a.m.
Mum is incensed with anti-binge drinking fervour. It is the *Times*'s fault for reporting the dangers of passive drinking. I said surely it was impossible, as you cannot get drunk from sniffing Taboo and black, just mildly nauseated. But she says it is the ensuing violence in pubs, and even a minute amount can affect anyone within a ten-mile radius with devastating consequences. She has a point. Last night I only had Diet Coke and ended up with a twisted ankle (in escape to freedom tripped over Fiddy (yappy miniature Pinscher, former lover of dog, passed out in hallway from drinking Crème de Menthe)) and

four burn holes in my T-shirt (Dane). Anyway, it has sent Mum over the edge in her anti-alcohol stance. She is writing to Mr Wilmott to demand that he include an anti-binge drinking lecture on his citizenship syllabus. She thinks he will be sympathetic given that his sister weirdy Edie is a recovering alcoholic. She will be disappointed. Binge-drinking is endemic at John Major High. Half the staff start the day with an Anadin and soon-to-be-broken vows never to touch the bottle again. Mr Vaughan (chief drinker) says it is due to the pressures of endless paper-work and SATs. It is more the pressure of having his supersized nipples illegally groped by Sophie Jacobs. Anyway, then Dad said what about passive drug-taking, i.e. he was suffering from shout-induced earache due to her being grouchy from the herbal Nytol last night. At which point had to leave the table as not-at-all passive violence threatened to break out over the coarse-cut marmalade. Luckily they have gone out now. Treena is doing Sunday lunch. James and I are excused on the grounds our immune systems are not as well-developed as Mum's and Dad's.

1 p.m.
Oooh. Doorbell. Maybe it is Sad Ed come to update me on his fake religious anti-sex ploy.

2 p.m.
Was not Sad Ed. Was Mellors. Aka Davey MacDonald! He

is not giving up in his pursuit of across-class love. (Or 'pervy nerd sex' according to Thin Kylie.) He said, 'Can I, like, have a word?' I said, 'OK.' He said, 'So, do you, like, want to go out, like, somewhere?' I said, 'Um.' Which admittedly is not very articulate but was transfixed by his many gold earrings, and slightly confused by all the 'likes'. Then he said, 'It's like, I like you, like.' At which point, temporarily lost all track of what he was saying. Luckily James was on hand to translate and said, 'Unbelievable. Billy Elliot is asking you out.' So I said, 'Um. I'll think about it. I'll call you.' And then shut door before he could do any more 'liking'. Which I know is utter cop-out. Especially as do not actually have his number. Though could probably get from Thin Kylie for a packet of B&H. But am now utterly torn. On the one hand, he would be utter experiment in Lady Chatterley across-the-divide love. But on the other hand he is flashing rat boy. This is how Princess Diana must have felt when deciding whether or not to snog son of grocer, and wearer of criminal leather jackets, Dodi Al Fayed.

At least James is happy. It is the closest he has been to the 'criminal fraternity' and he is mental with potential ASBO excitement. He says it is lucky that Mum is out but that he will be monitoring all my movements from now on and any breaches will be reported to the authorities, (i.e. Mum).

Monday 4

Mind has been temporarily swayed from Davey MacDonald conundrum by incredible news that Sad Ed is now ENGAGED! TO BE MARRIED! Apparently he popped the question during T4 yesterday. Although was not actual popping of question. More begging by Melody Bean following disclosure of his no sex before marriage rule. He is now utterly inconsolable. Pointed out that, on plus side, at least he is safe from her gropings until she turns sixteen. But he says that only gives him two months' grace. So said he could always actually tell her the truth, i.e. that not only does he not want to marry her, but that he never wanted to go out with her in the first place, it was a total sympathy thing and that in fact she physically repels him. He said, 'Yeah, right.' So said, 'How are you going to get out of it then?' He said he is going back to his depressives' favourite get-out clause, i.e. untimely death. He says by this time next year he will be but a postscript in history. He is overegging it. He will be lucky to get two lines in the *Walden Chronicle*.

. . . .

Tuesday 5

Shrove Tuesday i.e. Pancake Day
Not only is today Shrove Tuesday but is also apparently something called Super Tuesday. Which is very important politics-wise in America. (Although does not contain pancakes or indeed food of any sort and is mostly about

voting so does not sound that super to me.) Anyway, I know this because Scarlet is in complete overdrive and is in two-way communication with Hilary at all times via text. They are all worked up over whether Barack or Hillary (two ls, no definite penis) will win California, New York, and Utah. I said no one in their right minds would want to win Utah as it is full of morons, as she had pointed out only last week. But Scarlet said, 'Mormons, you moron. God, you are so politically smalltown.' She is right. This only highlights further why she is with left-wing Hilary and I am being pursued by no-wing Davey. How utterly ironic. And crap.

5 p.m.
Although maybe Davey MacDonald is actually potentially political. He could be like trade union leader for bricklayers or something.

5.30 p.m.
Except have just remembered he once tried to join BNP.

6 p.m.
Although admittedly it was so he could get cheap Fred Perry shirts off someone called Wiggy.

6.30 p.m.
No, that is still not good enough. Ignorance is no excuse. Look at the Cleggs.

Wednesday 6

Sad Ed is still engaged, i.e. he has neither told the truth, nor managed to kill himself in the last forty-eight hours, despite several attempts at the latter, including binge drinking water to burst his brain. Apparently all that happened is that he had to go to the loo seven times in music and has been referred to the nurse (aka school secretary Mrs Leech) with possible diabetes. Apparently his weight and excess sugar consumption are also key indicators. Asked him if he had broken the happy news to Mrs Thomas yet (wedding, not diabetes). He said no as she will probably encourage it. He is wrong. She is dead set on him marrying female version of Aled Jones, i.e. Welsh and chaste. Not sex-mad Goth from Bird's Farm estate. Plus he is mad if he thinks he can keep it a secret. Melody has already signed up four minigoths as bridesmaids.

Thursday 7

Went round Scarlet's for tea after school with Sad Ed. She and Hilary are all texted out after Super Tuesday and she said she needed the company of those with simpler intellectual needs. I said in fact my brain was a hotbed of conflicting intellectual thoughts, mostly brought on by this afternoon's philosophical discussion/row, i.e. what would heaven be like? (Probably not swirly marshmallow paradise, where everyone has rocket packs and X-ray vision as imagined by Reuben Tull.) Sad Ed just shrugged. He is glad to be anywhere that Melody isn't. All the wedding talk is wearing him down. Sad Ed says she is going for a *Corpse Bride* theme, with a black dress and raven-feather fascinator thing. I said is economical as she can wear it to his funeral instead. He said, 'God willing.' He is utterly determined. Am actually worried he might succeed this time. He says he is like Odysseus—trapped between two evils (i.e. the whirlpool of death and six-headed monster). Scarlet said he is not trapped by any evils, more caught up in his own web of idiotic deceit and cowardice.

Anyway, tea was utter disaster due to Edna's steam cleaning all kitchen cupboards without bothering to empty them first and all labels falling off tins. So now all food consumption is utter lottery, i.e. what Scarlet thought was asparagus soup followed by Ambrosia rice pudding (retro food of proletariat and therefore de rigueur in Labour households) turned out to be cannellini beans and condensed milk. Suzy does not mind. She says it is waste not, want not and refused to throw it away due to all the children starving in Africa. Scarlet said she would rather starve along with them. So Sad Ed had both tins. He said he quite liked it. Either he has killed his taste buds with too many Nice 'n' Spicy Nik Naks or it is a lie and he is hoping it is a fatal combination. Me and Scarlet had a bowl of cornflakes instead. Is nutritionally equivalent of cardboard, but at least is edible.

. . . .

Friday 8

The cannellini beans/condensed milk was not fatal. Though was not without serious side-effects. Sad Ed is very much alive and smelling. He has been banned from the common room and is in quarantine in a language lab until he is fresh again. This could be weeks. Sad Ed says he welcomes the solitude because *a*) Melody cannot find him, and *b*) Leonard Cohen, patron saint of depressive types, is playing Glastonbury, so nothing can dampen his good mood, ironically. Scarlet says she is boycotting Glastonbury. It is not Leonard Cohen. Or controversial rap star Jay-Z. She says she is suffering festival fatigue. There are too many pretenders out there now and the spirit of free love is being watered down with Boden wellies and private portaloos. She is right. I will boycott it too. Though more because do not want to repeat last year's Jack weirdness. Or wee in Pringles tube.

Saturday 9

Oh my God. Got visited by both Dean Denley and Davey MacDonald at work today. Am complete man magnet. Or rather midget and mentalist magnet. But, none the less, is progression on last year's drought. Dean came over in his meat-spattered apron (possibly actually white coat from dressing-up doctor kit, as has stethoscope drawn on pocket) to ask if I wanted to go to see someone called Bingo Bob play tonight at the Lord Butler Leisure Centre

(Jockey Wilson Suite). Said no thanks, as do not like country and western. Said is not country and western, is death metal from Billericay. But luckily, before he could use his powers of persuasion, Mr Goldstein demanded he remove himself from premises as pork traces were offending the vegans, not to mention his own Jewish sensibilities. Then, five minutes later, Davey MacDonald came in, not in meat-spattered apron, but in blue nylon Puma, which is possibly equally offensive, to ask if I wanted to watch Darryl Stamp beat up Ricky Stuart later. Also said no. On so many grounds cannot begin to name them. He seemed genuinely sad. Maybe he is actually sensitive under his mask of thuggishness. He could be potential rough diamond.

8 p.m.
Oh my GOD, he is Heathcliff. And I am spoilt rich girl Cathy. Who will ignore true love of gypsy type and marry for money and end up miserable. It is utter revelation. Think Davey MacDonald may well be ONE after all. Will phone Scarlet and Sad Ed for second opinion.

9 p.m.
Scarlet and Sad Ed not available due to various political/bridal commitments so forced to ask James. He says Davey MacDonald not Heathcliff but run-of-mill Whiteshot Estate pikey and that if he catches any more hints of me pursuing ASBO love he will be forced to

intervene. I said that was rich coming from someone who consorted with an O'Grady on a regular basis. He said he does not actually like Keanu. It is purely a means of avoiding getting beaten up and is more in the tradition of Guy Ritchie squiring Vinnie Jones. And yes he actually used word squiring.

. . . .

Sunday 10
11 a.m.

Hurrah, no French again. It is because Mum and James are gloved and helmeted up and busy researching gladiatorial skills on the computer. Mum does not know about James's TV ambitions. She thinks it is because he is doing ancient Rome at school. He is not. Nige thinks it is too bloodthirsty. They are doing grow your own crocus instead.

3 p.m.

James has fallen at first gladiatorial hurdle, i.e. fighting wild beasts. In absence of lions, he tried to wrestle with dog, causing surfeit of howling and scuff marks on lino. He has been sent to his room to think about the perils of aggression. The dog is on the sofa with a rich tea and a smug expression. It is not often that it is at the centre of a kerfuffle and is identified as victim rather than perpetrator of crime. Have told James he should rethink his hobby and find one that utilizes the skills he does have, as opposed to ones he has no hope of acquiring. But he said he is not a quitter and that, like phoenix, he will rise again, stronger and more powerful from the ashes of today's defeat. In fact is thinking of changing name from Gazelle to Phoenix. Am not sure which is worse.

Anyway, more importantly, have made decision to stop obsessing about the ONE. (Following extensive reading of Treena's copy of *Glamour* which she left here yesterday and which have rescued from recycling. Though have disguised inside *Accountancy Today* to avoid shouting from Mum.) Think maybe there is no Mr Right. Just Mr Right Now. Instead will have series of interesting lovers and will grow as person from each liaison in manner of Sienna Miller. (Though will not snog Rhys Ifans as he just looks dirty.)

Monday 11

Saw Davey MacDonald at school today, seeing how many times he could headbutt wall before wall collapsing/him passing out. All signs point to James being right. He is not Heathcliff. He is moron. Think will focus on seizing Dean Denley. It will be experiment in cross-height love. Which is almost Romeo and Juliet-like, if you think about it. We will both grow as people from liaison. Which would be excellent, in his case.

Also, am not going to tea at Scarlet's again. Had tinned tomatoes and custard today. Suzy is embracing the new

71

regime as an experiment in culinary taste and an exercise in using up all the stuff from the back of the cupboard. Bob, Scarlet, and Jack are not so forward-thinking. They are mostly existing on hummus and cereal.

. . . .

Tuesday 12

Am thinking philosophy possibly bad choice for AS level. Apparently there are NO right answers, there is only opinion. Which is why Mum does not agree with it, due to potential for free thought/getting marked wrong. James on other hand appears to be embracing it. It is his vast cavern of brain which welcomes subject in which there are endless answers to everything. He has read all my Kant ('too obvious') and is on Descartes now. There is no way he is not going to get into St Gregory's. He is freakishly geeky. Although he says he may not actually be attending secondary school at all as he is still aiming to fulfil his gladiatorial ambition. He is hoping to also incorporate philosophy. He says it will make him mentally superior and physically unbeatable. It will not. It will make him look like weirdo he is and he will still get hammering. He can't even outwit dog at moment.

. . . .

Wednesday 13

It is Valentine's Day tomorrow and in new experimental Mr Right Now style, am going to send several cards. It is

James's idea. He says I need to cast my net wide to ensure a good catch. He sends at least ten every year. Pointed out that he didn't actually have girlfriend so results do not bear out theory but he said, 'That's what you think.' Oh God. Think James might actually be stud nerd at St Regina's. Anyway, have drawn up shortlist and am sending them to Dean, Davey, and Reuben Tull. It is all-embracing group, to show am not in any way anti-chav and that can also overlook height issues and beliefs in laser-eyed dogs. Was going to send one to Jack as well. But *a*) Stones do not 'do' Valentine's Day due to it being made up. And *b*) he has made his views on me utterly clear, i.e. I am not snogging material any more. Which is sort of a shame. As he is utterly good at snogging. But he is not Mr Right Now. He is Mr Back Then. And he can't be only one in world to stir my (girl) mojo.

5 p.m.
Can he?

7 p.m.
Dad is not so excited. It is not the worry about Valentine's Day (he gets Mum the same thing every year, i.e. pre-approved box of Green and Blacks chocolate miniatures and card with Tate print on). It is that tomorrow is his refresher driving course, i.e. he is being forced to spend most romantic day in calendar with Mike Wandering

Hands Majors, aka Mum's not-so-secret admirer. He says he would rather swim naked in Grafton Centre fountain. James said Mad Harry once did that. Does not bear thinking about.

10 p.m.
Have added Justin to Valentine's list. To show that do not bear grudge and also because snogging your ex is also utterly allowed in the rules according to *Glamour*. Have borrowed emergency spare card from James. Has geek-theme, i.e. picture of embracing chess pieces, but he will think it is ironic. Possibly. Am not signing them anyway so is untraceable.

10.30 p.m.
Though what is point of sending them if no one knows who they are from? It is utter Catch 22.

10.40 p.m.
Will just put mysterious 'R' inside. Am like Zorro.

. . . .

Thursday 14
Valentine's Day
It has been an excellent Valentine's Day, card-wise, i.e. got fourteen. In fact is best haul since Year Two when Mrs Bunnet forced everyone to make cards for everyone else in fit of inclusiveness. Not sure they are all genuine

declarations of love. In fact think several are left over from 'do anything for drugs' rumours. But it beats James who only got eight. He is not too disappointed as he sent eleven, which means he is only £3.30 down overall. On the down-side, think my mysterious Zorro-style 'R' may be confused with both Ramona Fork in Year Eleven and recipient of one of my cards, drug baron Reuben Tull. Who spent two hours drawling on about how he must have been in an alternative reality last night because he sent a card to himself. He was not in alternative reality. He was just stoned. As usual. Also have no idea who mine are from. Except one, which is definitely Davey MacDonald's as, in true Retard and Criminal tradition, he had signed it. Sadly none of them are in Justin's illegible scrawl. But do not care about provenance as am not limiting myself to one man. Am embracing love itself today, in spirit of experimentation and general day seizing. (Though purely in philosophical sense. Am not Leanne Jones.)

In contrast Dad has utterly not embraced the spirit of anything. It is because he spent six hours driving around the Hockley one-way system with Mike Wandering Hands. Mum went to invigilate. Dad accused her of only going to ogle Mike but she said she went to ensure fair play and value for money. It is a good job she did. Clearly Mike Majors is no admirer of Mr Clarkson either as he told Dad off forty-seven times and said it is a wonder he is still alive or has a licence at all, and is a good job he has a role model to observe in Mum. At that point apparently Dad performed an illegal U-turn and emergency stop and stormed out of car. He only returned because Mum threatened him with divorce, or being transported everywhere in her Fiesta if he didn't. (He said he doesn't know which would be worse.)

James pointed out that, on the plus side, it is the last Dad will ever have to see of Mike. And now he knows what speed limit on motorway is (i.e. not 99mph, as previously thought). Mum agreed. Plus she distracted him with her Valentine's surprise. It was not heart-shaped cake or new underwear. Thank God. It is news of their new hobby and is guaranteed to cement their love, i.e. Saffron Walden Amateur Operatics Society. They are auditioning for major roles in this year's production of *Grease*. It is Marjory's idea. She has been banging on about it ever since she and Clive got to be backing dancers in *Chicago*. Which is horrendous thought. Also, am not entirely sure it will cement love as actors are always philandering, especially amateur ones. And fear a repeat of the whole Captain Von Trapp sing-off hoo-ha. But at least it means they are out of the house every Sunday afternoon for the foreseeable future. Plus they have a whole new social calendar, starting with a 'meet and greet' tomorrow night at the Seven Devils Lane home of perpetual lead actress (and ferocious lady golf captain) Margot Gyp.

Friday 15

Hurrah. Today was last day of school for a week. Can rest brain from complicated A level thought for seven days of hanging around town, hanging out watching crap telly, or hanging from Scarlet's loveswing (repaired and re-inforced). Apparently it is actually quite philosophical and experimental to lounge about and watch members of opposite sex, according to French philosophical genius and poet Baudelaire. It is called being a *'flâneur'*. Although admittedly his *flâneur*ing was in Paris and passers-by probably included Simone de Beauvoir lost in poetic thought as opposed to Keanu O'Grady trying to breakdance on head outside the Abbey National. None the less, am starting general air of French loucheness tonight, and taking advantage of Mum and Dad's operatic absence, by watching *À Bout de Souffle* and eating maraschino cherries from the tin with a spoon (donated by Scarlet who was offered them on toast for breakfast).

11 p.m.

Baudelairean evening marred only by dog deciding it doesn't like maraschino cherries after all and hawking one up on sofa (yet it considers cutlery edible). Luckily James is also master of all things stain-related and used Mum's arsenal of equipment to full effect.

Mum and Dad did not enjoy such laid-back evening of entertainment chez Margot Gyp. A spanner has been hurled into their romance-cementing operatic dream. It is

Mike Majors! He has also signed up. Though not to seal love, but more probably to engage in extra-curricular hand-wandering. Anyway he and Margot did an impromptu rendition of 'Summer Lovin'' and according to Mum he has 'quite the voice'. Dad said, 'Yes, if you like the thin, reedy sort.' I predict hoo-ha on a colossal scale come the auditions.

Saturday 16

8 a.m.

Have decided to continue air of French loucheness by seizing day with Dean Denley. Will corner him near meat bins on break and experiment, Sienna Miller-style.

6 p.m.

Ick. Have begun and ended brief growing-as-a-person liaison with Dean Denley. I do not care how experimental Sienna Miller is, I bet she never had to lift Jude Law up in order to kiss him. Dean did not seem to mind too much when I apologized and said I was just trying something out and possibly would never do it again. He just said, 'Rock and roll, Riley.' He is clearly under delusions he is fully-fledged music industry tart. When in reality he is undersized meat-mincer with a set of Fisher Price bongos.

No sign of Davey MacDonald on man front. Although maybe he is still trying to read Shakespeare sonnet that wrote inside Valentine's card. I know for fact he struggles with *Floppy the Hero*. Did see Reuben Tull in Waitrose car park at lunchtime though. Unbelievably he is Sad Ed's new trolley-herding apprentice now that Sad Ed has been promoted to chief herder (following Gary Fletcher's suspension for various crimes on freezer aisle). Reuben said, 'Nice smell, Riley,' in appreciative manner then rode off on trolley into darkness of Level One like Dick Turpin on Black Bess. But with enormous afro and singing 'Shine On You Crazy Diamond'. (Would like to say smell was classic Chanel No. 5, but was actually environmentally friendly drain cleaner, which Rosamund spilt on my shoes at tea break.) Told Sad Ed that am utterly amazed at Reuben's appointment and if Waitrose are desperate for workers maybe I should rethink my own employment situation. But Sad Ed said, in fact, Reuben is not last resort, but first choice for job. I said it's hardly rocket science but Ed said *au contraire*, there are several key skills to success, e.g. hair able to withstand extreme weather conditions, and ability to sidestep Year Nine skateboard pests who use spiral exit route for ollying etc. Plus he is happy to talk nonsense all day. This is true. When I left he was wondering aloud whether or not a man will ever be born with wheels instead of feet. Waitrose should start including mandatory drug tests for Saturday boys. May well write to Mr John Lewis to suggest it. Although it is improvement on Gary Fletcher whose topics of conversation were limited to radio-controlled cars and Janine off meat's breasts. Anyway Sad Ed is right. Would look like giant puffball, or Reuben Tull, if my hair was exposed to endless howling wind and damp of car park. And the nylon overall does nothing for complexion.

. . . .

Sunday 17

1 p.m.

Hurrah, Mum and Dad have operatics so can spend entire afternoon in bed in manner of French experimental type. Only dressed and alone. And reading *Penguin Guide to Houses of Parliament* instead of erotica. James is also pleased. He is planning a gladiatorial arena in the bathroom where he will attempt to remain under water for five minutes. Said did not think this was actually a gladiator challenge but he says he has thought about what I said about sticking to what he is good at, and is going to try to rewrite the rules to include his special skills.

1.30 p.m.

Lounging and drowning in bath attempts both banned due to alternative arrangement made by Mum to spend quality time with Baby Jesus, i.e. save him from axis of evil that is Treena and the O'Gradys next door. At least Grandpa is vaguely experimental type, i.e. he is ageing lothario with dandyish style of dress (though not always deliberate). Maybe will actually be quite French after all.

5 p.m.

19 Harvey Road not in any way French. Unless you count bottle of flat Orangina in fridge. Though Grandpa showing signs of being experimental. Had very lengthy discussion with him about benefits of pentapeptides. Thought he may actually be scientific genius for minute but Treena says it is not that. It is that he has been reading all her *Grazia*s and *Heat*s and is now also well-versed in waterproof mascara, St Tropez versus Fake Bake, and Jordan's 'boob nightmare'. Which is weird. Although suppose is good that he is educating himself in ways of modern woman. Is better than Grandpa Clegg who rang up in a panic about free radicals after seeing an Oil of Olay advert. He thought an 'army of Commies' was about to invade and that somehow face cream might save him. He is advertisers' dream, i.e. utter moron.

Attempted to have philosophical discussion about God with Baby Jesus in ongoing religious education role. But he more interested in James's gladiator antics, i.e. trying to catch him in fishing net. Although on plus side Jesus already utterly obeying one of ten commandments, and one of my New Year Resolutions, i.e. Thou Shalt Not Lie. He is happy to tell truth at all times, e.g. 'Who did that smell?' Jesus: 'I done it.' Or 'Who ate all the Wagon Wheels?' Jesus: 'Wachel.' Am going to have to overrule pro-God education for anti-Mum education, i.e. he is going to have to toughen up and learn the Riley rules if he, or any of us, are going to survive.

81

Luckily Mum too preoccupied to do any interrogation of Jesus today. She and Dad are all fired up with operatic potential. They have just a week to prepare for their auditions. Mum is going for Sandy and Dad for Danny Zuko. Have warned them that they should aim lower as *a*) do not want to step on toes of established company members, and *b*) they are not that good, or young. But all pleas have been in vain. Mum says it is high time Margot Gyp made room for new blood. Plus Mike Majors is also going for Danny and Dad says there is no way he is going to let him get his greased lightning anywhere near Mum.

. . . .

Monday 18
Half term

9 a.m.
Hurrah, it is beginning of week of *flâneuring*, following yesterday's interruption to play. Am going to start by lying in bed until eleven. Then may go round Sad Ed's for some moping. Then to Scarlet's for some hovering before ending with some idling outside Gayhomes (crap hardware shop, not homosexualist one). Excellent.

9.15 a.m.
Am out of bed. Mum says she does not care how French it is, I am not lounging about festering on laundry day and if I have nothing to do I can test her on lines while

she presoaks the pants. Declined. It is not the pants. It is Mum's version of Sandy. Who seems to have gained implausible Australian accent and insane smile. She has no chance. Will leave her to James.

9.30 a.m.
James also declined. He is devoting half term to gladiating. He is going to Mad Harry's to consume protein for day. Will go to Sad Ed's instead for early moping. He will not mind. Plus even if he still asleep is generally same effect, i.e. pale and quiet with occasional grunt.

9.45 a.m.
Sad Ed not in. He has gone to Cambridge with Melody to buy clothes, according to Mrs Thomas. This is an utter lie. Sad Ed does not buy clothes. He has had same T-shirts for four years. It is cover-up for illicit wedding activity. He has probably gone to choose his hypothetical tuxedo. Will go to Scarlet's instead for hovering.

10.30 a.m.
Scarlet not in. Apparently Suzy drove her to Cornwall yesterday to reunite her with left-wing love Hilary. Jack said I could come in and hover anyway but said hovering not same when no one else to moan at T4 with. So he said could just come in and have brunch (banned in our house for being *a*) American, *b*) a made-up word, and *c*) usurping elevenses in popularity). Was hesitant, as did not want to end up with vichysoisse instead of baked

beans but it turns out Edna's tin regime has been abolished. It is because Bob opened up Kitekat and said was last straw. Edna said she ate cat food in the war and was grateful. But Bob said if he can't eat filet mignon he is hardly going to chow down on scrag end and eyeballs. All tins have been donated to Pink Geranium Sheltered Housing (old people will eat anything as long as it is mushy, even cat food) and so had full (vegetarian) English breakfast brunch-style meal. Which was revelation as Jack is first man have met who can cook. Grandpas Clegg and Riley do not cook on principle (it is women's work, along with household cleaning, and purchasing of pants), and Dad does not cook on grounds that Mum gets too shouty when he does. Also Jack is only man whose breakfast conversation is not limited to tax (Dad), Ninja Turtles (James), or groaning (Sad Ed). Was tempted to ask if could stay for lunch too but remembered had *flâneur*ing to do in town. Jack says am welcome back any time though. Which is excellent as apparently he can also do Eggs Benedict (also banned chez Riley due to Hollandaise sauce being chief perpetrator of food poisoning, according to *Which* magazine). Plus we have nice time when we are not busy being all minty with each other about ONE issues. Experimentation is definitely way forward.

4 p.m.
Though do not think *flâneur*ing in town is. No one lost in poetic thought, only usual mental trances. Plus got

questioned as to reasons for lurking on bench by PC Doone, Marjory PI, and James (on shopping trip with Mad Harry and Mrs Mad Harry to buy fun fur for gladiator outfits).

. . . .

Tuesday 19

11 a.m.

Oh God. Have just witnessed horrendous sight. It is James and Mad Harry in furry leopard pants. Cannot believe Mum is not stopping them. It is operatics. It has taken over her life already. She is neglecting her child-rearing duties in favour of singing about someone called Sandra Dee who is 'lousy with virginity'. Cannot watch either display any longer. Am going round Sad Ed's. And if he not in will just sit in darkened corner of Waitrose car park. Reuben Tull may be stoned and think God is a futuristic Alsatian but he is marginally less disturbing.

4 p.m.

Was right about Sad Ed. He spent four hours trying to squeeze into a wedding suit in Moss Bros. Asked what he had gone for. He said his choice was limited due to his 'unique build', i.e. shortness and roundness, and he is going for pale blue and ruffles. He says it is exactly like the one Jamie Oliver wore when he married Jools. Said it sounds more like one Elton John wore when he married David Furnish and that pale colours will only accentuate his 'unique build'. Then he accused me of being unsupportive. At which point accused him of being idiot as he is not getting married in a baby blue suit or any suit for that matter as wedding is giant charade.

Spent rest of day reading *An Introduction to the European Union*. Which is not experimental, but is partly French, and at least does not feature schoolboys in fur pants or forty-somethings pretending to be lovestruck sixteen year olds.

. . . .

Wednesday 20

Thank God. James and Mad Harry have given up on being gladiators for time being. It is partially due to pant irritation (fake fur has brought Mad Harry out in genital rash) and partially due to total lack of gladiatorial powers. James says he is going to stick to philosophy for a bit. He is confident of being on par with Derrida by end of year.

. . . .

Thursday 21

Went round Jack's again today for brunch (scrambled eggs with parsley garnish). Asked how Scarlet was getting on in Cornwall, spiritual home of UKIP and all things backward. He said she is having excellent time and she and Hilary are busy converting the Cleggs to the cause. Said that was waste of time. Jack said they have given up on Grandpa Clegg who, according to Hilary, is

unreconstructed Thatcherite with Powellian ambitions (personally thought he was just moany old racist). But that they are making progress with Granny Clegg. Apparently Scarlet says she has been repressed by Grandpa Clegg's patriarchal regime and that she may look like a weak old lady, but that under the housecoat lurks the beating heart of a true suffragette. Said she is wrong and all that lurks under the housecoat is a saggy woman with a Viennetta habit. Which made Jack laugh. Although was not actually meant as joke. Is true.

Did not do any *flâneur*ing. Watched *Ugly Betty* repeats with Jack instead. Which is almost the same. Why oh why can I not meet someone like Henry, i.e. brainy, yet surprisingly good looking and with nice chest?

Friday 22

Have discovered reason for mysterious lack of Davey MacDonald activity. He is in Formentera with the rest of the MacDonalds. I got a postcard this morning. It says:

> Deer Rach
> Its well hot. Dad burned his nippel so bad a bit fell off. Wicked.
> Wish you was here,
> Davey ☺

I can safely say I do not share his sentiment, i.e. I

do not wish I was anywhere near Formentera, or the sight of his dad's 'nippel' scab. James has issued another ASBO-love warning. He tried to take it to higher authority but luckily higher authority too busy lip-synching to Olivia Newton John in mirror. I hope Dad is not this bad at work and neglecting his crucial paperclip stock-taking or whatever it is that he actually does in favour of doing Danny Zuko impressions at the water cooler. The shame.

6 p.m.
Apparently Dad is as bad. Mr Wainwright has threatened to promote Malcolm from IT above him if he doesn't stop knee skidding along the nylon carpet.

• •

Saturday 23
Still struggling at work with till of confusion. It has taken to using Hong Kong dollars instead of pounds. Rosamund says it has bad 'chi' and is going to burn a healing candle over it on Monday.

More worryingly, tomorrow is the big day, i.e. Saffron Walden amateur operatic audition madness. Mum and Dad did a full dress rehearsal before *Doctor Who* in front of specially invited audience, i.e. me, James, dog, and Riley senior household (i.e. Grandpa and Baby Jesus. Treena would have come but was down Queen Lizzie with her cousin Donna who is 'double mental'). Was awful. Is not

the singing, which is actually passable. Is horrendous attempts at being American teenagers, which is excruciating. Had to overrule honesty resolution when Mum asked for 'constructive criticism' (she does not mean constructive criticism, she means be nice). Said was truly groundbreaking. Baby Jesus and dog not so good at constructive criticism and sobbed/howled throughout proceedings. Grandpa Riley conveniently stunned into silence. Only person who actually enjoyed it was James who danced in the aisles (aka in between John Lewis nesting tables) in 'Greased Lightning', and actually shed tears during 'Hopelessly Devoted to You'. He has offered himself up as their manager to take them to new heights of stardom.

. . . .

Sunday 24
10 a.m.
Have gone back to bed. Is not French-style lounging. Is to escape audition madness downstairs. James is shouting 'fantastic fantastic fantastic' in demented John Barrowman fashion as Dad and Mum (in leather jackets, presumably left over from Clive and Marjory's bondage backing dancer *Chicago* stint) jive around the sofa singing 'I got chills'.

5 p.m.
Mum and Dad are back and are in vile moods. It is not

that they were awful (although Dad was, according to Mum, and Mum was, according to Dad) it is that Margot Gyp has fielded a ringer, i.e. she has persuaded Saffron Walden's only celebrity, i.e. the not-so-famous McGann brother, to try out. And if he is Danny, he will make sure Margot is Sandy, as he has been on waiting list at golf club for a year and it will seal the deal for membership. Dad says the dream is over. Personally do not think it ever really began. James Barrowman, on other hand, says he must never lose sight of his ambition and that a bit part in *Emmerdale* cannot compete with Dad's raw unschooled talent (it can). Anyway, it is all tenterhooks until next Sunday when the winners are announced. On plus side at least there will be no more horrendous 'wella wella wella uh'-ing for at least a week.

. . . .

Monday 25
Back to school

Am actually looking forward to school. It will be excellent for *flâneur*ing. Can just stand at nut dispensing machine in black vintage dress looking coquettish. Though not exactly sure what coquettish means. (Should probably have kept to French A level instead of politics. Politics not all cracked up to be. Seem to spend most of time trying to fathom point of Europe.) Will be enigmatic instead, i.e. look bored.

4 p.m.

Gave up on being coquettish at nut machine. Potential men too busy bulk purchasing Bombay Mix to respond to enigmatic antics. Scarlet said did not look enigmatic anyway, just looked retarded. Which is possibly why Mark Lambert offered me one of his 'tasty nuts'. As if I'd fall for that. Said hello to Davey MacDonald. But did not thank for card. Am still disturbed by scabby nipple image.

Scarlet is still insisting that Granny Clegg is not mental or bigoted by nature but is in fact a political powerhouse waiting to burst out of her elasticated trousers. Apparently she and Hilary went round several times last week (officially to restock Fray Bentos and unblock toilet, and unofficially to debrainwash her) and are slowly breaking through the layers of conservatism that have built up over the years from repeated exposure to Grandpa Clegg and the *Daily Mail*. Scarlet says I will be surprised at the new woman I see next time I visit St Slaughter. I doubt it. She will still have polyester slippers and tendency to say 'hooge'.

5 p.m.

Oh my God. Granny Clegg just rang to demand that Mum start boycotting the Jade Garden Chinese Restaurant in protest at Chinese occupation of Tibet. She says the Beijing Olympics is an historic opportunity to put the plight of the Tibetan people on the world stage. Scarlet

91

was right after all! Two weeks ago she thought Tibet was in Wales. I bet Grandpa Clegg is going mental. Although he probably supports the boycott. Not because he is sympathetic to Tibet, but because he is anti all foreign food. Anyway Mum has agreed.

7 p.m.
Oooh. Wonder if can persuade Mum to boycott sadistic dentist Mrs Wong on same grounds.

7.30 p.m.
Mum has declined. I said it was hypocritical to boycott one Chinese outlet and not another but Mum says she is not boycotting the Jade Garden because of Tibet. Or foreign food issues. It is because take-aways are evil, i.e. they are overpriced, trans-fat-ridden, and harbingers of e-coli. Whereas Mrs Wong is just overpriced.

. . . .

Tuesday 26
8.30 a.m.
Grandpa Clegg *is* going mental. He has just rung to demand that Mum has words with Granny Clegg over the arrival of a 'highbrow left-wing rag' at the breakfast table this morning. Mum said there is nothing wrong with the *Guardian*, bar the annoying Berliner size issue, and it might do him good to see other side of story for once. Grandpa said it is not *Guardian*, is *Daily Mirror*

and it has put him right off his Grape Nuts. Mum says she is not interfering in their relationship. The last time she did that was in 1995, over the infamous Judith Chalmers stand-off, and no one spoke to her for a month. Though frankly think that would be a bonus.

• •

Wednesday 27
4 p.m.
Philosophy ended in row again today. It is thorny issue of cloning and 'playing God'. Personally am not concerned whether people get to choose sex or hair colour of baby or clone them in their own image. Would mean end to unmanageable frizz etc., etc.

4.30 p.m.
Although possibly Mum would have chosen two Jameses instead of me. Or cloned herself and had a litter of small Mums. Oh God. World would be awful place with endless Cillit Banging or Googling. Am changing opinion. Is utterly allowed in philosophy. James is pro though. It is not that wants to clone self. It is dog. He wants to freeze it when it dies until it can be reincarnated as 'Hyperwolf'—part dog, part robot. Mum has refused. She says it's bad enough when it's alive, she cannot be expected to put up with its hairy expression leering out from the frozen peas when it's dead.

• •

Thursday 28

Is Dad's birthday tomorrow. And, as is leap year, is actual
official one, i.e. on 29th instead of substandard fake
birthday on 28th. But, more interestingly, is day when all
women are encouraged to propose to men, in stand
against traditional rules of romance. Scarlet says it is
media-manufactured nonsense and if she wanted to get
married, which she does not, because it is repressive act
that only perpetuates antiquated religious and patriarchal
mores, she would propose whenever she liked, instead of
waiting until GMTV offered her a slot to do it live on telly
just because it was 29th. She is right. Anyway have no
one to propose to. As usual. Although is excellent seizing day opportunity. Melody Bean should have waited
though. She could have got a free bridal makeover
thrown in if she'd done it in the studio with Kate
Garraway.

Friday 29

School is awash with seizing the day and general leap
year madness. Thin Kylie has proposed to Mark Lambert
and he has said yes! She did it outside the mobile science
lab with a glow-in-the-dark ring out of a packet of Coco
Pops. They are going to get proper ones from the Argos
catalogue later. Scarlet said it is pathetic and will be over
by Christmas when he snogs someone else or has fatal
minibike crash, and what was wrong with my eyes? Said

was despair at futility of it all. But was lie. Was utterly swept away by true chav romance. Sad Ed also happy. Though not at romance. He is just relieved that he has teen wedding rivals. He said Thin Kylie is bound to go for Wayne and Coleen style nuptials, which will detract attention from his and Melody's alternative ceremony. Pointed out there wasn't going to be a ceremony. He said 'Hmmm.' Said what does 'hmmm' mean. He said he thinks it might be easier to just go through with it and then get a divorce on grounds of non-consummation due to missing mojo. He is insane. Then missing mojo will be public, and Mrs Thomas, knowledge, and he could save himself humiliation, shouting, and colossal cost of wedding by just TELLING TRUTH NOW! He said I underestimate Melody's determination. Said I give up. The girl is mad though. Sad Ed is not that much of catch. I have seen his buttocks.

Dad not so seized with leap year madness. Although he is enjoying his heart-rate monitor (James) whilst watching *Lovejoy Christmas Special* DVD (me). Apparently it goes up massively every time Ian McShane appears. It is horror at mullet hairdo. He says he is saving Mum's present, i.e. celebration cake (wholemeal date and seed) for later. He is not. He is going to 'lose' it, i.e. feed it to dog.

march

FURRY
GLADIATOR →
PANTS

RESCUE
REMEDY

£20

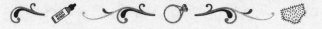

Saturday 1
St David's Day

Rosamund's candle-burning till chi remedy has failed. Till of confusion now not only unfathomable but has lumps of smelly wax all over it which means drawer now sticks, which means is also now till of death. On plus side, have only two weeks left until am debt-free. Hurrah! So can lavish money on fripperies instead of posting it into Mum's collection tin (WHSmith petty cash tin, locked, with keys stashed in unknown hidey hole) every week.

6 p.m.

Or save sensibly for my pension, as James has suggested.

. . . .

Sunday 2
Mothering Sunday

Mum utterly not excited by Mother's Day gift of packet of halva (on discount from Nuts In May due to partial packet breakage). Is because of operatic anticipation. I pointed out that it does not matter if she fails to be cast as Sandy as the most important role in the world is being a mother, which she already plays to great (and somewhat irritating) effect. James did not agree. He said mother-hood has stifled her ambition and thwarted her destiny and that this is her chance to find herself, and fame. He is still fully of belief that she and Dad are acting dynasty couple like Michael Douglas and Catherine Zeta

Jones. Or Chuckle Brothers. Which will be proven this afternoon.

5 p.m.

Mum and Dad are not acting dynasty. As predicted, main roles went to McGann and Margot Gyp. But is possibly more terrifying. They are Rizzo, the school slut, and hard heart-throb Kenickie. Which is most misled casting ever. Mum had not even seen a willy at age of sixteen, let alone got possibly pregnant by leather-clad stud. Marjory and Clive are the 'kooky' (i.e. fat) pink lady Jan and someone called Eugene. Who does not even get to sing. Which is more sensible all round. Mum is delighted though. She says it will be a real challenge to play the bad girl. Dad is also accepting defeat gracefully. It is not because he is relishing role. It is because Mike Majors is ugly rival gang leader Leo, i.e. not a stud. Pointed out that Leo gets to snog Rizzo. Dad not so graceful now. In fact is mental with Wandering Hands rage. Mum says he will have to rise above it as is only acting and no feelings are involved. Did not mention Jack *Bugsy Malone* stage kiss, when however hard tried not to let feelings get involved, was utterly swoony by end of it. Luckily James interrupted by reminding the Zeta-Jones-Douglases of other impending matter, i.e. secondary school admissions results are released online tomorrow. Mum has got the gloves and helmet out in readiness. She does not want to waste a minute of vital gloating time when James secures his place at St Gregory's

100

Girls, and future place in history as general boffin type, and Mad Harry ends up at Burger King Sports Academy.

. . . .

Monday 3

Tension at Shreddies table is utterly palpable. Mum is checking clock every few seconds. Although this is point-less as James has forbidden her to go online until he gets home from school so that he can share the joy. He has hidden Marigolds to ensure she does not cheat. Said she was not this het up when I was getting my place. She said James has more sensitive needs. He does not. He is just nerd. He is not worried though and has departed for St Regina's confident in the knowledge that he will be enjoying a state-of-the-art computer lab and hygienic toilet facilities in six months' time. Leaving me to endure germ-harbouring cracked bowls, and a Dell with a stolen shift key.

4 p.m.
The gloves and helmet are on. James is singing the *Star Wars* theme. The dog is jumping around like crazed crea-ture of hell.

4.15 p.m.
Gloves and helmet are off. Dog back under table chewing a shoe. A travesty has occurred. James has failed to secure a place at St Gregory's Girls and has been allocated to

substandard, unboffiny John Major High! Mum has already rung the council to point out mistake but Mr Lemon (formerly of housing department, now of education office) said it was actually not mistake and that is all down to catchment area and to please stop shrieking. James has stopped singing *Star Wars* theme, but is not completely despondent. He says his superior intellect will still out, even with broken locust tanks and second-rate teaching. Plus Mad Harry is going too. Mum has vowed to take it to appeal. And, failing that, move to Bishop's Stortford.

5 p.m.
Granny Clegg has rung. She says James's disappointment is inevitable consequence of abolition of grammar schools and catchments are fairest method in ultimately flawed system. Asked if she was reading script provided by Scarlet. She said no, she heard it on Radio 4 this morning! This is unprecedented news. Granny normally only listens to Pirate FM and shipping forecast (does not understand it, thinks it is mystical ancient language, plus it soothes Bruce). Maybe Scarlet was right and she is actually repressed Carla Bruni. Except in body of old woman.

· ·

Tuesday 4
8 a.m.
Mum is drawing up her appeal plan with military

102

precision. She has taken SatNav out of car to check exact distance door to door, and is also listing James's many and varied 'special' needs.

8.30 a.m.
Dad has rung to know where SatNav is as he is lost somewhere in Harlow and has been round same roundabout twenty-three times.

4 p.m.
Told Scarlet about James's school results. She asked how he is taking it. I said he is back to philosophical gladiating at moment as fallback in case his education now doomed. Scarlet said he is idiot because reality TV, game shows, and talent contests give the masses false hope that there is an easy way to money and happiness and that education is the only ladder out of poverty. I said except for Paul Potts. And Girls Aloud. And egghead Judith Keppel. So Scarlet thwacked me with a Grizzly Bar.

5 p.m.
She has a point though. James is no Cheryl Cole. He is one of the weirdos they let through just to humiliate them on live TV. And look at Granny Clegg. Prior to power of education she was borderline racist with Fray Bentos habit and now she is potential suffragette. Ooh, have had brainwave. Will elevate Davey MacDonald out of his council house by power of education. After few

months of political awakening he will be utterly Hilaryesque (one l, penis). It is brilliant. He is utter blank canvas, literature- (and most things) wise and I can mould my ideal man. Am like Mary Shelley and he is my Frankenstein's Monster. Hurrah! Will start tomorrow by agreeing to meet him out of school hours. Where no one can see us.

. . . .

Wednesday 5

Have arranged to meet Davey. Is out of school hours, but is very much in public. It is at party at football club hut on Saturday night, to celebrate Thin Kylie and Mark Lambert's engagement. Agreed on grounds that will be dark, and everyone will be drunk, so they will either not see us together, or be too busy trying not to be sick on dance floor to care. Also, have made clear that agreement is not green light to start groping my bra or pants region yet. He will have to pass tests first. He said he definitely does not have chlamydia because Leanne Jones got tested and she is totally clear. I said not that sort of test. Although is reassuring to know his penis is infection-free given that he has been known to wave it around in crowded areas. Though not so reassuring he actually said cholera not chlamydia.

. . . .

Thursday 6

Sad Ed has changed his mind about Britcher/Lambert

104

nuptials being welcome diversion. Melody is determined not to be outdone and is demanding a party of their own. Sad Ed has agreed as long as they don't actually call it engagement party. It is at Melody's on Saturday night. He is begging me and Scarlet to go as reinforcements. Said I had prior engagement at REAL engagement party, i.e. where givers are actually going to wed. He says if that's the way I feel then Scarlet can be best man. Have agreed to make appearance. Do not want to lose potential as best man, even if is only hypothetical. And am not man.

. . . .

Friday 7
Grandpa Riley has rung and is mad with excitement. He has been watching Crufts and thinks dog may actually not be hairy, valueless mongrel but pedigree Otterhound with star, and money-making, potential. He is booking it in for assessment with Official Otterhound Society (Essex branch) next week. He is making mistake. Dog is not pedigree. Is moronic mix possibly including orang-utan and amoeba.

. . . .

Saturday 8
6 p.m.
Could not concentrate at work due to impending political education appointment with Davey MacDonald. Not entirely sure that Thin Kylie engagement party is the

right setting though—chances of overdosing on bacardi and Hi-Tecs quite high. Rosamund has given me a bottle of herbal Rescue Remedy. Is not actual drug. Is just calming flowers etc. Have to put drop on tongue when am feeling anxious. Have had twenty so far. Thank God arranged to meet Davey at football club. James is already suspicious. He asked why I was going to celebrate such an ill-conceived union, i.e. Thin Kylie and Mark Lambert. Which even if is not divorce statistic in a year, has no hope of producing genetically superior offspring. He is genetics obsessed at moment. It is the dog cloning Hyperwolf thing. He is hoping to develop a method to isolate its eating gene and make a man who can eat an entire fridge. Anyway, said was celebrating seizing of day, not teen marriage per se, and that his attitude on eugenics was bordering on fascism. He said is not. Is just common sense. Did not mention Melody Bean and Sad Ed engagement party. The genetic implications there are quite scary.

12 midnight

Am home. Evening has been education. Though possibly not for Davey MacDonald. Have learnt several things:

a) Rescue Remedy does not work. Had taken fifty-eight drops by the time I got to the football club and was feeling sicker than when started. Then Davey saw me with pipette thingy in mouth and accused me of being on drugs. I said, *i*) not actual drug is only herbal, and *ii*) I would hardly think he minded. But

he said, *i*) is made-up then, and *ii*) he had never done any drugs, not even snorting iron tablets (briefly in vogue amongst more idiotic Criminals and Retards) because what is point when cider is cheaper and legal. Said was not strictly legal as he is only seventeen. He said actually no he is eighteen. Said no he is seventeen. He said no is eighteen as was kept down a year. Said is it dyslexia? He said no, is thickness. Plus the penis-revealing thing.

b) Alcohol does work. Had several halves of Magners, purchased by genuine older man, i.e. Davey, and was instantly calmer. And much better at dancing too.

c) Davey also not approving of teen marriage. I said exactly, as marriage is defunct institution, which is repressive to women, and does not even come with tax advantages any more (cunningly combining Scarlet's and Dad's theories on subject). He said, whatever, she will be bored in a year and trying it on with Liam O'Grady again. Said which one. He said all.

At that point said had to go to other engagement party, which also doomed, but not actually real, so not as bad. He said he would walk me. Said am modern woman and can walk by self thank you very much. He said am girl and can not walk on own unless look like Fat Kylie. Plus he needed to go to offie for fags.

Quite liked caveman approach. Although was worried his penis-revealing antics might rear their ugly head.

Literally. But walk was thankfully penis-free. Said he was welcome to come to party (as would be excellent opportunity to integrate him with best friends and let Scarlet use her powers of political education) but he said he'd rather watch Casey and Dane set fire to football club than goths and fat emos swaying to crap music. And anyway, wasn't Sad Ed gay? Said sadly not, as it would solve several mojo- and marriage-related issues, plus had been hoping for Gay Best Friend for years.

Said goodbye on corner of street. He tried to do kiss but managed to dart head to side so he only got mouthful of hair. He said, 'What's up, Riley, you weren't so shy before.' Said yes but was temporarily overcome with resolution madness and am not ready to seize day, (or Davey), again yet. (May take weeks, or months, before he is fully reborn. Have not even begun to deal with wardrobe issues.)

He has point about hanging out with goths and emos though. Melody Bean's dining room was like crowd scene from Tim Burton movie. But was not there for fun but purely to show face at fake engagement party. So can be fake best man. And pick up pieces when bridegroom admits to all fakeness and bride has meltdown. Though am worried about scale of potential meltdown. Melody Bean is marriage mad. Cannot believe Mr and Mrs Bean do not know what is going on. One of her bedroom walls is covered in cut-outs from *Brides* magazine. Which is only marginally less disturbing than the wall that is covered in Sad Ed cut-outs. Reuben Tull liked it though.

108

He lay on the floor staring at it through a pint glass until he got paranoid that all the Sad Eds were going to attack him and had to be talked down by Scarlet.

Sad Ed is also depressed at the scale of it all. The number of bridesmaids has gone up from four minigoths to twenty-three and Melody is also talking about arriving on the back of the black stallion with all the bridesmaids in a winged chariot. Said they will not fit in. He said that not point. Is that it is getting harder and harder to keep it a secret. Especially as Melody gave his home number to a catering company and they keep ringing to ask if he prefers traditional fruit cake or a chocolate profiterole pyramid. He told his mum it was just random market research calls. It is lucky he is glutton and so is entirely plausible. Asked what he preferred. He said profiteroles.

Sunday 9
2 p.m.
Sad Ed has been round all morning. Thought was to spend quality time with best friend (he is my second best friend, but I am his first best friend. Is excellent arrangement. For me anyway) but was only to escape Melody, her twenty-three bridesmaids, and the black stallion dream. He said he would not choose to spend several hours listening to my mother singing about being 'trashy and no-good' unless times were desperate. He is right. Is a horrifying performance. Just hope the director

(i.e. Russell Rayner, closet homosexual, golf club resident professional, once in Erasure video) has the talent, and endurance, to deal with her. Though fear not. Performance is only in eight weeks. Anyway, was productive, despite sound of James urging Mum to 'notch it up a level' echoing up the stairs. Told Ed he should suggest to Melody that they elope to Gretna Green instead. Which is like Las Vegas, but in Scotland. Is utterly romantic, money-saving, and, by definition, secret. Sad Ed says am genius. Hurrah!

Monday 10

Sad Ed says am not genius. Plan has backfired horribly. Melody has agreed to eloping idea, but, now that no planning of winged chariot or profiterole tower involved, she wants to do it on her birthday, i.e. next month. Have said sorry. But also that is not entirely my fault as am not idiot that agreed to marry her in first place to avoid dealing with missing mojo issue. Have volunteered services as best woman to make up for it. Said, as his first best friend, is least I can do. He said thanks but is not that easy as Scarlet, who is also claiming best friend status, has put herself forward for role. Said it was an outrage as *a*) I am actual best friend, and *b*) Scarlet does not even believe in marriage. He said, *a*) actually we are both equal best friends, and *b*) I said I was anti-marriage too. I said, *a*) that is slight shock and will be revising own friend list forthwith, and *b*) I was only parroting Scarlet's opinions and actually think marriage is ultimate romantic gesture, especially if also involves suicide à la Romeo and Juliet. He said Oh. Anyway he has gone home to draw up list of my and Scarlet's attributes so he can choose best woman to be best man. Will win obviously.

. . . .

Tuesday 11

8 a.m.

Mum is in bad mood. It is not *Grease*-related for once but is Delia Smith, original domestic goddess (as opposed to pretender Nigella who is just heaving bosoms and flashy gadgets), and her new 'How to Cheat' TV series! Mum, who is anti-cheating at any time says it is a symptom of the decline of the BBC, and society in general. James agrees. He says it is a betrayal and is writing to Mark Thompson (Director General of BBC) and Gordon Brown to complain. Said Gordon probably had more important things to worry about than tinned mince. As do I. Though is not economic decline. Is battle of the best men. Though am confidently expecting to triumph by double English. Will serve Scarlet right for stealing Hilary and forcing me to create my own.

4 p.m.

Am not best man yet. Sad Ed says it is a trickier decision than he thought. I said what is tricky about it? I am reliable, my hair looks good in weddingy up-do, plus am not likely to object at last minute due to militant feminist tendencies. Scarlet said, *au contraire*, she would overcome her desire to stop proceedings because supporting her *best* friend was more important. I said I thought I was her best friend. She said she has reconsidered following the Hilary hoo-ha and anyway she thought Davey MacDonald was my new best friend. Said he is not friend. Is social experiment. And how did she know about him anyway? She said Tracey Hughes (mum answers phone at police station) saw us doing the macarena at Thin Kylie's engagement party. Do not remember that. Must have blocked from memory. Anyway, at that point some of the new but unimproved Criminals and Retards set the fire alarm off (proving that it is genetically inbuilt) so had to shiver on the sheep field for half an hour and was too busy conserving energy to argue. But am now in shock as started week with two best friends and now have potentially none.

. . . .

Wednesday 12

Have made decision to downgrade Scarlet and bump Ed up to first best friend. Now he will have to choose me. Plus have stolen packet of Duchy Chocolate Butterscotch biscuits from cupboard as bribe. They are his favourites but Mrs Thomas does not buy them because Aled prefers macaroons.

5 p.m.

Sad Ed not swayed by upgrading or biscuits. Says is still racked by indecision and is like choosing between Morrisey and Leonard Cohen. Plus Mum now in forensic hunt for missing biscuits. I said was dog (habitual biscuit thief) but she says is not dog as he does not like butterscotch (but will eat brillo pad). Said was James. She said he is too short to reach cupboard. Plus he is joining in the hunt. Am not concerned. She will never work it out. Have carefully concealed trail of evidence, i.e. biscuits in Sad Ed's tummy and empty packet in Sad Ed's bag.

. . . .

Thursday 13

Scarlet trumped the Duchy Chocolate Butterscotch biscuits and brought Sad Ed a dozen homemade Nigella-recipe triple chocolate nut muffins (in contrast to Mum, Suzy is definite fan of heaving bosoms and flash gadgets). Cannot compete with that. Even dog rejected Mum's celebration seed cake. It dropped it on kitchen tile and caused minor cracking. Have resigned self to being second best friend and not at all best woman.

Also Mum still consumed with missing biscuit mystery. Dad is currently suspect Number One. Mum says it is not her he is cheating, it is himself, with his potential cholesterol issues. He says he is cheating nobody and is in fact eschewing all fatty products in bid to lose middle-aged paunch before playing decidedly non-middle-aged

Kenickie. She is not convinced and says he cannot have pudding. Is yoghurt. So no loss.

. . . .

Friday 14

An excellent thing has happened. In fact three excellent things. 1) Am best woman. Thanks to 2) Davey MacDonald, who may well be idiot savant after all as opposed to plain idiot. Bumped into him in oven chip queue at lunch and explained entire best woman hoo-ha and he said why not just have two? Mark Lambert is having Davey and Darryl Stamp. Is stroke of genius! Though possibly not for Mark Lambert—speeches will be potentially horrendous. And 3) We have all agreed to reinstate each other as equal best friends so there is no confusion any more. Is slightly annoying that Scarlet is also best woman. But I get to be ring bearer so am slightly more equal. Ha! Though mainly because Scarlet says she is allergic to any contact with non-precious metals.

On downside, Mum has identified biscuit thief, i.e. me. Was not cunning forensics though. Was Sad Ed, who came round after school and said, 'Got any more of those butterscotch things?' Mum said she cannot afford to lose entire packets in the current economic climate and offered him a digestive or a rich tea finger. He went home for macaroons instead. Have agreed to pay Mum £2.49 to cover cost of biscuits. Which means will not be debt-free

until 3 p.m. as opposed to 2 p.m. Is minor setback. Will still be cash rich by end of tomorrow.

• •

Saturday 15
6 p.m.

Hurrah. Am liquid again (cunning financial speak for having actual money). But debt-free status is not without potential threat. Mr Goldstein (of similar paranoid persuasion as Mum) is also concerned with economic climate and has issued a warning that there may be cutbacks in the coming months if Gordon Brown does not pull his finger out, i.e. compulsory redundancies. Is bound to be me for the chop. Rosamund is older, is not afraid of till, and has vast experience of herbal remedies and health-foods given that she is vegan and ailment-ridden. Plus she does not come back from lunch break with trolley-related injuries to fingers that mean she cannot lug lentil sacks for several hours. Is last time I let Reuben Tull push me down spiral ramp. All drugs have left him with inability to judge distance from wall. Sad Ed is far better herder. He is slower, but does not crash so frequently.

• •

Sunday 16
10 a.m.

Mum's recession panic is mounting following study of *Times* money section. She says banks are dropping like flies and she is thinking of withdrawing her life savings and keeping them in a shoebox. James has warned her not to regress to Clegg-style money madness. Pointed out that her security arrangements are stricter than Barclays.

2 p.m.
Mum changed mind about shoebox. Is not James's Clegg argument. Is because dog has eaten a twenty pound note that Dad had left out to pay window cleaner. Her window locks and alarms may be state of art but dog is most definitely not. Is complete security threat.

Grandpa, who was round for lunch, said to stop shouting at dog as is harmful to pedigree animals to be treated like ruffians. He is taking it for its Otterhound assessment tomorrow and says he is hopeful dog will be key to surviving downturn as will potentially rake in fortune from shows/stud fees. Mum says it is pointless as even if dog is Otterhound, which it is not, is worthless as *a*) is too disobedient to be in show, and *b*) has had genitals removed so cannot pass on pedigree. Grandpa says if that is case then he may well have grounds to sue Mum for lost sperm.

Did not get involved in absurd sperm wars. There is no point as dog will not pass test. Is not pedigree. Pedigree dogs do not look like Chris Moyles.

* *

Monday 17
St Patrick's Day
As predicted, dog is not key to fortune. Otterhound

Society (Essex branch) says it is in no way related to their superior breed as its face is too long, its legs are too short, and it has asymmetrical ears. Grandpa said that is only where Bruce ate a bit of one of them in a fight over a plastic octopus. But they were not moved. Felt bit sorry for dog having to listen to all its faults being listed. Grandpa said it did not mind as it was still chewing the liquorice toffee he gave it to persuade it to get on bus to Chelmsford in first place. Plus it is used to being called variety of insulting names, e.g. hairy idiot, moron, and prize pest, on regular basis.

. . . .

Tuesday 18

Philosophy today all about moral relativism, i.e. bad things for good ends, e.g. euthanasia. Mum very pro-euthanasia. Think she is keen to dispatch Cleggs asap. Mum not so keen on Reuben Tull's answer to moral right or wrong of achieving ultimate happiness, which was to put mind-altering drugs in the water system. She is pro-fluoride but think she would struggle with Ecstasy on tap. I said was not aiming to achieve ultimate happiness as pain is part of all great literature, e.g. *Wuthering Heights*.

Saw Davey at nut dispensing machine after lesson (not buying nuts, he does not consume healthfood, just watching to see who got the mouldy apple that has been in there for a fortnight. He has 40p on Alan Wong). Asked

what he'd been up to. He said, 'Bricks and stuff.' Gordon
Brown is wrong. A BTEC is not like three A levels at all.
I said I had been discussing whether pain was an essential
part of life and literature. He said, 'My mum's got them
sort of books.' So maybe is actually not in house full of
Chat magazine and *Gun Monthly* but library of Brontës and
Thomas Hardy.

. . . .

Wednesday 19

9 a.m.
Davey MacDonald not in house full of Brontës. He
brought in one of the 'pain' books for me. It is by Marquis
de Sade, i.e. is about sex. I said no thanks.

3 p.m.
Scarlet said I should have borrowed book. She says it is
eye- and mind-opening and is considered a literary classic. I said, 'Yes, by Suzy,' (who is great fan of 'pain' and all
things sex-related). She said in fact by entire forward-
thinking world. Have borrowed book after all.

7 p.m.
Mum has confiscated book pending its return to Suzy and
said if she finds me reading filth again she will have to
consider calling in reinforcements, i.e. Auntie Joyless and
her Christian army. I said it is considered a classic by
entire forward-thinking world. Mum said not in this

house it is not. Did not tell her it wasn't Suzy's. If she finds out about ASBO love experiment she will possibly implode.

. . . .

Thursday 20

Hurrah it is Good Friday tomorrow, i.e. no school. We are going to see *Juno*, which is compulsory viewing in common room. Admittance to saggy sofa is now strictly for those who can say 'homeskillet' with confidence. Mum is not happy as according to her sources (Marjory) it glorifies teen pregnancy and I will be possibly with child within minutes of watching. As if. There is nothing cool or in any way enviable about being pregnant at school. Look at Emily Reeve. She is still a stone overweight and her nipples will never be the same. Have asked Davey to come. Hopefully tale of geeky but brilliant types will seep into brain and he will be listening to the Moldy Peaches by Saturday instead of 50 Cent.

James not coming to cinema as is *a*) too young, *b*) of same mind as Mum concerning teen pregnancy films, and *c*) on revived gladiatorial duty with Sabre aka Mad Harry. They are going to do muscle building in James's bedroom. Am glad am not in house as is potentially terrifying. Melody Bean is not coming either. Sad Ed says there is no way he is letting her get ideas about babies. Said he was being paranoid as film will not in any way make intelligent teenagers want babies but he is not moved.

He has told her he is spending day writing his vows instead.

. . . .

Friday 21
Good Friday
6 p.m.

Oh my God, I *am* Juno: i.e. cool-talking music buff type. Although obviously am not pregnant. Though think life would be utterly more interesting if were. Even clothes did not look too sacky. In fact Topshop do maternity wear now so would possibly look better pregnant than not as wardrobe currently depleted due to previous debt. Plus washing machine chewed up one of dresses after time Jesus climbed inside to poke Rice Krispies through holes in drum. And Juno is excellent goddess name. Like Venus or Dido. Whereas Rachel is utterly dull. If do get pregnant will call daughter Juno. Or possibly Olympia.

Davey MacDonald not entirely in agreement about seminal nature of film. In fact slept through most of it. Possibly as is first movie he has seen that is not either *a*) cartoon or *b*) involving Steven Segal and enormous weaponry. Plus he was up late last night revving cars on Barry Island. Scarlet not thrilled about his presence. She says he smells of chav, i.e. Burberry Brit. Said that was very non-mass-embracing of her but she says it is not non-mass-embracing just that she is allergic to non-organic perfume. Pointed out that at least he met us at

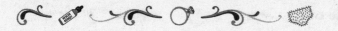

cinema and did not squish into sick-smelling Volvo. Though perhaps would have killed off vomit odour finally. Its persistence is staggering.

Got home to find Gazelle and Sabre (aka James and Mad Harry) on sofa under blanket with cups of Lucozade (and strict instructions not to spill any on floor on pain of death). James said they were merely replacing lost joules from all the muscle-building and under the blanket their biceps were bulging magnificently as we spoke. Did not look in case they were also wearing furry gladiator pants but got truth from Dad who said Harry strained his groin after two lunges and James got bitten when he tried to weightlift the dog. Is lucky Mum was out at Marjory's having a character building Pink Ladies pyjama party (aka thermal nightgown party and no actual slumber involved due to Marjory having the spare room redecorated and a general aversion to zed beds).

7 p.m.
Mum is back from pyjama party. Said it was somewhat early for a hard-drinking hard-smoking girl gang. Mum said Frenchy (aka Mrs Noakes (bad perm, calls trousers 'slacks', works on Waitrose deli counter)) wanted to get home for *Gardener's World*.

. . . .

Saturday 22
Jack was at work today. It is because Rosamund has

gone to Wales for Easter. Not for egg-based celebration but to tend to mother's many ailments. He asked what I thought of *Juno*. Said it was forshizz excellent. He nodded and said, 'So what's with you and Davey MacDonald then? Didn't think it was his type of film. Or that he was your type of boy.' I said *a*) nothing is with me and Davey MacDonald it was just one trip, and *b*) how do you know if it is his type of film, have you even seen it? He said *a*) you also took him to Thin Kylie's party, and *b*) yes I have. So I said *a*) are you keeping tabs on me? *b*) Davey is a sort of social experiment, am trying to create perfect combination of political awareness and brawn, and *c*) what's your favourite line? He said *a*) As if. Scarlet told me, *b*) why can't you just let Davey be Davey? and *c*) where Mac Macguff says, 'Good mood, bad mood, ugly, pretty, handsome, what-have-you. The right person is still going to think the sun shines out of your ass.' Then he went off to stack the glucosamine before could reply.

He is wrong anyway. Cannot let Davey be Davey. Do not fancy him enough in current form. He is completely un-Paulie-like. Plus the best bit is where Juno says, 'Being pregnant makes me pee like Seabiscuit.' Even Davey laughed.

Would be nice to find someone who thought sun shone out of my ass though. Even with my uncontrollable hair and impossible mother.

Sunday 23
Easter Day
10 a.m.

Hurrah, it is Easter Day, i.e. licence to eat cheap chocolate in vast quantities, as opposed to the rest of the year when bars of Green and Blacks are broken into small squares and doled out one at a time like a scene from wartime rationing. And Mum and Dad are at operatics this afternoon so even exhortations to be sensible and save some for tomorrow will be null and void. Plus, after years of experience, can safely say that is better to do all in one go because after a week you cannot face any more hydrogenated fat without feeling sick and so is waste as dog always gets it. Only have three eggs though—from Mum and Dad, James, and Baby Jesus. Granny Clegg obviously too busy listening to Radio 4 and reading *Das Kapital* to go to Trago Mills for cut price sweatshop confectionery.

4 p.m.

Have another egg! Is not from Scarlet (boycotting Easter due to Cadbury's moving factories to Far East) or Sad Ed (ate one he was going to give to me in emergency low-sugar episode during *The Wire* last night). Is from Davey MacDonald. He brought it over after lunch. Luckily Mum and Dad were busy at Rydell High with Marjory PI and James was at Mad Harry's doing a gladiatorial egg challenge. No idea what it involves but suspect they will fail, as usual. Davey was definitely angling to come in. But feared Mum would use spooky sixth sense and sniff out presence of chav somehow, so restricted access to front garden only. He said it was 'well nice'. Compared to his, which is mostly concrete and a bit of leftover car, I suppose it is. But was only small talk as obviously neither of us interested at all in shrubbery or pea gravel. Was delaying tactics for kiss. But did not want to do kiss. On several grounds. Mostly that do not fancy him and am scared mojo will not move. So said had to go and sorry for not getting him an egg then shut door in panic. Experimenting with Mr Right Now is more complicated than thought. Is shame about failed Dean Denley thing. At least he likes The Doors so half the challenge is done.

5 p.m.
As predicted James failed his gladiatorial challenge, i.e. eating fourteen crème eggs and half a giant Toblerone. He has been sick twice and is now in bed. Said did not think chocolate-eating was actual part of TV show. He said it is weight gain programme. Mum's diet is too balanced and he has not bulked up at all since January. Then he had to be sick again. So no bulking up there either. Hope he is better by tomorrow. It is his birthday and he likes to be fighting fit for examination of gifts. Have got him DVD of *Spartacus*, i.e. actual real gladiators, as opposed to idiot eleven year olds in furry pants. Or lycra-clad pinheads on Sky One.

Monday 24

Easter Monday

10 a.m.

James absent from birthday breakfast table (featuring special celebratory real tablecloth, as opposed to usual wipe-clean surface). He has been compromised by yesterday's egg consumption. Though has told Mum it is norovirus. Birthday outing to Mole Hall Wildlife Park to see exciting new exhibit of flamingo postponed until further notice.

2 p.m.

Have delivered invalid's lunch of Marmite on crackers to James. He asked where Mum was. Said she was antibacterially cleaning surfaces to avoid cross-infection.

5 p.m.

James has emerged from sick bed and is on sofa with Dad and dog watching *Spartacus*. Mum has installed precautions including emergency bowl and plastic matting. And she has had three Yakults in last hour. Said James should admit to egg mania and put Mum out of her misery. He said *au contraire*, she lives for hygiene emergencies as it gives her a chance to show off her skills. He is possibly right.

7 p.m.

James revived by gladiating film. Both he and Dad claiming to be Spartacus. Said neither of them looked at all like

Kirk Douglas. James gave me withering look and said am cinematic heathen. Am getting tired of being accused of being emotionally and filmically illiterate etc., etc. Am utterly versed in all matters creative and brain-based. And am right about Spartacus. If anyone is Spartacus, it is dog. It has cleft in chin and absurd hair.

. . . .

Tuesday 25

Saw Davey in common room at lunch today. He was not on saggy sofa (due to refusal to say forshizz every other word), was in kettle corner preparing nutritious meal of microwave cheeseburger. Think possibly losing battle experiment wise.

. . . .

Wednesday 26

4 p.m.

Common room, and country, has gone mad for French first lady Carla Bruni aka Mrs Sarkozy. She is living proof that you can be political, poetic, and look like supermodel. I bet Lembit Opik is kicking himself for not aiming higher and only going for Cheeky Girl. Maybe I am not Juno after all but am destined to be Carla Bruni type, i.e. brainy, with legs to die for, and ability to play more than 'House of Rising Sun' on guitar.

5 p.m.

Although am only 158 centimetres and cannot even

play 'Bobby Shaftoe'. Will stick to Juno. Short, average-looking, and prone to mishap.

5.15 p.m.
Although even she can play guitar. Is obviously essential instrument. Will ask for one immediately.

5.30 p.m.
Mum has refused on grounds still have clarinet gathering dust in cupboard and three recorders in James's bedroom being used for God knows what (answer: pipes of pan during Elvish phase). Said was utterly committed and would not cease practising until had secured record deal à la Kate Nash. She said I said that about the clarinet, and flower pressing, and the majorettes. Which is true. But said was different this time. But Mum says there are to be no new hobbies until economic climate on upturn. Said what about operatics. She said that is different as does not involve purchase of expensive props or costumes. They are all being recycled from *Chicago* and 1996 production of *Showboat* (the mind boggles). Will ask for guitar for birthday instead. Will still be into it in August as is not passing phase but definite commitment.

· ·

Thursday 27
Have gone off guitar. Scarlet says is passé and ukelele is instrument of moment. Do not want to play that as may

be instrument of moment but also is instrument of embarrassment. Look like mental giant holding one of those. Dean Denley could take it up though. On him it would look relatively normal. Whereas he still has to sit on three cushions to do the drums.

Also Granny Clegg has rung. It is Carla Bruni. She is causing hoo-ha in St Slaughter. Not literally. Do not think state visit includes visiting former disused playgrounds and a Spar. Is that Cleggs are split in their support for poetic/political first lady, i.e. Granny Clegg is very much for and Grandpa is against. He is against all things European. And feminist. And all poetry, unless it is of 'hilarious' limerick variety. Granny says she is tiring of his backward attitude and is minded to move into the spare room with Bruce. Mum told her not to overreact and that she has put up with his jingoism, and feet, for fifty years, so a few more won't make a difference. Granny says she is not so sure. But has agreed to wait a week when Carla will be safely out of country and political wives will be back to wearing Hush Puppies and Marks & Spencers instead of Chanel and Louboutins. Plus Hilary is coming to Scarlet's for the holidays so her personal Karl Marx will be off limits. She will be back to the *Daily Mail* and Viennetta in a fortnight.

Am reinspired by Granny Clegg's torment though. If she can be awakened then there is hope for Davey. Will recommence experiment forthwith.

. . . .

Friday 28

Last day of school

But not yet. Davey is going to Sciathos for a week. Why is it that Riley household travel arrangements consist of Cornwall once a year, and that is usually torturous, whereas Britchers, O'Gradys, and MacDonalds of world spend half of lives enjoying exotic foreign climes, e.g. Florida, Bahamas, and Benidorm?

Davey said he would write. Have said do not. Even with Mum busy handjiving all week, James will come down on me like tonne of bricks.

. . . .

Saturday 29

Jack was at work again today. Pointed out to Mr Goldstein that I do not take endless days off to tend to my ailing Welsh mother (although she is so fortified with vitamins and Yakult cannot remember last time she was actually ill). Mr Goldstein said *a*) she not in Wales, she is in Sudbury at Vitamin D conference, and *b*) economic downturn is beyond his control. Jack said is not true. Mr Goldstein says it is, she got the bus at eight this morning. Jack said not the vitamin conference, the belief that he has no ability to sway financial destiny, and is mistake to sack workers as business will be compromised and income will fall even further. In fact what he needs is to raise game. Mr Goldstein said is not a game. Is serious business. And went back to pricing up Buzz Gum.

129

Think my fate as one of jobless millions is sealed. Will start search for alternative employment next week in anticipation of gloom. Is better to resign than be sacked.

. . . .

Sunday 30
Summer Time begins (i.e. clocks go forward)
11 a.m.
Thank God have one less hour of Sunday. Think twenty-four is too much. Already have had to endure Mum and Dad practising Rizzo and Kenickie snogging scene over Fruit 'n' Fibre, and James getting dog to pull him round garden on gladiator chariot, aka Toys 'R' Us plastic sledge. Is house of idiots. Am almost glad to be decamping to Riley senior establishment this afternoon.

4 p.m.
Was right. In surprise reversal of fortunes, Whiteshot Estate in fact far more educational than Summerdale Road for once. Grandpa very au fait with Mr Right Now theory, as has been reading all about it in *Cosmo*. Said did not think Treena got *Cosmo*. He said she doesn't. He has started buying as beauty news is of superior quality to *Glamour*, plus is full of sex. Anyway, Grandpa says am wasting time trying to mould Davey MacDonald. Should just accept him for what he is, i.e. man candy, and use him for his body, like Jennifer Aniston and Vince Vaughn. Said did not like Grandpa using words like 'man

130

candy'. He said 'shag bunny?' Said not to use any words at all.

Grandpa right that Davey MacDonald does in fact have nice body, due to brief and ill-fated stint as ballet dancer. But still do not think want to 'use' it. Am not shallow user. Am more interested in beautiful mind.

4.15 p.m.
In combination with six pack and thighs of steel.

5.15 p.m.
Just hope can find beautiful mind in there somewhere among desire to melt stuff and eat Monster Munch.

. . . .

Monday 31
Like Hilary, now fully installed chez Stone. Had forgotten quite how muscly he is. In brain and body departments. Is utterly depressing that he is Scarlet's man candy. Is not shag bunny, have asked her and she said she is making him wait to test his commitment. Maybe if she makes him wait too long he will seek solace with me. Hurrah! Then will not have to create my own Hilary. Am going over later to discuss division of best woman duties. Will test waters by doing some French lounging. Would be utterly experimental to share boyfriend. Look at Dylan Thomas. He was doing it with Keira Knightley and Sienna Miller.

4 p.m.

Scarlet has instructed me to stop staring at Hilary as makes me look retarded. Plus she says am not Keira or Sienna but am bit-part jealous maid-type who cannot admit is actually better suited to stable boy.

On plus side, best woman duties are as follows: co-ordinate outfits (Scarlet). Check train timetable to Scotland (me). Getting married is cinch. Do not know why people make such a fuss.

Tuesday 1

April Fool's Day

9 a.m.

Awoke to 'hilarious' April Fool breakfast of gruel with suspicious black things on top. Have not eaten. Have gone back to bed until Mum is back from whatever it is she is doing and has shouted at James for meddling where he is not wanted, i.e. food management.

10 a.m.

Was not April Fool. Was new recession-busting regime, as declared by James. There is to be no more luxury muesli or Duchy Originals marmalade. It is health-giving porridge and 'fresh, wild fruits of the forest' (aka some partially defrosted blackberries from the bottom of the freezer) from now on. Said temporary economy drive possibly threatening permanent hygiene drive and they need to think long-term. But James says he has taken over control of the kitchen while Mum concentrates on her glittering stage career. Plus he says if gladiating fails he can be TV chef à la Jamie Oliver instead. He cannot. There is no way anyone would fantasize about him in their kitchen naked. Ick. Have done involuntary shudder at thought. Will escape to Riley senior household to wish Grandpa happy birthday. And avoid potentially minging lunch. James is going food foraging, in hope of unearthing truffles behind compost heap. Will be futile. Only things lurking behind there are slug trap and semi-digested tennis ball.

4 p.m.

Have given Grandpa Riley *Vogue*, *Marie Claire*, and *Chat* as birthday present (emergency purchase from Mr Patel's) so he can learn about peplums, Somalian refugees, and the woman who got anaphylactic shock from her Primark pants. Is essential this season reading. Got home to discover that Mum has regained control of kitchen. She says James is to be admired for his economy-drive skills, but not for his food foraging ones. There are no truffles, and lunch (nettle soup) resulted in borderline hospital emergency after James fell in nettle patch. He is now lying on plastic sheet on bed covered in layer of antihistamine cream, listening to *Harry Potter* CD. We have got liver for tea instead. Which is peasant-like and utterly economical. Plus does not sting.

. . . .

Wednesday 2

9 a.m.

It is utterly depressing. Am sixteen years old and should be at prime of style iconness, i.e. in black lace and Agent Provocateur underwear à la Daisy Lowe. But instead wardrobe consists entirely of M&S pants, grey T-shirts, meat lorry vintage dress, and rejected St Trinian's outfit, i.e. have NOTHING to wear to Sad Ed's wedding. Plus still have no money to buy anything due to frittering last week's wages on Grandpa's glossy magazine habit.

Although, traditionally, groom has to buy best man

outfit. Is brilliant plan. Will go to Waitrose and demand money from Sad Ed so do not show him up at altar.

3 p.m.

Sad Ed says there is no way he is footing bill for vintage Chanel dress. Or any dress for that matter. He is saving everything so he can stage his own disappearance after wedding and start a new life as Irish recluse. Or pay someone else to kill him as he is spectacularly rubbish at doing it himself. On plus side, have put name down on list for Saturday job at Waitrose. Is forward thinking back-up move, as advised by mad-eyebrowed Chancellor Alistair Darling, in case Mr Goldstein and his lentil emporium do not weather the economic storm long-term. Although will possibly be offered job within week as there were only two names above mine and one of those was an O'Grady. Plus I saw Reuben Tull crash his trolleys into a blue Lancia. I said that was hardly successful herding but Sad Ed says the Lancia belongs to Cormac Costain who owes Reuben fourteen pounds and an MGMT ticket so it was in fact expert handling as it totally looks like a scrape from the Yaris parked next door and Reuben will be blame-free.

* *

Thursday 3

Thank God James is off food duty and we are back to Cheerios and Shreddies. (Waitrose own brand though, i.e.

practically povvy. Have suggested Mum changes her supermarket of choice to Lidl but she says things are not that desperate yet.) James is still sticking to the gruel and old fruit regime though. He says it is what gave Madonna her muscle definition. Asked where he got that dubious fact. He said Grandpa Riley and his oracle *Grazia*. Am going to Scarlet's in minute for economy drive wardrobe planning. We are going to raid Suzy's vast closet of vintage designer wear. Is utterly brilliant plan as is bound to be full of OTM 1980s finds. (No idea what OTM stands for but Grandpa says is essential fashion speak and has replaced fashion-forward, which is totally last season. But then he also said I should embrace harem pants, which, as any fool knows, are not to be worn if are midget with hips, so am not entirely convinced of his role as withering non-Chinese Gok Wan man.)

4 p.m.
Am still outfit-less. There has been a crime against fashion chez Stone. It turns out that Suzy has been victim of fashion 'gurus' Trinny and Susannah, who took umbrage at her 'hot hippy' look during their turn on her sex sofa and sent a minion round to 'streamline' her wardrobe. All the spangly bust-revealing stuff has been replaced with severe capsule wardrobe more befitting TV star. So we have had rethink and are going shopping in Cambridge next week after I get paid. Scarlet is depressed though. She says Channel 5 fame is messing with Suzy's socialist

ideals and she will be joining golf club next. Said that would never happen and suggested a swing in the bat chair and some T4, but not even *Friends* could cheer her up. And was one where Ross bleaches teeth, so things really bad.

Friday 4

There has been another gladiator-related incident at 24 Summerdale Road. James and Mad Harry are dressed in their leotards and furry pants and have been attacking each other with 'pugil' sticks, i.e brooms with pillows tied around the end. But their aim is less than expert and they have broken a Hobbit figurine and bent Des Lynam's head in a funny angle. Plus the dog is wedged under bed in fear. It sustained no less than three body blows. Although is possibly its own fault for trying to eat pugil stick mid-action. Mum is redoubling her school appeal panic. She says if both menaces end up at John Major it will be all over for James and he will end up in Dartmoor like cousin Leonard (swarthy relative of Grandpa Clegg). Am inspired by Mum (and slightly panicked at hazy memory of cousin Leonard, who ran own father over in tractor) and am redoubling academic and Nuts In May work efforts, i.e. will be so dedicated at lentil-face, Mr Goldstein will offer me extra shifts and management position by end of tomorrow. And when am not triumphing over till of insanity, will study ceaselessly to better chances in life.

5 p.m.
After Paul O'Grady show.

. . . .

Saturday 5
8 a.m.
Am fully prepared for new pro-work ethic attitude. Am wearing business-like outfit, i.e. St Trinian's but with minor adjustments, e.g. impenetrable black leggings instead of fishnets. And have prepared list of suggestions to revamp Nuts In May, e.g. on-premises thai massage (luring in demographic currently absent from sesame seed aisle, i.e. meat-consuming and impressionable forty-something men) and, for the women, buy one get one free offers on slow sellers like chemical-free sanitary towels. In fact think am maybe candidate for *The Apprentice*. Alan Sugar would be lucky to have someone with my combination of business acumen and knowledge of nine-teenth century literature.

10 a.m.
Have been sacked. Did not even get to tell Mr Goldstein about the genius BOGOF offer as he ordered me into the stockroom the minute I walked in the door. I said I was sorry that the credit crunch was affecting his Fruesli sales but that if he gave me a second chance I would more than prove my £2.85 an hour worth. He said is not crunch, is treachery. Mrs Noakes told Mrs Dyer (unconvincing dye

job, fat feet, smells of Yardley) who told Mrs Goldstein (wife of hunchback, i.e. Esmerelda) that I had begged for a job on the toiletries aisle, i.e. his main competitor, claiming I could not tolerate third world working conditions any longer. Is possibly true did say something like that. But on understanding that was in confidential employment-type meeting. Not engaging in idle banter with badly permed, loose-tongued town gossip. James says I should look on the bright side, i.e. I get to spend quality time in the bosom of loving family. Said Mum and Dad are next door pretending to be sex-mad American teenagers, the dog is fighting a cushion and do not fancy look of James's furry pants either. Although suppose at least will not have to beg for next Saturday off for wedding.

Will go and lie down on bed for bit. And prepare self mentally for arrival of Mum and her shouting. She makes Alan Sugar look meek. Will come up with genius financial recovery plan and baffle her with words like subprime and spreadsheet.

10.15 a.m.
Will just watch bit of T4 first though. Is true there are some advantages to being one of jobless millions.

2 p.m.
Mum not at all happy about sacking. Cousin Leonard mentioned again. Nor is she happy about my brilliant idea

that she pay me to give her private drama lessons. (Was only suggestion had time to think of due to incisive documentary on Justin Timberlake. Did not know he had dad called Randy. Is interesting.) Mum said her talents do not need honing, they are already polished and primed for action. (She is wrong. Her rendition of 'There Are Worse Things I Could Do' is brimming with irony.) Said, on bright side, it meant I could concentrate on my AS levels and earn my fortune in the future with my ability to repeat large swathes of Jane Austen dialogue or name the most marginal constituency in Scotland. She said was not swayed and am being sent out to tramp the streets on Monday begging for work. It is utterly Dickensian. Am Oliver Twist. James has asked to join me but she says child labour is illegal. Notice it does not stop her paying him to comb dog and delimescale bath on weekly basis though.

. . . .

Sunday 6

Went round Scarlet's to mope about being victim of economic crisis. She less than sympathetic. Said not victim of economic crisis but of schoolboy error of saying anything to Mrs Noakes other than 'A pot of olives, please.' Also she and Hilary busy on phone being outraged at Olympic torch being processed around country in flagrant disregard for Chinese crimes against working poor etc. And outraged at Suzy's apparent lack of outrage. Scarlet is

142

right, she has definitely gone off the boil, socialism-wise. She is baby-mad. There are ovulation charts and thermometers all over house. Took my temperature. Was forty-one degrees. Had panic that was going to melt but Jack said was false reading as was using in wrong orifice as is uber-sensitive bottom one. Had bigger panic and washed mouth out with entire bottle of Listerine.

At least Jack understanding about my employment issues. He said it is all utterly anti-workers rights and by the sound of it I could take Mr Goldstein to a tribunal. (He not party to conversation about libellous gossip with Mrs Noakes.) Did not want to disappoint him, left-wing wise, so said to be fair did not like job that much and think will be better off elsewhere in long run. Is very nice of him though. He offered to boycott store and refuse all stand-in shifts from now on. Said did not want him to suffer financially because of my misfortune. (Or idiocy.) Then he said Suzy is on lookout for personal assistant type person if I need extra income. Said is very kind but would possibly prefer to hack up lamb shanks with Dean the Dwarf for seven hours a day than listen to Suzy talk about pelvic floor exercises. He said is fair point. Both he and Scarlet have turned it down already.

7 p.m.
James is in mourning. It is also Olympic torch related. He says Konnie Huq (his all-time favourite *Blue Peter* presenter, also potential future wife (in his dreams)) has

lowered herself by carrying the torch and ignoring plight of Tibet. Said was impressed by his new-found politicism. He said it is all thanks to his mystical guru. Asked who mystical guru was. Is Granny Clegg. Mum not so inflamed with mystical guru wisdom. She says it is bad enough having to listen to her talk about the miracle of Blu-Tack let alone the Chinese class system. Had to leave room at that point as this information was relayed to me in absurd accent with much hand-on-hipping and eye-rolling. It turns out that Dad and Mum are following in footsteps of Dustin Hoffman and have taken up method acting. They are trying to stay in character as Rizzo and Kenickie at all times. Is completely unbearable.

. . . .

Monday 7
9 a.m.
Am happy to be sent out on Dickensian job hunt. Trudging the dusty cobbles (aka gum-soiled concrete) will be breeze compared to having to witness Mum 'smoking' cigarette (HB pencil) whilst eating pancake stack (Waitrose drop scones). Said Rizzo would still be in bed now, not, in fact, consuming nicotine or heart-congesting breakfast. But Mum said, 'I gotta get ma jobs done, sweety-pie.' Think she is confusing Rizzo with someone from *Gone with the Wind*, or possibly Peggy Mitchell, but did not risk pointing this out. James is already in his room for suggesting she tones down the make-up.

4 p.m.

Is utterly depressing. Saffron Walden like Poland, i.e. land of no opportunity. No wonder everyone is moving to Sawbridgeworth. Tried at no less than three establishments (Gray Palmer, WHSmith, and Boots—all other shops on proscribed list (mine) due to things like being called Gayhomes or (Mum's) containing too many Kylies). But none are taking on new staff until the Christmas rush, i.e. September. Went back to Waitrose to see if have moved up on waiting list but in fact am two places down. Said that was outrage, but Mrs Noakes said is all utterly fair and merit-based, i.e. Alan Wong has previous experience with fish (he has a tank of piranha—toothy fish favoured by dentists) and Rebecca Hooton is dyslexic, and they are down on their minority quota since Lawrence Gavell (enormous head, no qualifications) left to be beet picker. Am doomed to poverty.

Oooh, am excited now. Poverty is good for literary chances. Will be utterly like J.K. Rowling, i.e. writing by candlelight in scabby café. May well get notebook and sit in Mocha immediately!

5 p.m.

Have remembered still cannot afford wedding outfit. Let alone fritter 70p on skinny mochalatte (i.e. Nescafè and a Cadbury's Highlights mix). Am depressed again.

Tuesday 8

11 a.m.

Hurrah. My Frankenstein's monster (aka Davey aka Hilary to be) is back from his week in Sciathos. He has sent me a text saying to meet him outside Smeg Launderette and Mr Patel's 2 (aka Mrs Patel's) at half one. He has got a present for me. Is probably hideous stuffed donkey or bottle of undrinkable and illegal liquor. Still it is thought that counts and once have schooled him he will be purchasing only Chanel No 5 at Duty Free. Is odd that MacDonalds are not suffering credit crunch issues. Although they are used to shopping in Lidl so it is business as usual. Will not tell Mum where am going. She is busy doing method acting with Jan (i.e. telling Marjory Lakeland catalogue is 'swell') so will not even notice I am missing. And James is round Mad Harry's attempting wall climbing challenge (scaling garage), so am not at risk of capture by their anti-ASBO love patrol.

3 p.m.

Was not hideous stuffed donkey. WAS in fact Chanel No 5. Well, actually Chantel Numero 5, i.e. fake purchased from man with huge moustache on beach, but is a step in right direction none the less. Said thanks and even gave kiss on cheek. Am aiming to move to centre of face, i.e. lips, millimetres at a time so is not too much of shock to system. Did not get to stay long though, despite invite

146

to 'go for a burn in Lambo's wheels'. (Translation: ride recklessly around the estate in Mark Lambert's Toyota, which appears to be held together with No More Nails and parcel tape.) Was because have got text from Scarlet demanding to know whereabouts. Said was on Whiteshot Estate. She said HAVE U BEEN MUGGED? Said NO AM WITH DAVEY. She said IS AS BAD. Then she demanded that I leave environs of Whiteshot Estate and walk forthwith to her house to resolve urgent wedding dispute with Melody (GET ARSE HERE NOW MELODY MENTAL). I then suggested that Jack, Hilary, or Sad Ed could act as negotiator in proceedings (ASK MEN) but apparently Hilary is refusing to be involved on grounds of wedding being non-progressive, Jack is refusing to be involved on grounds of it being non-sane, and Sad Ed is not man due to missing mojo. She did not text this, she rang, as was getting too complicated and threatening to aggravate her text thumb issues. Anyway, apparently Melody wants me and Scarlet to wear same dresses, as her bridesmaids now whittled down to six (which is still too many, but is compromise on twenty-three anyway). But Scarlet says Best Men are superior and outfits must reflect this. Agreed to go round at four as am excellent deal broker. Maybe could be like United Nations ambassador and secure peace in Middle East. Hurrah. Have invited Davey to come with me and get taste of socialist lifestyle. He said would meet me there once has burned up and down the estate a few times.

5 p.m.
Did not broker excellent deal. When got there dispute already settled by Scarlet's favoured 'who can shout loudest' method. We are going to Cambridge tomorrow to purchase superior Best Man wear. Pointed out only had seven pounds fifty to name so will not be entirely superior but Davey said, 'I'll borrow it you, I got a monkey for offloading the Kawasaki.' (Translation: I'll lend you the money, I have made £500 for selling on a lime-green motorbike.) Scarlet rolled her eyes and said 'Whatever.' She is only annoyed as Hilary will not buy her clothes as it is too patriarchal. That is problem with socialist love. Whereas sexist ASBO love means I will be able to purchase excellent vintage Best Woman outfit and be better Best Woman. Hurrah.

5.15 p.m.
Although is NOT love. Obviously. Is experiment.

* *

Wednesday 9

10 a.m.
Am fully prepared for arduous day of wedding outfit purchasing, i.e. have eaten double Shreddies for energy and have reread *Vogue* to focus mind on prize. Scarlet, Jack, and Hilary are picking me up in the non-sick-smelling car of the people. Said was surprised Hilary has even agreed to accompany us. She says he is only coming so he can

acclimatize to seat of learning (St Slaughter to Cambridge could induce massive culture shock due to lack of tractors, rain, and processed foods). And Jack is only coming because the Nissan Micra is leaking black fumes in not at all polar-bear-friendly way and is at fat Len Viceroy's being fixed. He will not let Hilary drive Beetle. He says it requires a special touch. It mostly requires shouting at and thump on dashboard.

Have texted Davey to come too. Is only fair as he is funding purchase. Have not told Scarlet that yet though. Will be excellent surprise. Have not told Mum either. Though not as am preparing it as excellent surprise (it would not be), is because she has gone to Wandlebury Wood with James and the dog to forage for wild herbs. They have taken *Observer Book of Shrubs* to avoid any near-death experiences. I did point out that was not sure Rizzo would go yomping around wood looking for sorrel, i.e. is not wholly in character, but Mum says she going to wear Pink Lady jacket under cagoule.

5 p.m.
Have got outfit. Is utterly vintage-look chiffon tea-dress from Topshop. Am practically Kate Moss! When suck cheeks in and squint at mirror. On downside Scarlet is wearing exactly same. But she had to pay for her own. Whereas mine is token of love. She is not at all happy with Hilary. He got minty with her for going into Topshop in first place due to possible sweatshop/non-organic

issues. And then, when we tried dresses on, and did practice Best Woman walk in shoe section, Davey said, 'You look skill, Rach.' Whereas Hilary just shrugged and said, 'True beauty is on the inside.' I think Scarlet is beginning to regret her choice of lover. At least Trevor got swoony over her in her vegetarian leather goth coat. Political prowess is nothing when it comes to raw bat sexuality.

Got home to find James and dog being sick in downstairs toilet and patio respectively. Apparently they both dared question the authority of the *Observer Book of Shrubs*. Asked how this travesty had occurred under beady eye of Mum. James said stiletto heel got stuck in bog. But Mum said Rizzo possibly couldn't even read so was in character at least.

Oooh. Maybe Mum/Rizzo swap is good thing, i.e. Rizzo would embrace Ribena and Wotsits etc. Will just go and ask.

5.15 p.m.
Or not. Apparently even Rizzo understands the perils of chav snacks.

. . . .

Thursday 10
10 a.m.
Have just bumped into Thin Kylie on wall. Was taking dog for walk and not concentrating as wall is usually

danger-free zone at this time of day due to scheduling of Jeremy Kyle/Trisha etc. But apparently their Sky is on blink and Fiddy needed poo. So had to endure sex-related questioning as follows:

KYLIE: 'Are you, like, shagging MacDonald?'

ME: 'No.'

KYLIE: 'You should. He is, like, totally good in bed. His thing is bent though so just keep your eyes shut.'

ME: 'Uh, thanks.'

KYLIE: 'Him and Lambo are over mine later. You have, like, totally got to come, innit. Whippy's bringing his van so we can get 99s for nothing.'

ME: 'Well, I . . . '

KYLIE: 'Nice one.'

ME: 'OK. I have to go now.'

KYLIE: 'How come your dog can shag with no balls?'

ME: (Yanking dog away, who is trying to conjugate with Fiddy, who is mid-poo in gutter) 'No idea.'

Is true. Is complete mystery. Sad Ed has got two and he has no stirrings and the dog is gonad-free and is at Fiddy every chance he gets. Is ironic. Or possibly depressing.

Anyway, more worryingly, am now haunted with hideous images of bent penises, Mr Whippy's 99 cones, and potential chav orgy situations. Oh God. What have let self in for? Experiment is not working at all. Cannot breach two worlds. Is like Elizabeth Bennet trying to go out with Phil Mitchell.

10 p.m.
Thank God. Did not have to do anything untoward with
anyone's penis. Although have consumed four 99 whips,
which is almost as bad in Mum's book. In fact, evening
vaguely amusing, i.e. watched Davey doing some *jetés* as
dare across the laminate floor. It is utter shame he got
thrown out of Royal Ballet. He is very athletic and almost
swan-like in his grace. Although not so much when he
skidded on DVD box (*Resident Evil*) and crashed headfirst
into display cabinet of glass fawns. Kylie says Cherie will
go mental as she has been collecting them out of back of
Mail on Sunday for months. Personally think he has done
Cherie, and world, favour.

Also, have invited Kylies, Mr Whippy, Davey, and
Mark Lambert to Sad Ed's secret wedding. Actually is
more that they invited selves as Kylie is wedding-mental
at moment. Did not explain about missing mojo though.
As it is they all think he is gay. His unresponsive penis
would seal the deal.

Am totally bridging two worlds after all. And har-
moniously integrating them in manner of peacekeeping
type. Am like Gandhi. Or Gabriella in *High School
Musical*.

10.30 p.m.
Not that have seen *High School Musical*. It is just what have
been told.

. . . .

152

Friday 11

Only one day to go now until joyous union of Melody Rapunzel Bean and Edward Arthur Thomas. Though Sad Ed not at all joyous at moment. He has been lying on my bed emitting low moaning noise for several hours. Did point out to him that there is obvious way out of this mess. Sad Ed said web now too entangled to tell truth. I said not that obvious and, *au contraire*, I meant that Sad Ed could revive his mojo, reverse his 'no sex before marriage' claims, and do it with Melody tonight. He said he had thought of that but not even fantasizing that Melody is actually Susan out of *Neighbours* had any discernible effect on pants area (thank God). Said on plus side he will be unable to consummate marriage so will be null and void anyway. Sad Ed just moaned some more.

7 p.m.

Sad Ed has finally left, resigned to his fate, but slightly more cheerful due to the Duchy Lemon Thin I procured from James's secret stash. (He is also taking advantage of Mum's Rizzo-related lapse in larder security. Not for consuming purposes (he is still on poverty-style porridge diet) but so he can sell them in playground for 10p each. He has amassed 70p so far. Said it was hardly going to solve economic crisis. He said it is just beginning of his fortunes and even Bill Gates started small and he is confidently expecting to rival McVities by the end of the year.) He did not give them up without fight though and demanded to know precise nature of Sad Ed's woes. Said his willy does not work. Just hope James does not offer to 'mesmerize' him into action with his Ninja skills, like he did with bust.

11 p.m.
Scarlet has just texted to ensure that I have done best woman duty and checked trains to Scotland. Said yes. To be fair have not. And not entirely sure where Gretna Green is. But will be simple. Will just buy tickets to Edinburgh and get taxi. Endless military checking spoils atmosphere of romance. I bet Madonna didn't spend hours on phone to Network Rail making sure that she could get a connection to Skibo Castle.

. . . .

Saturday 12
9 a.m.
Hurrah. Is brilliant am not working. Especially when have rich admirer to fund wardrobe. Am already wearing dress and hair is in elaborate beehive thing, as styled by Thin Kylie. Though drew line at emergency spray tan and bikini wax. There is no way am letting her turn me into Jodie Marsh again. Also do not want to aggravate Mum further. She already suspicious as to why *a*) Thin Kylie up at 8 a.m., *b*) Thin Kylie invited into bedroom, and *c*) why we wearing 'cocktail outfits'. Told her it is annual sixth form anti-war, save-the-whale, non-alcoholic charity cocktail

morning. Is made-up but sounds ridiculous enough to be plausible. James not so easily duped. He eyed me with air of positive mistrust over his gruel. Luckily he is going with Mum, Dad, and Mad Harry to London to see West End version of *Grease* (following educational and tedious tour of no less than four museums) and will not be home until midnight. By which time we will be back from Scotland, Sad Ed will be married, and I will be snogging my home-made Hilary, i.e. Davey MacDonald. Have decided today is day. Admittedly he is still not very progressive. But am imbued with wedding fever and he did look almost Heathcliffish at Kylie's yesterday. If Heathcliff had worn a baseball cap and fake Evisu jeans.

Have pointed out Mum and Dad are mad going to see the professionals though. It can only reveal their own shortcomings. James said, *au contraire*, he is hoping they will be talent spotted during the audience participation bit and asked to join the cast. He is over-optimistic. Or just idiot.

9.30 a.m.
Can see wedding car, aka the non-sick-smelling car of people! Jack is driving me, Scarlet, Hilary, and Sad Ed to station. Davey is going with Kylies in Mr Whippy's van and Melody and bridesmaids are catching Viceroy bus. Hurrah, this is it! In just a few hours Melody Bean will be Mrs Sad Ed. And I will be breaching British class system and engulfed in experimental ASBO love.

155

1 p.m.
Wedding did not go entirely to plan. Am not in Gretna Green. Am in totally non-Scottish 24 Summerdale Road (unless you count a packet of Highland Shortbread, now in James's biscuit stash). And am not engulfed in love, ASBO or otherwise. Is all fault of James. Although James says is all fault of self and failure to adhere to resolution and be honest about feelings.

Events unfolded as follows:

9.45 a.m.
Non-sick-smelling car of people arrives at Audley End station and decants occupants all attired in full wedding regalia. Bar Hilary who is wearing black shirt and unhappy scowl.

9.55 a.m.
Mr Whippy's van arrives and decants occupants, all attired in full wedding regalia, but also full of Nobbly Bobblys and Reef.

10 a.m.
Sad Ed notes lack of bride, or bridesmaids, or indeed any sign of Len Viceroy's supercoach.

10.30 a.m.
Not-so-super coach arrives, having had to stop three times on Sparrow's Hill to let bride vomit on verge. Was

nerves. Not alcohol. Bride demands to see birthday present from groom. Groom admits forgot was birthday in wedding panic.

10.35 a.m.
Bride calls wedding off due to crapness of groom. Groom says 'great'. Bride collapses in heap in car park. Groom has panic and tells her his love is present to her. Bride announces wedding back on. Rachel Riley announces groom is muppet.

10.40 a.m.
Thin Kylie vomits on bonnet of ice cream van. Was not nerves. Was alcohol.

10.45 a.m.
Wedding party agrees is time get show on road and sends travel co-ordinator, i.e. Rachel Riley, to ticket office to buy tickets to Gretna Green.

10.50 a.m.
Rachel Riley returns sans tickets having been informed it will *a*) cost £248 each, and *b*) take nine hours and six changes due to engineering works at Peterborough and Doncaster. Wedding party shouts at travel co-ordinator.

10.55 a.m.
Mr Whippy offers to drive wedding party in van. Wedding party attempts to squeeze in amongst Magnum boxes.

11 a.m.
Wedding party emerges from van with coating of raspberry syrup and scattering of hundreds and thousands. Rachel notes is almost confetti like.

11.05 a.m.
Idiot savant Davey MacDonald says he will commission fat Len Viceroy to drive party to Scotland with his Kawasaki money. Rachel Riley kisses Davey MacDonald on cheek (but at least five millimetres closer to lips than last time).

11.10 a.m.
Wedding party boards supercoach.

11.11 a.m.
Coach does emergency stop due to obstacle. Len Viceroy does emergency swearing. Travel co-ordinator Rachel Riley sent out to investigate nature of obstacle.

11.12 a.m.
Obstacle identified as Mr and Mrs Thomas, aka Sad Ed's mum and dad, lying in road, engaging in last-ditch attempt to pervert course of marriage.

11.13 a.m.
Wedding party unboards coach. Sad Ed attempts to explain self. Mrs Thomas says, 'Aled would be turning in his grave.' Rachel Riley points out Aled Jones not dead.

Mrs Thomas gives Rachel Riley withering look. Rachel Riley vows to keep mouth shut.

11.15 a.m.
Sad Ed demands to know how Mr and Mrs Thomas found out about secret wedding. Mrs Thomas admits to having informer. Sad Ed demands to know identity of informer. James Riley appears from behind ticket machine with red A4 ring binder and Mad Harry.

11.20 a.m.
Rachel Riley demands to know *a*) why he not at home with Rizzo and Kenickie preparing for nerd-a-thon, *b*) whereabouts of Rizzo and Kenickie, and *c*) what is with folder?

11.25 a.m.
James Riley says, *a*) he got lift with Mrs Mad Harry, *b*) they on way right now to catch 12.14 to Liverpool Street, and *c*) is dossier of evidence against Sad Ed and Rachel Riley. Though was only back-up as bet Rachel Riley did not alert marriage authorities in Scotland with official two weeks' notice.

11.30 a.m.
Scarlet demands to know more about marriage authorities and period of notice. James Riley explains Scottish law in mind-boggling detail. Rachel points out that they

159

didn't show that in *Hollyoaks*. James explains difference between soap operas and real life, i.e. nor do they show pooing due to it not being of dramatic consequence unless is dysentery-related and essential to tropical disease plot.

11.35 a.m.
Melody Bean demands to know nature of dossier of evidence. James unveils transcripts of conversations between Rachel Riley and various other members of wedding party concerning *a*) Sad Ed's missing mojo, *b*) fakeness of wedding, *c*) annoyingness of Melody Bean.

11.37 a.m.
Melody Bean faints and is carried by horde of bridesmaids into Mr Whippy's van for reviving cider barrel lolly.

11.40 a.m.
Davey MacDonald calls James Riley 'nosy little knob' for spying on Rachel Riley. James employs Mum's favoured 'sticks and stones' routine and threatens to reveal Rachel Riley's evil intentions. Rachel Riley threatens James Riley with actual sticks and stones. Davey MacDonald offers James £50 of Kawasaki money to reveal evil intentions. Rachel warns James not to succumb to bribery. James says, 'Needs must in these hard times,' and tells Davey MacDonald that Rachel does not fancy him, he is just pawn in her political game.

11.45 a.m.

Davey MacDonald points out he 'ain't no sodding prawn'. Kylies escort him to Mr Whippy's van, which departs complete with an ice-cream man, four chavs, six brides-maids, and Melody Bean.

11.50 a.m.

Mrs Thomas ushers Sad Ed into Mini Metro. Metro departs with 'Walking in the Air' coming from windows and Sad Ed's rotund face pressed against glass in defeated manner.

12 noon

Jack suggests rest of wedding party also departs before arrival of Rizzo and Kenickie.

12.01 p.m.

James and Mad Harry depart for station shop to spend Kawasaki money on Polos, Quavers, and copies of national rail timetable.

12.05 p.m.

Non-sick-smelling car of people departs for Saffron Walden in silence. Possibly in reverence at dream being over. Possibly because Scarlet not talking to Rachel over train issues, Hilary not talking to Scarlet over non-progressive issues, and Jack not talking to anyone over idiocy issues.

It is all utterly depressing. Am back to where started. And am utterly annoyed with James. Do not know why he persists in gladiator ambition, he is much more suited to being nosy detective type. He has obviously been hiding Ninja-style in nooks and crannies, trying to overhear conversations. Or possibly just listening in on other phone, as learned from Mum in pre-Rizzo days.

Plus it is a waste of my Kate Moss-style best woman dress. Even Jack agrees. When I got out of the car he said, 'Davey was right. You do look skill, Rach.' But is meaningless unless have someone to rip it off me in frenzy of experimental love.

1.30 p.m.
Though at least have house to self. Even dog appears to have been farmed out for day.

1.45 p.m.
Dog not farmed out. Was trapped in airing cupboard. Life is just one endless disappointment. Usually involving dog sick and shouting. At least James has promised not to tell Mum and Dad though. Am not strong enough to endure their wrath at me engineering teen marriage. Or ASBO love. Plus he has not asked for anything in return. Is selfless brother. Am lucky to have him.

. . . .

Sunday 13

Am still depressed. Is partly Davey MacDonald hoo-ha
and partly Rizzo and Kenickie hoo-ha. Mum and Dad are
infused with West End musical fever and are in *Grease*
overdrive. Have already witnessed full-scale rendition of
'You're the One That I Want' (complete with James as
Danny Zuku stand-in and dog as Sandy) and is only nine
a.m. Am going over to Sad Ed's. Aled Jones is bearable by
comparison.

6 p.m.

Sad Ed not depressed for once. Despite being grounded
for two weeks and having Bontempi organ confiscated
as punishment for anti-Aled secret wedding plans. Is
because, despite humiliation, has had lucky escape from
being tabloid fodder. And Melody Bean fodder. Scarlet
also there. Though not so philosophical. Apparently
Hilary decided she is not the woman he thought she was
and has ended their left-wing love affair. He retrieved
Nissan Micra from Fat Len and drove back to Cornwall
yesterday afternoon, in cloud of anti-polar bear fumes. So
she is utterly single too! BUT, in interesting twist, she says
is not devastating as Hilary did not stir mojo like Trevor!
I said what about het-up phone calls? She says is political
talk that is stimulating. Not Hilary. Which is odd, as on
paper he is her ideal man but in fact her mojo is far more
interested in weedy-armed bat boy. But is too late as he is
still going out with minigoth Tamsin Bacon. We have all

been in utter denial. It is lucky I did not mould a new Hilary if he is so disappointing mojo-wise.

Mum and Dad are back from operatics and are also visibly disappointed. Is not mojo-related. Do not think they ever had them in first place. Is because Margot Gyp aka Lady Golf Captain aka Sandy and Russell Rayner aka gay golfer aka director did not take on board any of their suggestions for show improvements. James says they will regret refusing to move with times and has offered to set up a rival production, but Mum says she has nothing left to give. Rizzo has drained her emotionally and physically. Thank God. Maybe will be able to eat breakfast without having to pretend am stuck in episode of *Happy Days* from now on.

• •

Monday 14
8.30 a.m.
Mum is revived Rizzo-wise and is back with vengeance. She is determined to outshine Margot and prove her mettle as leading lady for next year's production. James says he is delighted she is thinking long-term. Asked what next year's production was. Is *Hair*. Which does not bode well, anything-wise. Thought of Mum and Dad in tie-dye, or worse, nude, singing about the age of Aquarius is terrifying. Thank God am going to school. Will be breeze compared to insanity of 24 Summerdale Road.

4 p.m.

School not quiet retreat had hoped for. Am now in unholy trinity of hatred along with Scarlet and Sad Ed. Nowhere is safe. D Corridor is full of armed and dangerous Retards and Criminals, C Corridor is minefield of Melody Bean minions, and canteen out of bounds due to proximity of goth corner. Not even the common room can provide sanctuary. Fat Kylie has warned me if any 'boffins' even put one toe over the boundary of BTEC corner we will be 'totally, like, dead, innit'. Plus now have A levellers on back as well as no one can use CD player or leaky microwave and we have to suffer 50 Cent and smell of idiotic BTEC microwave experiments (oranges, Mars Bars, shoes) all day. I begged for mercy but Thin Kylie says no one messes with their men and I should stick to my own kind. Said I no longer knew what own kind was. She said, 'Knobby weirdos like fat boy' (i.e Sad Ed). Is utterly depressing. Was trying to break down barriers. But walls now even higher. And will possibly be actual walls if Mark Lambert and his BTEC bricklaying skills get their way. Plus am social pariah. Like leper. Or Nigel Moore, who has impetigo (not potato blight). Sad Ed says is small price to pay for freedom. But he has iPod and underactive nasal capacity.

* *

Tuesday 15

Saw failed experiment, i.e. Davey, at the nut dispensing

machine today. Tried to hide behind gaggle of maths geeks but they move too quickly and in pack, like cockroaches, so was not at all camouflaging. He said, 'I ain't gonna deck you or nothing, Rach.' Said thanks. I offered to pay him back for best woman dress. Even though have no money and no job. But he said, 'Keep it. Anyway, the Kawasaki was nicked off Ducatti Mick so, like, you owe him not me.' So not only am social pariah, but have been wearing illegally gotten goods. Am utterly gangster's moll. Or ex-moll. Am not telling Mum. Or James. He will only use information to own advantage. It turns out he actually not selfless at all but storing up secret knowledge about failed elopement in order to blackmail me into his gladiatorial idiocy. He has demanded that I join his troupe. He has already got stage name for me. Am Amazon. Said what about Mad Harry? James says he is taking time off duties to recover from pugil-stick inflicted injuries and recoup his strength, and James needs replacement fight companion. Suggested dog (aka Hyperwolf) instead but apparently dog not keen. Plus paws too small to hold pugil-stick. Have given in. But only if can choose own stage name. There is no way I am being named after website. Will possibly be Mantis. Or Black Widow. Which sound sexy as well as menacing.

· ·

Wednesday 16

Thank God. Mr Vaughan has announced an A level

theatre trip to see *Macbeth*. Have signed up immediately. Am not going to try to transgress any class, social or other barriers ever again. Thin Kylie is right. Need to stick to own kind. Though obviously not 'knobby fat weirdos'. Not that Sad Ed knobby fat weirdo. Though still has man boob issues, i.e fat. And suicidal tendencies, i.e. weird.

5 p.m.
Mum has asked if she can come on theatre trip for inspiration. Have pointed out it is Shakespeare, i.e. not involving any Cadillacs, pyjama parties, or dance-offs. But she says she is thinking of basing 'her Rizzo' on tortured Lady Macbeth. Said trip overbooked already. Do not want Mum infesting coach with her health-giving snacks and cagoule.

Thursday 17
When will common room class-war end? Had to endure CD of Wildcats banging on about getting your head in the game nine times during free period. Sophie Microwave Muffins actually had to be taken to Mrs Leech with symptoms of nausea. Is like Middle East. And leaky microwave and CD player are in West Bank. Though at least A levellers still in control of Jerusalem, i.e. saggy sofa. Sad Ed tried to enter Gaza Strip (i.e. stain-ridden blue carpet) to retrieve half a Snickers, but got pelted with

honey-roasted cashews. I bet Jamie Oliver didn't think of potential ammunition issues when he invented nut dispensing machine. Crisps are far less dangerous, missile-wise.

· ·

Friday 18

Class war has escalated. Scarlet sneaked into Gaza Strip when BTECers distracted by sheep versus Criminals and Retards hoo-ha on field outside and microwaved their *High School Musical* CD. But then Thin Kylie trumped her with Ministry Of Sound mix, which has a bass line that actually made teeth hurt. Mrs Leech had to come upstairs to common room and threaten to turn electricity off as a piece of plaster fell off ceiling and narrowly missed her head. She not so worried about head though, more concerned at its actual target which was packet of ginger snaps, now irretrievably in state of crumbs. Head boy and girl, i.e. Jack and non-smelly Oona, have said enough is enough and have tabled peace talks on the saggy sofa before registration on Monday. Do not rate their chances though. BTEC 'peace' ambassadors are Fat Kylie and Mark Lambert who employ violence as first, and often only, resort.

· ·

Saturday 19

Am inspired by Jack and Oona's historic stand against

168

oppression (and also sick of being broke) and am going to seize day and demand rise in pocket money from Mum and Dad. £3 a week is utter poverty pay. Cannot even buy *Vogue*. Am like Dickensian workhouse orphan. Although not actual orphan. Or in workhouse. But am poor. Anyway, am confident of success as have special secret weapon. Is James and sidekick Google, who have printed off evidence of national pocket money average, i.e. £6.30 for under-12s (i.e. James) and £9.76 for sixteen year olds, i.e. me. Will be rich beyond compare by this afternoon.

11 a.m.
Had forgotten Mum also now au fait with Google. She immediately donned helmet and rubber gloves and produced conflicting evidence that pocket money dependent on myriad factors including academic background, level of household chores, and average cost of wheat. According to her calculations, am lucky to be getting £3 and any more querying of *a*) her absolute power, or *b*) her money management skills will be met with a reduction, and penalties. James asked what penalties might be. Mum said that counted as *a*) querying absolute power so he is down 20p already. Am going to have to employ Plan B.

11.15 a.m.
Forgot have not got Plan B. Will write one immediately. Once have watched relaxing T4.

1 p.m.
And eaten thrifty lunch of soup and roll.

2 p.m.
And lurked in Waitrose car park with Sad Ed.

4 p.m.
Still have no Plan B. Will do brainstorm with James. He excellent source of scientifically proven ideas.

5 p.m.
James's ideas not so scientifically proven as hoped. List as follows:
1. Become champion gladiator,
2. Revive ancient art of alchemy, i.e. creating gold from base metals,
3. Discover buried treasure.

Pointed out he and Mad Harry tried alchemy before and only succeeded in creating enormous mess. Plus his gladiatorial career showing no signs of moneymaking success at moment. In fact, they are financially out of pocket following purchase of fake fur for pants. He said what about buried treasure? So reminded him of Grandpa Riley's ill-fated phase with the metal detector when he became convinced there was ancient Saxon gold buried under Mum's lupins. All he got was a Norwich Castle Museum badge and a hefty shouting.

5.15 p.m.

Oooh. Have had idea though. Grandpa Riley may be key to restoring Riley fortunes after all. Will offer to revive babysitting career!

6 p.m.

Grandpa not key to restoring fortune. He says the credit crunch is biting hard at the residents of 19 Harvey Road. (It is not the credit crunch. It is his magazine habit.) He pointed out that theoretically, as am god-mother, should offer to look after Jesus for nothing but benefit of his moral betterment. Said these were hard times. And also long words for Grandpa. He said is due to *Economist*. Said glad he upgrading from *Chat* magazine. He said he is not, he bought it by mistake because it had Cheryl Cole on the cover (was story about financial planning in music industry, not Ashley Cole betrayal, as he had hoped). Anyway, best he can offer is £1.50 an hour. Have refused. Is worse than Mr Goldstein. Will have to search for other babies. Preferably rich ones. Ooh, maybe the not-so-famous McGann man has some small McGanns that need minding while he is busy being Danny Zuko. Will ask Mum to ask him at operatics tomorrow.

Mum says she is not asking any favours from the entrenched hierarchy. Plus I can barely be trusted not to cause stain-making chaos at 24 Summerdale Road, let alone a celebrity household, which is bound to have ill-advised pale carpets and too much faux suede.

. . . .

Sunday 20

9 a.m.
Thank God is Sunday, i.e. is practically illegal to work. So do not have to feel guilty about being jobless and generally aimless in life.

10 a.m.
James has, yet again, shattered my aimless dreams, i.e. he has reminded me I have gladiator practice this afternoon. Have resigned myself to fate. Though maybe will be champion gladiator after all and make thousands from endorsing cleaning products and questionable convenience foods.

6 p.m.
Am not champion gladiator. Though on plus side, James has also admitted this is case and has excused me from practice in future. He says even Hyperwolf (now official name for dog) has more natural skill than me. Is because I broke shed window with pugil-stick and fell off 'wall of doom' (aka patio surround) nine times.

Also, Dad is in vile mood. It is because Mum and Mike Majors had to rehearse their kissing scene this afternoon. Mum pointed out that the whole purpose of kiss is to make Kenickie jealous so is utterly brilliant acting. Dad says Leo would not have said, 'Thank you, Janet,' afterwards. James asked if was authentic, i.e. did they use tongues. Mum said tongues is unhygienic. So there is still a glimmer of Janet Riley under the chain-smoking Rizzo façade.

7 p.m.
Mum has demanded James stops calling dog 'Hyperwolf'. She says dog confused enough as it is after the Otterhound incident and cannot cope with any more identity issues. Plus it sounds mental.

Monday 21
Is historic (and frankly unbelievable) day in John Major High common room. BTECers and A levellers have signed tentative peace agreement allowing mutual access to West Bank (leaky microwave and CD player). Plus the walls of Jerusalem, i.e. saggy sofa, have been toppled. BTECers get the cushion with the spilt Yazoo and A levellers get the one with Um Bongo. So is utterly fair.

Tuesday 22
Scarlet is inspired by the BTEC/A leveller peace accord in the common room and is determined to take class war one step further (plus she is bored now that she is not consumed with multicultural love). She says she is going

to lead boycott of golf club until they reassess their ancient and misogynistic rules that mean women can only tee off on Mondays, Wednesdays, and after two on a Sunday, and are banned from wearing trousers except during particularly inclement weather conditions. She says she is guaranteed success because Suzy came on this morning and baby failure is bound to make her want to throw herself into causes left, right, and centre. And Suzy can use celebrity status to gain publicity. Said not sure publicity will be entirely favourable, given *Walden Chronicle*'s past coverage of Suzy. (e.g. election drug and lesbian in closet scandal. Metaphorical closet. At least think it was. With Suzy, can never be sure.) Scarlet says she is not concerned with tinpot local rags, which all perpetuate the twisted agendas of their small-time small town owners. She is aiming for broadsheets and broad minds, i.e. the front page of the *Guardian*.

. . . .

Wednesday 23

Scarlet's anti-golf club campaign has suffered celebrity endorsement setback. It is Suzy. Apparently her status as non-fertile Myrtle not as invigorating as Scarlet had hoped and she says she not able to actually do any boycotting as will be too busy exploring alternative routes to motherhood. Scarlet pointed out she is already a mother, twice, and maybe she should just get another cat, but

Suzy says she cannot suckle a kitten (not legally anyway) and besides it is her human right to have another baby. Scarlet says she is undeterred and will find other famous and enlightened women to swell the ranks of the masses. Or failing that, just shout louder.

Sad Ed has offered his services to swell ranks. Scarlet pointed out that *a*) he is not famous, except for crap suicide attempt, plus *b*) he has penis so not actually discriminated against. But Sad Ed said *a*) penis malfunctioning so might as well be woman, and *b*) combat trousers and beanie hats are banned from the clubhouse as well so he is discriminated against as an artistic being.

- -

Thursday 24

Have found woman to swell ranks of fight against oppressive golf club. Is Mum! Not so much because is enlightened but is because she is anti Margot Gyp. Scarlet says cameo in local operatics is not quite level of celebrity she was hoping for but I pointed out her excellent credentials fighting the scourge of dog poo. Plus she is wife of club member so she will be whistleblowing insider. Like Russell Crowe fighting the evil tobacco industry.

Scarlet has agreed and is going to write to *Guardian* immediately. Mum is going to be spellchecker. So she is invaluable in several ways.

- -

Friday 25

11 a.m.

There has been a setback in the common room peace accord. It is the appearance of a suspicious spillage on the Um Bongo cushion. Sophie Microwave Muffins has accused Fat Kylie of deliberately soiling our side of the saggy sofa with Cherry Tango. Fat Kylie says it was not her, it was Bat Boy Trevor with his fake blood (i.e. Ribena Strawberry). The maths geeks have biopsied the cushion and taken it to Miss Mustard (lab assistant, not Cluedo character) for further investigation. Until then, the saggy sofa is out of bounds to all sides and we are having to squat on the Gaza Strip, aka blue carpet, which is stained beyond all recognition so no one is claiming it at moment.

2 p.m.

Lab results are in. Stain was neither Cherry Tango nor Ribena Strawberry but had high cranberry content, i.e. was Sophie Microwave Muffins' Ocean Spray anti-cystitis remedy. She has been forced into humiliating climbdown and banned from sofa for a week. The goths are jubilant. They say it is a blow to both the Plastics' domination of the Um Bongo cushion and the BTECers perpetual repression of 'bat people'.

Saw Scarlet get a bit teary during Trevor's speech. I said is it because she is stirred by Trevor but is too proud to seize day and declare undying love. She said no. It is because a piece of celebratory flying raisin got in her eye. It is a lie. Trevor is her mojo-stirring destiny. She just needs to be honest with her feelings. She has learned nothing from the whole Hilary/wedding/Davey MacDonald debacle.

. . . .

Saturday 26

Bumped into Jack in town today. Was actually in Waitrose car park having utterly philosophical discussion with Sad Ed and Reuben Tull, i.e. 'are goats actually evil?' when Jack beeped horn of non-sick-smelling car of people and offered me a lift home. (He and Edna are job-sharing as Suzy's PA until she finds someone who can fulfil all roles. Jack is doing shopping as Edna cannot be trusted not to purchase Nestlé products or multipacks of pink wafers (rogue biscuit, substandard to HobNobs in every way).

Anyway he has offered me a job. Well, not actual job, as will not get paid, is more work experience. It is to be a life model for his A level art portrait. I said, 'No way, pervy,' but he said I can totally keep my clothes on. It is not about nudity, it is about capturing the essence of the person within. So then I said, 'Why me?' He said, 'I don't know. You're just interesting, Riley.' Which admit was kind of disappointing. Was hoping for, 'Because you are utterly Pre-Raphaelite beauty and I am undone at the sight of you.' But was better than, 'I asked Scarlet and she told me to bog off,' which was expecting. I said I was actually quite busy, timetablewise, what with the golf club campaign and my AS levels, and all my extra-curricular philosophical activity. He said, 'What? Hanging out with the Hair Bear Bunch and talking about farm animals?' Said, 'Actually Reuben is very enlightened when it comes to philosophy, his eyes have been opened to higher plains of experience.' Jack said, 'No they haven't. He's just smoked too much weed again.' Which is possibly true. Then he said, 'Look. It'll only be a couple of hours on a Sunday for the next few weeks. Just think about it.'

So am thinking about it. And think it might actually be quite good. Admittedly Jack is not Lucian Freud. But this is good thing as do not want to end up looking like wonky minger. And being a muse is utterly Kate Mossish. Even if he does not think I am Pre-Raphaelite beauty nor is undone. Though what is undone? Is it magical clothes falling off because someone so mojo-stirring? Is odd.

5 p.m.
Not that want him to be undone.

6 p.m.
Do I? Oooh, what if he is my destiny? Maybe I should do it and seize day (i.e. artistically-charged atmosphere) and see if our clothes magically fall off.

7 p.m.
No. Muses do not actually do it with artists. They are just vessels of endeavour. Or something like that.

8 p.m.
Except Colin Firth was totally in love with Scarlett Johansson. Oh my God. I am the girl with a pearly earring!

8.15 p.m.
Possibly.

. . . .

Sunday 27

Jack has rung to ask if I have given any thought to being life model. I said there were a lot of considerations to weigh up. He said, 'Christ, if it's that hard, I'll ask Oona.' Is clear am not girl with pearly earring at all but just one in list of potential muses. So said yes. Do not want to be out-mused by former smelly bisexual. Am going to start next Sunday. At worst will be cheap Christmas present for Mum and Dad, i.e. portrait of beloved first-born.

6 p.m.
Though by Christmas may well need two portraits. Operatics is not love-inducing activity at all. Got home to find them more divided than ever. Is because not-so-famous McGann has been offered Lenor advert and

Margot is having to emergency recast Danny. Dad says he is in with a chance but only if Mum rethinks her golf club boycott. Mum said she is not rethinking boycott and anyway part will go to Mike Majors who plays off scratch and compères annual salmon sandwich quiz night. Which proves why a golf boycott is necessary. Seized on Mum's zeal and gave her Scarlet's *Guardian* letter for spell checking.

Monday 28

Mum has finished letter. Is not just spell checked but totally rewritten. With fewer uses of word 'hegemony', no swearing, and a lot more punctuation. Will post on way to school. Am sending it to Julie Burchill at *Guardian*, John Kampfner at *Independent*, and Deirdre Roberts at *Chronicle*. Am not telling Scarlet about last one. Is my own completely brilliant plan. Am adding paragraph to point out that is paper's chance to cast off its reputation as reactionary and ineffectual and become forward-thinking paper of the people. Hurrah!

Tuesday 29

James has come home with devastating news from St Regina's. Headmaster Nige has banned the maypole demonstration this year. Partially due to fear of injury risk and partially because it is non-embracing of

Muslims, Hindus, and other minority religions. James pointed out that there are no Hindus at school and only one Muslim, i.e. Mumtaz, and she is thrice area maypole champion. But Nige is unmoved. He says the maypole is staying in the cupboard along with the apple bobbing bowls (drowning potential) and hula hoops (just rubbish), and there will be a non-denominational assembly about rabbits instead. James says it is political correctness gone mad. He is just disappointed because last year Keanu managed to weave Maggot Mason into a multicoloured cocoon and he had to be cut free.

. . . .

Wednesday 30

There is no sign of any golf club coverage in today's *Guardian* or *Independent*. Mum does not mind. She says she has too many other battles on hands. It is more May Day related hoo-ha. But this time at other end of country, and PC spectrum. It is not to do with non-minority-embracing maypoles. It is to do with annual St Slaughter non-minority-embracing 'Darkie Day' (i.e. ancient racist celebration whereby local types black up faces and chase hobby horse around streets). Granny Clegg is refusing to don the boot polish this year and instead is joining the Nuamahs on their anti-racism reusable carrier bag stall. Grandpa Clegg (who is fan of both racism and non-environmentally friendly Spar bags) rang to demand that

181

Mum has word with Granny Clegg and remind her who wears the trousers in the Clegg household. He picked wrong day though as Mum was most definitely wearing trousers (non-golf-club-approved Marks & Spencers linen) and told him to belt up. Grandpa Clegg then demanded to speak to Dad but Mum pointed out *a*) he has no jurisdiction in these (or any) matters, and *b*) he was not even wearing trousers as was limbering up for dance practice in bedroom. Grandpa said, 'This family is going to the dogs,' and hung up. He is right about dogs though when it comes to Dad. There is nothing at all progressive about man in pants doing grapevine along landing carpet.

CONDOMS

MACBETH

Thursday 1

9 a.m.

Scarlet is not at all happy at the continuing lack of press coverage of our golf club boycott. She says the broadsheets are missing a trick as the story has all the elements of left-wing front-page news—sexism, sport, children of Channel 5 celebrities with heaving bosoms. I said there was still the front page of the *Walden Chronicle* to hope for. But Scarlet said, *a*) we never sent them a letter, and *b*) anyway only old people and my mum read it, so would be pointless.

4 p.m.

The golf club is in the *Walden Chronicle* after all! Though not on front page but on page 7 between a story on mini roundabouts and an advert for manure. Plus is not exactly pro-boycott coverage was hoping for. Headline is 'Youths Swing Nine Iron at Century of Sporting Tradition'. Which makes it sound as if hoodies are marauding on the course with a set of Pings. Which we are not (although Scarlet had suggested this for publicity stunt). Scarlet is outraged. Reminded her that only old people and my mum read it so is not utterly destroying. But do not think she heard me as she too busy demanding to know who wrote to paper in first place. Said it was habitual *Chronicle* reader Mum. Which is technically true, i.e. she drafted letter. Scarlet said this is last time she does any power sharing with a Lib Dem.

Mum is also outraged. As is James. Is not so much coverage, is that paper has misspelt 'rabid' as 'rapid', which makes Margot sound fast (positive), as opposed to mad (negative). Dad is only one who is happy. He says at least there is no evidence of Riley family involvement in the boycott and he will still be in with a chance of getting lead role. He is fooling himself if he thinks that is only barrier to stardom. His lightning is less than greasy.

7 p.m.
Granny Clegg has rung. Apparently Grandpa Clegg has surpassed himself in both his racist tendencies and idiocy. They had run out of shoe polish so he used a can of black Hammerite from the garage. Except it was not washable emulsion. Was permanent gloss. Granny says she has been at him with white spirit but he still looks like a coalman. She is thinking of buying some pink emulsion to try to return him to 'normal'. Mum has begged her not to.

Friday 2
Mum and Dad are both in vile moods. It is because Dad secretly emailed Margot offering to assist her in fighting the masses but Mum (who now has gatekeeper access to all email accounts) saw the evidence in his outbox and has accused him of undermining her authority.

So Dad accused Mum of undermining his privacy but James accused Dad of undermining Mum's IT education. Left before I got accused of undermining anything. Unlike dog who managed to eat the flashing mouse in all the hoo-ha and got accused of undermining everybody.

Scarlet is still depressed about her failed campaign. I said it was unlike her to give up so easily in the fight against oppression and look at Granny Clegg who is still resolute against the boot polish despite selling no reusable bags and having a husband who looks like a mentalist. But Scarlet said Granny Clegg is still in her political infancy whereas she has been active for sixteen years and is suffering fatigue.

. . . .

Saturday 3
10 a.m.

Scarlet has just rung. She is revived, campaign-wise. It is because she has been talking to Edna about her dead husband Stan who was a flying picket in the miners' strikes. She says we need to set up a picket line in the golf club car park and shame/bully members into submission. Did not ask her about how we are going to fly. Even though wanted to. Air power would be excellent special weapon to befuddle all the Pringle-wearing types. Anyway, whatever it is, we are doing it on Captain's Day, which is crucial golf tournament, like FA cup final.

11 a.m.

Thank God did not ask Scarlet about flying pickets. Flying does not actually mean we have wings. It is something else altogether, according to James. Politics A level definitely paying off, i.e. at least am curbing desire to ask stupid questions!

. . . .

Sunday 4

11 a.m.

Am getting used to life as long-term unemployed, i.e. reading important literature (*Times* Style section) and watching seminal documentaries (Girls Aloud tour secrets). Do not know why anyone moans about it. It is utterly self-improving and enjoyable. Do not even have to put on make-up or wash. So is economic too. Am almost annoyed at effort it will take to walk to Jack's later to be life model. Although at least just have to sit still and can probably also read/watch TV during process.

11.05 a.m.

Have just had thought. Do not want to be immortalized with unfeasibly large hair, no mascara, and stained Brownie T-shirt. Will have to wash after all. And plan wardrobe. This is life-defining moment after all.

11.45 a.m.

Am halfway there, i.e. am clean and hair visibly less

terrifying, but am not dressed. Cannot decide on what look want to go for, i.e. casual top and denim mini, or best woman dress. What if portrait ends up in National Gallery? Do not want hordes of tourists laughing at Mickey Mouse T-shirt, which may be over by next year, or even next week. On other hand, do not want Mum getting minty about picture of me wearing stolen goods. Maybe should have asked Jack to pay for special outfit. And hair products.

12.00 noon
Have gone for holey vintage dress. Is timeless look. And has interesting story attached, i.e. Granny Clegg's sister and the meat lorry. All great art has interesting story involved. Have done full make-up as well. Want to be renowned for Mona Lisa-esque smile, not Grandpa Clegg-esque dark circles. In fact am feeling utterly muse-like. Think Jack will definitely be inspired!

4 p.m.
Jack definitely inspired. Though with few minor adjustments, i.e. less make-up. And more clothing. He said he was hoping for a less formal feel, and it is not about external trappings, but what is inside. Which was possibly nice way of saying 'you look like mad transvestite and will fail exam if paint that' (which is what Scarlet actually said). So ended up in one of his Led Zeppelin T-shirts with limited Touche Eclat and no lipstick. Plus he told me to stop

pulling faces and just be me. Was not pulling faces. Was trying to be Mona Lisa, i.e. enigmatic. And said was worried that if am too much me he will fail as will look like portrait of Robert Plant, who everyone knows is dead and so cannot pose for Annie Leibowitz, let alone art A level. But Jack said to stop being paranoid. Plus Robert Plant not actually dead. Just looks bit like it.

Did not get to read. Tried to but Jack said he did not want copy of *Grazia* in picture. Said he was being snob but he said no, he just cannot do shiny magazine effect very well. Did not watch TV either as was *Will and Grace-A-Thon* and Scarlet's snorting not conducive to atmosphere of contemplative artistic genius. So in end we left den and went up to his bedroom which is TV and Scarlet-free. Although is also sofa-free so had to lie on his bed. But he says it is a classic pose, as is relaxing. Which at first was a bit hard. As was in enemy territory, i.e. boy-smelling bed (in boy-smelling T-shirt). But then Gordon and Tony came in and sat on feet, which was nice and warm and relaxing (cats, not Labour supremos—they would probably just argue about trade deficits which would be utterly non-relaxing, not to mention painful, and surreal). In fact two hours disappeared weirdly quickly. I said I did not mind doing overtime, but Jack said he had drum practice. And, anyway, it is best not to rush these things. Which is true. Although normally he is uber-fast painter like Rolf Harris and can do cartoon dog in less than two minutes. Did not mind though, as all in all was excellent experience and came home feeling utterly Kate Mossish. Am no longer idle unemployed. Am muse. Which is not same thing at all. Is important and potentially fame-making. Look at pearly earring girl.

Dad not so inspired by potential fame. He did not get role of Danny, despite his illicit wooing of Margot. Mike Majors got role. Dad says only consolation is that at least his wandering hands will not be anywhere near Mum now. Mum not so circumspect. It is because PC Doone has been promoted to be gang leader Leo, so she will have to lock tonsils with him now, and he has a moustache and gingivitis. Thank God the show opens on Thursday. By this time next week it will all be just an unhappy memory.

* *

Monday 5
Bank Holiday

Do not know what is wrong with this family. Bank holidays are meant for legitimate lazing around and snacking, yet have thrice been disturbed and told that if I have nothing better to do then I can usefully take dog for poo/wash Passat/umpire a gladiatorial match. Have declined all. Anyone would think I am unemployed! When in fact am busy being muse. Did point this out to Mum but she said there is nothing muselike about watching *Hollyoaks* repeats and eating Cheerios out of the packet. I bet Mona Lisa did not have to put up with this.

Thank God is double philosophy tomorrow when will be in presence of expanded brains and creative thinking.

. . . .

Tuesday 6

And drug-addled trolley herders.

Lesson was on whether external world is real, e.g.

1. Do objects exist when no one is watching them (yes, duh);
2. How do I know if I am dreaming (because hippogryphs are not real and there is no way you are going to fly on one in real life).

But apparently my common sense approach is in minority as Mr Knox says, in fact, instead of saying, 'I can see a desk in front of me,' it is utterly legitimate to say, 'I am having a desk-like visual experience.' So then Reuben Tull spent rest of day in happy trance claiming he was having a school-like visual experience.

Think Mum was right after all. Philosophy is just encouragement to stoners. May well write to Gordon Brown to complain. Or suggest to Mr Wilmott that he restricts intake to those not inclined to believe in mythical beasts. Thank God tomorrow is theatre trip, i.e. utterly highbrow and with no potential for desk-like visual experience nonsense. Plus *Macbeth* is all about powerful and ambitious women, i.e. is utterly feminist.

. . . .

Wednesday 7

Theatre trip was completely brilliant. It was genius political version with Macbeth and Mrs Macbeth wearing Tony and Cherie Blair masks and Gordon Brown as Macduff. Though not sure who funny man with accent and tights was supposed to be. Maybe Harriet Harman. Anyway was utter allegory of self-destruction of New Labour. I bet Scarlet is depressed she chose Economics over drama. Economics is just maths for the overambitious. Plus it is taught by Mr Waiting who has bad ties and distracting mole on nose.

Do not quite see how it is completely feminist though as Mrs Macbeth went mental and died. Plus the witches were wearing corsets. Which got sections of audience all het up. But luckily was sitting next to mojo-less Sad Ed who just sighed wearily and ate another packet of Maltesers.

Anyway, it has set a high standard for theatrical experience this week. I fear Saffron Walden Amateur Operatic Society's *Grease* will find it hard to meet the bar. Especially as their director is not Trevor Nunn type but gay golfer, and their set has been designed by Mrs Noakes.

. . . .

Thursday 8

Scarlet says *au contraire* Economics is full of drama, intrigue, and back-stabbing. She is kidding herself. Last week they spent two hours on the introduction of the euro.

Got home to find that 24 Summerdale Road had mysteriously transformed into *X-Factor* style boot camp, i.e. Mum and Marjory limbering up on the stair rail in headbands and legwarmers, James issuing military instructions regarding 'jazz hands', and Dad and Clive doing something messy in the bathroom with Brylcream and a tube of Maybelline Dream Matte foundation. Even the dog will be glad when this is all over. It is confused by all the strange goings on. It actually tried to attack Dad and Clive in potential burglar madness when they emerged from 'make-up' with excess of grease, overly brown faces, and madly applied eyeliner. Offered to hose them down but James says under the harsh glare of stage lights they will actually look normal. He is wrong. He might as well put Grandpa Clegg and his Hammerite up there.

Friday 9

There is air of dramatic tension over Shreddies table. Mum and Dad are not speaking. Though have ascertained through series of complicated hand gestures and post-it notes that this is to preserve vocal cords rather than due to any Mike Majors or Margot-related hoo-ha last night. James said in fact dress rehearsal went without a hitch, bar Mrs Wong getting left in green room in overture, though this may have been deliberate. And the general feeling amongst the crew is that this is the show to beat all shows, even the infamous 2002 production of *Oklahoma* which included real life cows and a wind machine. Pointed out that James is not, in fact, crew, but he said Barry from Radio Rentals electrocuted himself yesterday and he is now assistant assistant stage manager. He gets to turn on the house lights. Said, 'Dream big.' But do not think he got the *Juno* reference. His cinematic experiences are limited to *Lord of the Rings* and *Finding Nemo*.

Am not going to show tonight though. First nights are notoriously messy. Will wait until show has bedded in, i.e. tomorrow. Plus then if anything goes wrong, it doesn't matter so much as most of audience will be drunk due to happy hour in the Siam Smile (formerly the Dog and Bucket, owned by Les Brewster and former sex worker wife Ying) every Saturday from five (currently on the waiting list for one of Mum's complaint letters due to it *a*) being pro binge drinking, and *b*) lasting two hours so bad maths and a breach of advertising law).

* *

Saturday 10

9 a.m.

Mum and Dad are not talking again. Though this time think it is Mike Majors-related rather than vocal cords as Mum has also shouted at dog for trying to sit on washing machine (it likes vibrations). Will ask

assistant assistant stage manager in charge of light switch, i.e. James.

10 a.m.

James said there was a minor incident last night when Dad forgot his lines and Mike Majors had to play two parts, which made him look a bit insane. Mike has told Margot he is sick of 'carrying dead weight' and that if Dad does not shape up in the matinee then maybe his understudy should step in for tonight's crucial performance. Asked who understudy is. It is Mrs Wong. James said there is nothing to worry about as Mum is going to devote morning to rigorous testing. Plus it is utterly normal for creative theatricals to 'run hot'. Said it is something to worry about and show had better be good as Scarlet and Sad Ed are coming tonight and do not want them rolling round aisles in hysterics, which is what usually happens. James said, 'Believe, sister, and you will see the magic.' Am not hoping for magic. Just something that will be able to live down at school. Plus there is the after show party to worry about. If it is anything like our one for *Bugsy Malone* it will be fraught with sexual scandal. Though possibly no one will measure their penis with Mr Wilmott's ruler.

5 p.m.

Grandpa Riley and Jesus have just been round on way

back from matinee. Asked if they had enjoyed it. Grandpa said yes especially the bit where the witch got squashed by a house. Although Jesus got scared when the Oompa Loompa people did their menacing dance. Am now more worried than ever.

6.15 p.m.
Am slightly less worried. It turns out that Grandpa went to see 5th Guides (Baptist) production of *Wizard of Oz* by mistake. He just rang to ask if Mum was OK as she was looking a bit peaky, and possibly short, in the perform-ance. Asked him which role he thought Mum was play-ing. He said Dorothy. Said no, that would be Lydia Briggs who is eleven. Would have thought the braces and ginger hair gave it away.

Maybe it will all be OK after all. Maybe I am worrying over nothing and Mum and Dad do have talent. Yes, I should have faith in parents. They always have faith in me. Even when I decided wanted to be Darcy Bussell. Actually that's not true. Mum said was waste of money as had two left feet and grace of elephant. But I know deep down she thinks I will triumph one day.

6.30 p.m.
At least she had better do.

12 midnight
I was right the first time. The operatic dream is over,

drowned in the flood of tears, and crushed by the weight of Sad Ed falling off chair in fit of hysterics.

It is totally not Dad's fault though. Mike Majors started it. He was the one who tripped over Dad's blue suede shoes and ended up crashing Greased Lightning (Rory De'Ath's racing car bed) off the front of the stage, sending two pink ladies flying into orchestra pit and injuring Russell Rayner on Moog in process. But James said the worst of it was backstage during the interval when Mike accused Dad of deliberately wearing overlarge footwear to present a tripping hazard. Dad said he was not wearing overlarge shoes, he just has overlarge feet and that if Mike couldn't control a chipboard Chevvy then he was in no state to be in charge of a fleet of Ford Fiestas. James said he is not entirely sure who said what next, but Dad and Mike ended up on floor in horrifying wrestling display and Russell demanded that the understudies get prepped. Except that Mrs Wong was still unconscious from death plunge into orchestra pit and only other person who knew all Kenickie's lines was James. So second half had so many disturbing implications actually had to lock self in toilet, shut eyes and hum quietly to self until show finished. Suspect Mum wishes she could have done same.

Amateur operatics is clearly lethal for mental and actual health. Suspect it is statistically more dangerous than Formula One. On the plus side, the after-show party has been cancelled so at least only one

marriage hangs in the balance at the moment. Thank God the show is over and things can go back to normal tomorrow.

. . . .

Sunday 11
Whit Sunday
10 a.m.
Hurrah. As predicted was awoken to the nostalgic sound of antibacterial spray being squirted on every available surface. Rizzo has finally left the building. Dad is still not up though. James says he is suffering classic 'after-show comedown'. Asked what symptoms were. He said he is groaning intermittently and bowels are bit dicky. Said it sounds more like classic hangover to me. James said *au contraire*, it is like war vets who still hear the hammering of machine gun fire. Dad's inner brain is probably still resonating to the sound of 'Beauty School Dropout'. Said more like Mum shouting, 'Lift your feet up, Colin.' James then shook head in annoying patronizing manner and said he didn't expect someone like me to understand the delicate mind of a poet. He is a moron. Also evidenced by the announcement that he is giving up on gladiating for good and is going to pursue a career on the stage following last night's public debut. He says he has had a taste of glory and it aroused strange feelings. Oh God. Maybe he has found Sad Ed's mojo.

Anyway, he is wrong about not having delicate mind

199

of poet. I am utterly fragile. Like Sylvia Plath. Or Amy
Winehouse. At least Jack must think so as am off to do
more musing this afternoon. Hurrah.

5 p.m.
Have had excellent afternoon of muse activity, i.e. lying
on Jack's bed with cats on feet listening to Editors CD. He
said he was sorry to have missed the show yesterday. I
said not really unless he enjoyed ogling car crash am
dram. Anyway it is clear he understands that I am the
Riley with creative leanings as then he said I would make
an excellent Rizzo. Which is true. I am utterly tortured
but witty.

5.15 p.m.
Or maybe he means sluttish and cheap.

Dad was up went I got home. So clearly he not as delicate poet as James assumes. Or else he could no longer
bear Mum's moaning. I suggested that maybe it was time
he returned to tried and tested methods of obtaining
extra curricular enjoyment, i.e. golf. But Mum said there
is no way Dad is picking up a four iron again until there
has been regime change in the clubhouse so we are back
to square one. The only Riley to have enjoyed experience
at all is James, who is currently in his bedroom reading
John Barrowman's biography aloud to the dog. He is
determined to be the youngest boy ever to play Hamlet. I
feel sorry for him. It is like ghosthunting, Ninja Turtles,

and gladiating all over again. He is heading for certain disappointment.

Monday 12

Grandpa Clegg has rung to moan. It is not Darkie Day-related. It is Gordon Brown and his decision to withdraw troops from Iraq. Grandpa is not in agreement and wants him to shovel more in instead. Although in bizarre contradiction he said what Britain needs is a good dose of someone like Saddam because at least you know where you are with a dictator. He is mental. Asked him how the gloss paint was. He says he picked most of it during *Heartbeat* but there are persistent patches on his forehead and ears.

Tuesday 13

Granny Clegg has rung to moan. It is not Darkie Day or Gordon Brown. It is Grandpa Clegg. As usual. She says he has signed up to join the Cornish Revolution and is being sworn in at secret ceremony tomorrow. She said she has pointed out to him that Cornwall is economically dependent on the EU and Brussels but he is having none of it and claims the county can just live on ice cream and pasties and does not need anything from a bunch of 'sausage-eating frogs' (assume he thinks Germany and France combined to form gigantic stalking continental force). Said do not think there is anything to fear as it is just horde of straw-chewing pasty-wavers who will cower at the first sign of opposition from Westminster. She said are you sure? Asked her who else is involved. She said Denzil Junior from the Crazy Car Warehouse (Denzil Senior having choked to death on a sherbet lemon, as predicted by hip of doom) and his friend Pig Gibbons (pork farmer, excess facial hair, smells of slurry). Said point proven.

. . . .

Wednesday 14

Yet another phone call from the realms of idiocy, i.e. St Slaughter. This time it is Grandpa Clegg. Apparently he is now a fully fledged member of 'Trelawney's Army'. Was worried initiation might have involved menacing 'hazing' activity like running naked through streets or drinking pint of sheepdip but apparently Pig Gibbons just made him swear on a copy of *Jamaica Inn* that he would die for his county, and never buy Plymouth Gin (from Devon, so enemy liquor). Asked him when he is going on manoeuvres with rest of battalion. He said they are meeting round Denzil's tomorrow to sing mining songs and eat fairings. I said it did not sound very army-like. Grandpa said on the contrary (he does not say *au contraire* due to *a*) not liking French, and *b*) not speaking any language bar English, and not that very well) it is Cornish fodder for the troops and he is also anticipating getting his first

go on a gun. Which does not bode well at all. He is bound
to shoot himself in leg and end up in tabloids looking like
gullible yokel that he is.

. . . .

Thursday 15

Thank God. Trelawney's Army does not actually involve
any real guns. Unless you count Denzil's anti-pigeon
water pistol (£4.99 from Trago Mills). Granny Clegg
rang to revel in Grandpa's disappointment. She said he
was hoping to be hunting tourists on the moors this
afternoon. Instead they just sat around moaning about
up-country ways. I said he usually likes nothing better
than to moan about foreigners (anyone from over
Tamar is foreigner, even Dad). She said it is true, but he
has got Magnum madness now. I said Magnum madness
is not real, is made up by Walls to sell more ice cream.
But she said it is completely real according to Maureen
Penrice, whose son is in army, and is not ice-cream-
related but is obsession with Clint Eastwood-style
weaponry.

Mum is also tetchy. It is not Magnum madness. It is
potential irresponsible sex madness. It is because apparently a new anti-sexually transmitted disease drop-in
clinic is opening at the back of the Costcutter. I said this
was a good thing, given evidence that sex education in
schools is not working (widespread belief that can catch
syphilis from lower school toilet seats, Primark Donna

203

belief that cannot get pregnant if have sex standing up). But Mum says presence of genitally-compromised people will bring down tone of whole area and house prices will plummet and we will be in grip of recession. Said recession complicated economic phenomenon, according to Scarlet, and not usually caused by sex clinics, but Mum not in agreement. Nor is Marjory next door. She is going to stake it out with her digital camera and photograph all the culprits. (She is back to PI duty after her brief stint as fat pink lady. It is a wonder we survived without her spying services.) I said that was invasion of privacy and would not help in battle against underage sex or gonorrhoea. Mum said it is a small price to pay and anyway the threat of Marjory with a camera is enough to put anyone off sex. Which is true.

. . . .

Friday 16
The saggy sofa is awash with anti-sex disease drop-in clinic excitement. It is not at potential to be declared disease-free. It is that there are rumours that they hand out free condoms. The maths geeks are already planning a mass 'drop-in' to secure a supply. They are going to sell them in their own anti-sex disease shop (aka the Upper School toilets) for 50p each. The only person who is not excited is Sad Ed of missing mojo fame. He said it is like waving a packet of Starburst at a diabetic.

. . . .

Saturday 17

Went to see Sad Ed at lunchtime to try to cheer him up about sex clinic menace. But his trolley herding was even more morose than usual. It is because he had a driving lesson last night and Mike Majors is refusing to let him take his test yet. Reuben Tull offered to give him 'something for his nerves'. But according to Mr Wandering Hands, that is not the problem. It is more lack of concentration, inability to find fourth gear, and persistent belief that the kerb is further away than it actually is. He said it is two kicks in two days as being told you are bad at driving is devastating mojo-wise.

The ongoing missing mojo mystery is completely depressing. It is not just Sad Ed who is suffering though, it is Scarlet and me too. This was supposed to be year of seizing day and experimenting love-wise. Instead have just got dumped by future prime minister (Scarlet) and future prison statistic (me). When will we be stirred into love? James says it is all just a matter of oxytocin levels, they have proved it with voles. But voles do not have dress sense or guitar ability to consider. One vole is the same as the next. It is different for living breathing poetic people like me and Scarlet. (Though possibly not for Leanne Jones who is vole-like in her willingness to do it with anyone as long as they have £2.50 and a chart CD. She will be at anti-sex drop-in clinic on weekly basis.)

Sunday 18

And Jack. Have just realized that he has not gone out with anyone since the whole Sophie Microwave Muffins hoo-ha last year. Yet he has excellent dress sense. Plus he can play drums. Will ask him at muse session later what is going on, mojo-wise.

5 p.m.

It is universal affliction! Jack is also mojo-compromised. I asked him why he wasn't going out with anyone and he said none of the girls in his year do it for him. And he isn't going to waste his time with Mrs Wrong. Or try to change them into Mrs Right because that never works. You either love them or you don't, from the very start. Which think was possible dig at Davey MacDonald hoo-ha. But ignored. As, to be fair, he is right. Then he asked if I was doing any more experimenting. Said was concentrating on exams and had no time for affairs of the heart. Or mojo.

Maybe there is something in water after all, as well as fluoride. Though not mind-altering but mojo-altering. Grandpa Riley says in the war the Navy officers put bromide in his tea to keep his mojo down. But it didn't stop him as he only drank liquorice water. He is delusional. He was only seven when World War Two broke out and closest he has been to Navy is pedaloes in Margate.

· ·

Monday 19

The saggy sofa is extra saggy under anti-sex disease clinic disappointment. The maths geeks did their mass drop-in at lunchtime and it turns out there is a monthly ration of ten condoms per person. Fat Kylie said it must be 'run by mingers' if they think ten times a month is normal. So clearly there is nothing in the water. At least not in the Whiteshot Estate supply.

Marjory is also disappointed at her sex surveillance. She said most of the customers seemed to be respectable looking young Asians with clipboards, who were probably doing a survey. Did not tell her it was utterly non-respectable maths geeks on mission to flog cut-price condoms to sex-mad Sixth Formers. I said surely she should be jubilant at clean-living Saffron Walden. But James says *au contraire*, Marjory lives for scandal. It is the price you pay for being a private eye: you spend your life trying to eradicate crime and deviant behaviour, but without it your existence is meaningless. Is like Mum and dirt.

Tuesday 20

Marjory is revived and is mad with sex scandal excitement. Apparently four mystery men went into the anti-sex drop-in clinic today. She has photographic evidence and is going to enhance them digitally on the computer later, with the aid of her helmet-wearing assistant Mum.

They are hoping to have positive identifications for the *Walden Chronicle* by tomorrow's print deadline.

. . . .

Wednesday 21

The sex clinic mystery has been solved, and without the aid of Marjory's photofit software. It was not four mystery lotharios with compromised genitals. It was one sex-crazed Mr Whippy and his 99 cone. Fat Kylie was holding court on the Yazoo cushion this morning with story of how Mr Whippy tried to fool authorities with his armoury of disguises (i.e. four different hats). Asked if it had worked. She said no, she thinks his unmistakable aura of sex gave him away. It is more likely the lingering smell of chemical ice cream. And attempts to actually use 'Mr Whippy' as one of his pseudonyms. Scarlet said she thought Fat Kylie's Catholic beliefs forbade her to use contraception. Kylie said it was a tough decision but Dr Braithwaite (huge hands, lazy eye, bottle of whisky in desk drawer) says he is imposing a three-abortion limit due to NHS underfunding. It is not underfunding. It is overshagging. Have told Marjory. She is not bothering to contact *Walden Chronicle*. The whole town is already aware of his sexploits. There are still grainy CCTV videos doing the rounds of him and Leanne Jones on Barry Island, featuring the unforgettable sight of her buttocks glowing eerily in ice cream van headlights.

. . . .

Thursday 22

Am feeling utterly ravaged by credit crunch. The lack of employment prospects is seriously compromising my potential for day-seizing experimental love (and potential use of anti-sex drop-in clinic), i.e. have no new clothes bar illegal best woman outfit plus hair is in desperate need of cut. Curl volume now reached epic proportions and is complete health hazard, i.e. things get stuck in it, e.g. four locusts, a pencil sharpener, and a Chomp bar (although think some of them possibly inserted by Mark Lambert during assembly). Have begged Mum for funds (i.e. £40) for a restyle at Toni and Guy in Cambridge but she has compromised on £15 for a wet trim at Curl Up 'N' Dye. Said that is not compromise, is punishment, as is where Thin Kylie sweeps up clippings on a Saturday, and she is still minty with me about meddling with Davey so would end up maimed with thinning shears. Or worse. Mum said beggars can't be choosers and said she could always go round edges with the kitchen scissors. Also declined. The last time I let her do this she made me wear salad bowl as guide and ended up looking like lampshade. Though James got worse deal. He opted for a risotto dish and was positively monk-like for several months.

Friday 23

Hurrah, is last day of school. And for once, do not have life-changing exams to revise for. AS levels are not actual exams, according to Dad, but just spurious inventions of government, designed to boost England in OECD rankings. Mum and James, who embrace testing of all kinds, are not in agreement, but they are too busy concentrating on Boffin Boy's upcoming SATs to impose the usual rigid revision timetable. Mum is pinning her appeal hopes on him getting unprecedented 100 per cent and being inundated with requests from head teachers begging her to allow them to accommodate James's freakish brain.

4 p.m.
Am utterly going to revise for exams. Mr Wilmott gave Year Twelve his annual half-term exam rally assembly this morning (i.e. AS levels are not made-up, despite what Mrs Leech says, and should be taken seriously etc.) but, this year, he has added a menacing credit crunch theme, i.e. if you don't pass them, you will be completely at bottom of job queue and could face a lifetime of benefits and misery. He is wrong. Mark Lambert will be at the bottom of the job queue. And Caris Kelp who eats glue. But am worried none the less. Am already struggling to find work, despite having several GCSEs. Though being muse will be excellent on CV. Maybe should let Mrs Noakes in Waitrose know. I could be useful on toiletry aisle as inspiration, look-wise.

Have solved haircut issue though. Mum has found a recession-busting device on the internet that you attach to the Hoover and it gives you an even trim all round. She is mad with excitement as not only is it economical, but it tidies itself up immediately and is therefore her holy grail of gadgets. Said it did not sound too promising, but she says it is infallible, according to Mrs F from Puckeridge. Asked who mysterious Mrs F was. She said is author of glowing online testimonial. I said I hoped Mum's new found internet skills are not compromising her usual rigorous appliance appraisal skills, involving *Which* magazine, and instore testing. But she says it is that or the bowl method. Have agreed to hoover hair. Device is due to arrive tomorrow. So at least will be trimmed in time for portrait sitting. Jack said if hair got any bigger it would compromise Jimi Hendrix poster in background, which is essential part of composition.

. . . .

Saturday 24

10 a.m.
The Hoover device is here! Mum is going to do all of us, including the dog. Have suggested James is guinea pig, as his hair is not essential, muse-wise. He said, *au contraire*, he is minded to grow it and go for a Lee Mead rock opera look. Mum said over her dead body. But she has agreed to let him go after Dad, who is itching to do some putting practice. Mum said she hopes it is just hypothetical and that he is not hoping to put practice into practice. He said, 'Would I lie to you?' Which James then pointed out is,

211

technically, not an answer. But Mum was too busy whirring her Hoover device to get into semantics.

11 a.m.
It works! Dad and James are utterly shorn and do not look either mental or in pain! James said the buzzing was actually quite pleasant and has asked to go again. Mum said no as she needs a tea break before tackling her trick-iest customers, i.e. me and the dog. It is not our fault we are cursed, follicularly.

11.30 a.m.
The dog has been done. It is revelation. Have never seen it look so tidy. Dog is also in shock. It has been staring at self in mirror for several minutes. Is my turn now. Am almost excited. May well take device to school and offer cut price trims on saggy sofa. Will put BTEC hair and beauty, i.e. the Kylies, out of business in a week! Hoover is tidier, quicker, and does not call people 'lezzers'.

12 noon
There has been a Hoover-related hair accident. Am too weak to communicate. Am going to lie down in dark and pray for world to end. Or hair to grow. Very quickly.

1 p.m.
Oh God. World has not ended. And hair is as bad as thought. Have not got even trim. Have weird two

centimetre-short patch on back of head and rest of hair is just as absurdly huge as before. It is because hair got clogged in rotor and had to be cut free. Mum has offered to even it up with scissors but said do not want her lack of styling skills near hairdo ever again. She says it is not her fault if the device cannot cope with my level of matting. I said it *is* her fault as mental hair is totally the Clegg gene, look at Grandpa—if he doesn't keep it under a centimetre long he looks like midget Monty Don.

2 p.m.
James has come in with grave look. He says he has dissected Hoover haircut gadget and has evidence he would like to present to all parties.

2.30 p.m.
Mum is jubilant as hair accident not caused by user error or rogue Clegg gene. It was due to sticky substance concealed in hairdo, which James says can only be attributed to negligence on part of haircutee, i.e. me. Asked for sample of sticky substance to identify provenance.

3 p.m.
Ha! I am jubilant as sticky substance proven to be partially cooked sultana from last night's spotted dick, cooked by none other than Mum. So if her suet were not so claggy, sultana would have been sliced like butter by vicious rotor blades.

213

3.30 p.m.
Have just seen back of head in mirror and am unjubilant.
Oh God, is going to ruin already compromised image at
school. Plus career as muse. Do not know any muses who
have inexplicable baldy bits. Am utterly unfanciable. Jack
will never be inspired by me again.

4 p.m.
Not that Jack fancied me.

. . . .

Sunday 25

Am still depressed hair-wise. Plus have barely slept due to
recurring dream about being swallowed by a Dyson,
driven by dog. Mum says I am overreacting and that
patch is only size of a small potato and can be concealed
by cunning arrangement of ponytail or plaits. Said patch
more size of Granny Smith apple and anyway ponytail
would mean Jack having to redo entire portrait. James
said is not Granny Smith, is Cox's Pippin-sized, but that if
that is all concerned about then am being idiot as patch is
at back of head and assume portrait is frontal. Said had
had enough of fruit hair madness and fact that bald patch
not in picture is not point. I will know it is there and Jack
will know it is there and, therefore, I am unmuseworthy.

5 p.m.
Have had weird muse session. On plus side, Jack not at

all uninspired by hair after all. He said it just added to my unique appeal (aka weirdness). So lay down on bed. But then Jack put on 'Dark Side of the Moon' to aid relaxation, in case was still stressed by hair trauma. Which is ancient concept music favoured by Reuben Tull types, as is like strong drug and sends you to sleep. Although Jack says it is also seminal, guitar-wise. Anyway, it worked, as was so relaxed by plinky plonky sounds actually fell asleep. But when I woke up, Jack wasn't painting any more. He was just sitting watching me. And even though totally had Led Zeppelin T-shirt still on, felt oddly naked. Plus also know am hideous when sleep due to tendency to drool so apologized for spit and potential snoring. But he said was not hideous. Was just peaceful. Then didn't know what to say to that so just said, 'If you're done can I see it?' But he said he is not done. He needs another session next week. So groaned and said fine.

But the thing is I didn't feel groany. I actually felt pleased. Oh God. Think might fancy Jack again. Am so confused by all day seizing and experimenting can't tell any more.

5.15 p.m.
Have just seen hair in mirror. Am utterly unlovable. Day seizing definitely out until hair grows. Which could be months. If not years.

215

Monday 26

Spring Bank Holiday

Thank God is half-term so can hide in bedroom revising instead of being object of hilarity in common room for having 'spazzer head'. No wonder Einstein was so brainy with hairdo like that. He had to just sit inside learning, out of harsh glare of world.

James is also holed up in his bunker, though is through choice, rather than due to image issues. (He is permanently nerdy so bad hair would have no effect.) He has drawn up a strict SATs timetable, with scheduled wee breaks and a health-giving snack every forty minutes for optimum brain performance. Asked what the silver stars represented. He said that is scheduled creative time, during which he and Mad Harry will rehearse. I said rehearse what. He said for Beastly Boys. It is his new boy band. He says he is hoping it will revive the ailing fortunes of the House of Riley, and be a stepping stone to his stage career. Like H out of Steps. I said only fortunes that are ailing are mine. Plus H is pants. But James says according to *Financial Times* the office supply sector is suffering in the current anti-waste paper climate, which means Mr Wainwright will be looking at ways to tighten his belt and offload excess baggage. I said Dad is not excess baggage. But James said a computer, or possibly monkey, could do Dad's job and he will struggle to find a new one with his medieval qualifications and then we will have to sell house, but, due to stagnation in the market in Uttlesford, and sex clinic, we will be forced to downsize to a more C2DE community like Harlow, losing our fourth bedroom and the all-essential stormporch. At that point left as was more depressing than an afternoon listening to Leonard Cohen with Sad Ed.

On plus side have spent four hours rereading Nietzsche. On downside, it is still as confusing as it was six months ago.

. . . .

Tuesday 27

Am doing English revision today. It is far less complicated and does not require struggling internally with issues like whether famine is proof that God does not exist, or whether we should put drugs in the water. Will reread *Pride and Prejudice*.

11 a.m.

Or possibly just watch DVD instead (borrowed from Marjory, with strict instructions to keep out of consumption range of dog) as is utterly same thing plus can ogle Colin Firth in wet shirt.

2 p.m.

Oh God, think maybe Jack is Mr Darcy and we are just going round being sarky to each other, oblivious to our overriding mojo attraction.

3 p.m.
No, Jack not Mr Darcy. He does not ever use word 'ardently'. And cannot imagine Colin Firth ever drumming along to 'Teenage Wasteland'.

4 p.m.
He might be Jude the Obscure though. Which means I am cousin Sue. Oh God. English more confusing than philosophy.

5 p.m.
Have just had thought. Maybe I am not anyone. Maybe I am just me. Maybe I need to stop reading too much into novels and just do what Mrs Buttfield tells me, i.e. memorize Brodie's notes. And if that fails, do what Suzy tells me, i.e. write pertinent quotes on thighs.

6 p.m.
No, that is even more depressing. I have to be someone else. Otherwise English Lit, and life, is pointless.

· ·

Wednesday 28
Is politics revision day. Politics is not fraught with issues of existentialism, or whether or not I am William Pitt or Gladstone. There is no way I am anyone in politics. They are all odd looking and wear criminal outfits.

4 p.m.
Although maybe am suffragette Emmeline Pankhurst. Am totally pro women's rights—look at golf club boycott. Plus she had vast curly hair.

4.15 p.m.
Though probably not with sultana-related bald patch on back of head. Am disguising it with permanent ponytail. No one need know until am fully hirsute again.

. . . .

Thursday 29
Drama day. Cannot revise for drama. Either have talent. Or do not. And I utterly have it, as evidenced by B in my GCSE and standing ovation at end of *Over the Hills* (*Sound of Music*-based school musical involving battle of bands and nuns in lingerie), though that might have been to do with Fat Kylie bursting out of corset. Anyway, am not worried as have definite something. Unlike James. Have just sat through Beastly Boys rehearsal. Is horrifying. Particularly their version of 'I Kissed a Girl'.

Luckily Scarlet interrupted to remind me and Mum that it is golf club boycott day on Saturday. She says half of Walden will be there, as well as potential celebrities to embarrass into action. Asked who. She said the not-so-famous McGann is definitely back from Lenor advert. And there is a chance he might bring the bloke who does the Comfort advert, who also was once on *Strictly Come*

Dancing with Bruce Forsyth, who is celebrity golfing legend! Asked if Suzy would be using her celebrity status (or heaving bosom) to sway them into changing sides but Scarlet says she is apparently otherwise engaged today, probably with a C-list willy. Mum is not joining us either. It is not in any way penis-related. It is because she will be escorting James and Mad Harry to Kart Mania for Maggot Mason's birthday party. I said couldn't Mrs Mad Harry do it. She said Mrs Mad Harry did Keanu's and is still picking gum off the car upholstery so it is only fair. Thank God one of the Riley women has principles and is sticking to them, i.e. me. Treena has no principles. She goes out in leggings.

. . . .

Friday 30

Mum has begged James to give up Beastly Boys. She says she cannot endure any more renditions of 'You Raise Me Up' (featuring Mad Harry lifting James aloft like prize trophy). James has warned her she may regret her lack of faith when we are living on a diet of benefits and transfats on Whiteshot Estate. Mum said there is no way Dad is going to lose his job as he is the only one at Wainwright and Beacham (Hogg has defected to Parker Pens) who knows how coffee machine works. Plus now that he has given up golf, she can reassign his colossal membership fees as emergency credit crunch funds. So in fact we are not on poverty line after all. But we are still not getting any more Duchy Originals Chocolate Butterscotch thingies as they work out at 25p per biscuit whereas digestives are 3p. And rich tea fingers are 1p.

4 p.m.

Oh my God! Dad has not given up golf at all! There are no membership fees to be reassigned because he handed them over to Margot Gyp yesterday, along with his £30 entrance to the Captain's Day cup. Mum is labouring under false illusions. Dad said he only told me because of impending caddy crisis. It is that his usual bag-mule Malcolm has a Star Trek convention in Knutsford so he is caddyless for tomorrow's competition. He has begged me to do it instead. I said, as he knows only too well, I am utter suffragette, i.e. am boycotting golf club due to evil anti-women rules, and will not cross the threshold of the clubhouse, let alone tramp around eighteen holes with a load of ironmongery on my back. Suggested James as alternative. He said he cannot ask James as he cannot be trusted not to tell Mum. So said is true, but my lack of allegiance to Mum is overridden by my political ideals. So Dad said he will pay me £50. Said yes. Scarlet need never know. Will call in sick to boycott and sneak onto fairway via sewage works. Political ideals are all very well if your mum hands out pocket money like sex tips. Mine is repressed in every possible way.

Saturday 31
9 a.m.
Hurrah. The plan is simple. As all brilliant infallible plans are. Mum and James are already safely on their way to endure several hours of madness and e-numbers at Kart Mania. Dad is already warming up on the practice tee. And I will be joining him via the ditch next to the sewage works (aka poo factory) shortly. Then, as soon Dad has sunk his last ball, or whatever it is, will ditch Pings, and hat, and join Scarlet at front for shouty picketing. So in fact am killing two birds with one stone—principles and pocket! Have told Scarlet that am having hair shame crisis and may be late due to having to fashion intricate plait work. She says she understands, and it is a woman's right to feel confident in herself as much as it is to wear hideous golfing trousers and hit balls pointlessly round hillocks. Which is good point. We are possibly fighting for cause we don't actually like. As golf is utterly mental. But all sports are equal in eyes of suffragettes.

9.05 a.m.
Except water polo. Which should not be played under any circumstances.

9.10 a.m.
Or snooker. Which is not even a sport. It is just spotty men in nylon waistcoats playing giant bagatelle. Anyway, point is, plan is excellent. Nothing can go wrong.

4 p.m.

Except had not factored in the following crucial circumstances:

1. Keanu would try to off-road his go-kart.
2. Manager of Kart Mania would suspend all preliminary heats whilst Keanu is recaptured (halfway along B1053, where he had stopped at garage for Wall's Feast).
3. Party would be banned from Kart Mania for life, forfeiting the Grand Prix, and buffet luncheon (sausage rolls and Capri-Sun).
4. James would persuade Mum to go to boycott after all (in theory, so she can take political stand, in reality in case midget impresario Louis Walsh shows up to play round with old friend Bruce Forsyth and he can give impromptu performance of 'I Kissed a Girl' and be signed to Sony for a three-album deal).
5. Boycott would get bored with standing around in car park, getting toes run over by Mercedes X-classes, and decide to storm fairways and throw themselves in front of golf buggies, suffragette- (and Mrs Thomas) style.

Was awful. Tried to do Keanu-style getaway by hijacking golf buggy, but was impeded by Sad Ed (on his lunch hour) sprawled in front of me. He claims I tried to kill him. I said he should be grateful as he could be first ever golf-related suicide but he says if he is going to die in car

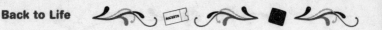

crash, it had better be à la Marc Bolan, i.e. crashing into a tree in a psychedelic Mini, not squished by a mini milk-float. Plus I had got tyre marks on Waitrose property and might be liable for a fine.

Luckily Scarlet was too horrified at cunning twist in events to shout about my betrayal. It is that Suzy was at golf course after all. But not at boycott. She was in a four-ball with Bob and the Braithwaites from Number 11! Worse, she was wearing unfathomable pink triangle jumper and plus fours. Scarlet went mental and demanded the number for Childline and immediate fostering but Suzy threw herself on ground (now littered with bodies, like some WWI killing field) and begged for mercy. She said she and Bob had only done it for the sake of the family. It turns out Suzy's hot flushes are not valium-related, they are early menopause and she can't have any more babies, so they are going on the adoption register instead and were trying to make themselves look like good parent material. Then Scarlet was racked with remorse, and injustice at world, and said that Suzy and Bob were best Mum and Dad and they do not need golf, because all their special skills mean they are bound to be given babies (am not sure am in agreement with this as do not think ability to perform abortions and knowing location of G spot is necessarily good parenting but did not say anything as did not want to draw attention to self now that Scarlet happier with Suzy). So Suzy flung off her jumper and said she was going back to the right, or left, side of the picket line. As did Bob, and several other golfers including the man from the Comfort advert. Though this was possibly due to fact that Suzy now wearing only plus fours and balconette bra. At which point Margot Gyp went purple and had to be carried to leather banquette in clubhouse for emergency Dubonnet.

Anyway, then everyone decided to give up the peaceful-ish protest and go back to Bob and Suzy's for hummus and olives as golf is ridiculous sport after all and unworthy of attention. They are going to focus on the darts club, which has a topless calendar behind the bar. I would have gone but Scarlet said I needed time to reflect on my Thatcherite self-interest before I am allowed to take a seat at the hummus table again.

Mum did not go either. It is because she has decided to make dramatic Suzy-style U-turn. Though, thank God, this did not involve removing any clothing. It is that she is going to join the golf club. She says on reflection, the clothing rules are sensible and, quite frankly, she does not want to play at the same time as the men because they are loud, smell of too much cologne, and never replace their divots. Dad has begged for alternative punishment but her mind is made up. She is going to be fitted for brogues tomorrow.

So now am back at home listening to Beastly Boys sing 'Holding out for a Hero' for the seventeenth time, have had £50 confiscated by Mum as a lesson in something or other (possibly deception, or bad driving), plus have

lingering odour of faeces on shoes due to slight slip along sewage short cut. So all in all, not brilliant day. The only plus point is that Jack was not there to witness it or he would be sacking me as muse for sure. According to Scarlet he was too busy fiddling with his etchings. Think this is literal not metaphor. Although, in that house, anything is possible.

GOLF
CLUB

Sunday 1

Today is my last muse session with Jack, potential rock genius, anti-war foreign secretary, and future Damian Hirst. And am feeling slightly odd, i.e. stomach is bit jumpy again. Think it is because it is utterly the end of an era as exams start tomorrow and then Jack will be leaving in few months for university. It will be weird not having him around. Had not really thought it before as am used to him always lurking in background. But will miss him. And possibly not just as friend. Will put to back of mind though. Must think of art above self and ensure final session is peaceful celebration of painting, which is more important than mojo issues.

5 p.m.

My career as muse is over. Am utterly sad. Plus last session not peaceful celebration of painting. Was fraught with tension. Mostly mine. Think I covered it up OK though. Although Jack not too happy with me lying on hands as made me look a bit like mental patient or corpse. But was essential emergency method to prevent me flinging self at Jack across his gouache board as mojo definitely stirred! Is typical. Mojo is completely out of step with current affairs as is too late now. At least will not have to see him until the end of exams party now so will not be tempted to embarrass self on saggy sofa.

Also am annoyed as Jack will not let me see portrait. He said he needs to do a few finishing touches in private and then I can see it in the end of term exhibition after it has been marked. But think he is lying. More probably, painting is hideous and he is scared I will shout at him and possibly sabotage A level.

. . . .

Monday 2

Scarlet is also depressed. It is nothing to do with her misdirected mojo. It is related to issues of democracy. It is because her political ambition has been thwarted twice in the space of two days. Not only is her anti-golf campaign utterly over. (She says it is a voluntary decision not to waste her lobbying energy on pointless ball games. Though is possibly more to do with restriction order banning her or any member of Stone family from within 200 metre radius of clubhouse or fairways.) But now, Mr Wilmott has decided to ban head boy and head girl elections. Instead they will be appointed by powers that be, rather than wasting weeks, and valuable stationery, whipping up the Upper School into election frenzy. Scarlet says he is being utterly fascistic. But he said he is being sensible because the common room is already factionized anyway, and he does not want full-scale conflict breaking out. (Personally I thought the saggy sofa peace accord was holding quite well despite breach last week when Fat Kylie sat on Um Bongo cushion. Is not her fault buttocks spread over two territories though. Actually it is her fault. Due to excess chip consumption. But was not deliberate anti-Jerusalem act.) Plus he says he is tired of candidates offering budget-breaking sweeteners to win votes. He is still trying to fund Oona's free tampons and membership of Greenpeace. Scarlet demanded to know which powers that be, aka evil dictators, were going to make the appointments and on what criteria. He said him and Mrs Leech and they will pick someone with broadly popular appeal, who can unite the A levellers and BTECers. Or at least not drive either side mental. Scarlet said it is utterly against the underdog and we will end up with plastic prom queens instead of dynamic political personalities. Though personally think it is not bad idea as at least it rules out single-issue candidates like maths geeks who wanted calculator ban and compulsory lunchtime chess. Or Scarlet, who was going to enforce toilet paper ration and maximum one flush a day. Is not fair on Big Jim who has been known to block toilet with outgoings.

Tuesday 3

Is historic day, on several counts. Partly because Barack Obama is official democratic candidate for American election. Saggy sofa is mad with multicultural-embracing excitement. I bet Gordon Brown wishes he wasn't so pasty-faced now. Complexion, and greasiness of hair, are not aiding him in his time of trouble.

Also, more importantly, was last ever philosophy

lesson today. Was actually sad as has been enlightening year, in sense that now know that anything goes, philosophy-wise. For example, today discussed whether forgeries were art or mere craft. Thought was obvious, i.e. Tracey Emin = good, Woolworth's poster = bad. BUT it turns out that is possible that a brilliant fake might be just as good as the real thing. After all, who is to judge which has greater artistic value—Boyzone or Westlife. So maybe my Davey MacDonald experiment was not so mad and my fake Hilary would have been as good as the real thing. Except that am clearly not very good forger as end result still resembled joyriding chav. Though was possibly subject matter and should have picked someone who could name three members of cabinet. Or at least knew where Houses of Parliament were.

Maybe I will find another Jack though. Maybe somewhere out there in my future there is another long-haired, drum-playing, political-minded artist, who will make me feel all breathless when he kisses me. Is heartening to know that all is not lost.

. . . .

Wednesday 4

Scarlet is not in agreement about the clever fake thing. She says, however good a copy is, it will never be worth as much as the real thing, look at Pepsi Max and Diet Coke. She is just annoyed because Trevor is still canoodling with Tamsin Bacon, who has modelled her entire life and wardrobe on Scarlet. She says she is the original and best. But think she is overestimating Trevor's discerning taste. He would be happy with anyone with black nail varnish and a plastic bat.

She is revived head girl-wise though. She says she is going to prove herself a friend of all parties, i.e. A levellers and BTECers, so that she will shine out as ideal candidate. Although initial attempts to infiltrate the Yazoo cushion were less than promising, i.e. Thin Kylie who told her to get her 'lezzer arse' off their side before they 'caught gayness'.

. . . .

Thursday 5

Exam season has begun. Though not mine, thank God. Is James. He is positively mental with SATs anticipation. He is flying in the face of advice from headmaster Nige though, who told Year Six that SATs were not a test of intelligence but of being able to parrot statistics, so not to get worked up at all. Instead he is obeying advice of Mum, who says if he does not excel then he will be joining generations of Rileys in the ranks of the average. I hope she is not including me in that equation. Though possibly is. She still hasn't forgiven me for the nine out of ten I got in spelling in Year Four when I put a silent p in triceratops. Let alone my several Bs at GCSE.

4 p.m.

James is home and is jubilant. He says it was all complete breeze and is confidently expecting offers to roll in from Eton and Rugby within weeks of results being published. He is pest. Now will have to do extra well in AS levels or will be outshone yet again by hobbit-worshipping moron.

. . . .

Friday 6

Granny Clegg has rung. She and Grandpa are at opposite ends of the nylon-carpeted front room again. It is because Grandpa wants to rename their house Pasty Manor in honour of his newfound Cornish Revolution allegiance. Granny says if it is going to get a new name at all it should be Herbert House, in honour of Mr Benson who is sole Labour councillor in Redruth environs. In fairness, either is better than its actual name Belleview, which is misleading as there is no view other than Hester's battery chicken shed/holiday cottage and windswept rec, both of which are less than belle. Mum said not to worry as Grandpa is armchair fascist, i.e. will not actually do anything, just likes ranting about it from comfort of broken Parker Knoll.

. . . .

Saturday 7

Granny Clegg has rung again. She is mad with anti-Grandpa fervour. It is because, in her absence (she was at Trago Mills with Hilary buying cut-price tinned

234

tomatoes), he left the broken Parker Knoll, and he, Denzil, and Pig Gibbons have redecorated the front of the house. Not only has a 'Pasty Manor' sign been nailed to door, but they have painted a Cornish flag on the cladding with what was left of the Hammerite. Asked how Grandpa was looking these days. She says he still has generally dirty look about him, and for some reason his ears are particularly stubborn. Said ears are mirrors of his soul. Granny said she thought that was eyes. I hope not. His eyes have look of murderer. Anyway, Granny says it is war now. And if he is going use underhand and non-democratic tactics, then so is she. Grandpa says as man of house he was merely taking executive decision. But do not think men who wear string vests as outerwear and have Hammerited ears count as executives.

Sunday 8

Mum is playing her first round of golf today, after two o'clock, and in approved skirt, gloves, and appalling pastel jumper. Dad says she is mad to be investing in kit before she has even tried the game as she will probably give it up when she realizes she is not going to be Seve Ballesteros, like most amateurs. Mum said *au contraire*, *a*) the jumper is from 1986, *b*) she borrowed gloves from Marjory (though they are not strictly for golf, they are for Jenga), and *c*) she is only playing to improve her fitness and co-ordination skills, and does not have any pretensions to professionalism. This is a lie. Mum does not do anything half-heartedly. Even her washing up is competition standard. Plus she has enlisted James as caddy. Dad says he asked first but James says he will do both, for double pay and injury money. Said that was unfair seeing as Mum and Dad are sharing clubs but James says caddying is one per cent lugging bag and ninety-nine per cent brain power, i.e. being highly tuned to your player and knowing instinctively which club they will need so will be doubly taxing. He is wrong. It is just bag carrying. And possibly argument defusing.

On plus side it means have house to self for afternoon to practise philosophizing for tomorrow's AS exam. Need peace and quiet to ponder questions of existence, and possibility of laser-eyed dogs. Hurrah. Am actually looking forward to revising!

3 p.m.
Revising not as productive as anticipated. Mostly due to presence of non laser-eyed but definitely peace-shattering dog, which decided to take advantage of lack of visible authority and chew a hole in James's beanbag chair. (Formerly quarantined in attic due to potential fire hazard issues, now out of quarantine having being sprayed with flame retardant. Though possibly life-threatening due to hideous chemical content.) Have hoovered up most of beans but bag looking bit deflated so have inserted some of James's old toys inside to bulk it up and

sellotaped hole. He will never notice. Cannot remember last time he played with naked Will Young.

4 p.m.
Mum is back from the fairway and is jubilant. She got two birdies and an eagle. Said did not think point was to brain wildlife but James said is golf jargon and means she is utterly a natural. Dad not so jubilant. He says not only are his peaceful Sundays in the company of men over, but he is also losing authority in the only area in which he could confidently claim to be better than Mum. He says it is all affront to masculinity. I predict mojo issues. Though am hoping Mum and Dad do not actually have sex so will not be in any way marriage threatening. Cannot cope with Cleggs and Rileys on verge of marital breakdown. Is like week's worth of Jeremy Kyle.

5 p.m.
James has sustained a beanbag-related injury. He threw himself backwards on it and got stabbed in the right buttock by Will Young's microphone. He has filed official complaint with Mum about beanbag sabotage. So have filed one back about misuse of furnishings, i.e. that according to her rules, they are to be sat upon only, and under no circumstances to be used as crash mats or climbing frames. We have both been sent to rooms with punishment tea of cheese and crackers. It is utterly unfair. He should know better than to engage in gymnastic leaps

inside the house. Plus how am I supposed to excel philosophically when have only had Ryvita and Pilgrim's Choice for sustenance.

5.10 p.m.
Though possibly should not have put Will Young inside bag. Is lucky did not also insert Dalek though. The potential of injury by sink plunger attachment is horrifying.

. . . .

Monday 9
8 a.m.
Am feeling utterly clever and philosophical. In fact, think undernourishment may be useful as am quite floaty-headed and possibly experiencing higher levels of perception. Will skip Cheerios to be sure though, i.e. feed them to dog. Mum will never know.

3 p.m.
Lack of food not quite as genius-inducing as thought. Had dizzy spell in exam hall (aka Mrs Brain's custard and cabbage-scented canteen) and had to go to Mrs Leech for medical attention, i.e. five French fancies and a party ring. Then had complete sugar rush and finished exam in thirty-five minutes instead of allotted two hours. Though is possibly fine and just means have excellent grasp of consequentialism.

3.30 p.m.

Although probably should not have just answered 'yes' to 'Is there always a right answer?' Also, Mum now worried have anorexia due to exam stress. It is because dog coughed up Cheerios on nest of tables during *The Archers*. I said was just first-day nerves and will be consuming hearty breakfast from now on. She says I had better do or she will be booking me in for a session with school psychiatrist (aka Mental Morris) faster than I can purge a digestive.

Tuesday 10

8 a.m.

Have eaten health-giving breakfast of Bran Flakes, two pieces of granary toast and Marmite, and banana. So will definitely not faint in politics exam. Though may possibly need to go to loo several times due to extreme fibre content. Is lucky Scarlet not in charge of toilet paper yet.

3 p.m.

Hurrah. Exams are over for this week. And totally excelled self today with brilliant treatise on how rapid reaction force is totally not same as standing army. Think would be excellent politician in fact. Or better, could be celebrity lobbyist like Bono. Scarlet says it is not merely question of being good on paper and that politicians need the three Cs: 'charisma, charm, and connectability'. But that is rubbish. Gordon Brown has none of the above, and Alistair Darling just has mad eyebrows.

• •

Wednesday 11

James has come home from school with exciting St Regina's related news. It is the annual Year Six leavers' trip. Headmaster Nige has instigated a change to itinerary, i.e. instead of the usual four days ingesting fried food and then throwing it up on rollercoaster at Butlin's, they will yomp around Epping Forest going 'back to nature'. James is mental with anticipation. It is because he thinks it will be utterly like *I'm a Celebrity* . . . and he will be devouring spiders and wrestling crocodiles to win his dinner. Mum is not so overjoyed. She has reminded him of his phobia of pooing on anything but fully-cleansed and flushing porcelain and says £145 is a lot of money if he is just going to whinge to be picked up after six hours because he needs a number two. But James claims his Ninja brain training and gladiatorial strength has cured him of poo issues and he will embrace portaloos and even holes in the ground and it is complete man-making style challenge. Mum says she will think about it. Frankly think £145 is cheap to have James off your hands for six hours, let alone four days.

• •

Thursday 12

There has been more marriage-wrecking madness in St Slaughter. Granny Clegg has had her revenge for the Hammerite Cornish revolution flag. She has 'mutilated Bruce' (according to Grandpa Clegg). Thought this might be some strange celtic ritual like cock-fighting but it turns out she just got him done. Grandpa says she used under-hand tactics and 'her and that commie, Chalky' dog-napped him. But Granny says, *a*) he is not a commie, *b*) his name is Hilary, and *c*) it is not her fault that Grandpa was down the Farmers Arms with Denzil and Pig Gibbons eating pickled eggs and plotting to take over the world at the time. Grandpa says Hilary has brainwashed her and that a few months ago she couldn't even bear to cut Bruce's toenails in case he yelped and now she is happy to lop off his crown jewels. He has begged Mum to stage an intervention and release her from the cult. Mum says the Labour Party is not a cult and that preventing Bruce perpetuating his idiotic line any further is an act of community-minded charity. And also to stop eating pick-led eggs or he will get trapped wind and have to have it manually released like in 1984. All of which are true. But am concerned that Mum is not taking the Cleggs' dishar-mony seriously enough. I fear Granny has climbed ladder of education and is fast moving out of realms of Grandpa's world of idiocy. She has not bought Fray Bentos for over a fortnight.

Friday 13

8.30 a.m.

Bruce has gone missing. Apparently Granny let him out for a wee during the *Today* programme and he has not been seen since. Grandpa Clegg says he has gone to search for his missing testicles. But Granny Clegg claims mysterious Friday 13th forces may have spirited him away. Which is promising, marriage-wise, as she clearly still has one foot firmly in the realms of mentalism, even if she does listen to John Humphrys.

4 p.m.

Told Sad Ed about Bruce. He says he sympathizes. He has lost its mojo and is clearly wandering through his lonely existence in search of meaning. I said I do not think Bruce thinks that deeply about anything and probably just went after one of Hester's chickens or got shut in the launderette again. But it is sad none the less.

5 p.m.

Bruce is back. He was not chasing poultry. Or getting trapped in industrial washing machine. He was on the 8.35 bus to Bodmin. Granny Clegg demanded to know why Mr Rabbet (bus driver, ferrety face, known as Bugs) had let him on without a ticket, but he said animals ride free on Badgerline. Plus he fancied the company. (Do not blame him. Usual customers make Pig and Denzil look attractive.) Apparently he got off at Somerfield, walked

242

towards the prison, and was in the queue for the 3.05 return. Maybe the removal of his mojo has allowed rest of brain to expand and he is now genius dog!

Saturday 14

Bruce has shut himself in washing machine again. So is not genius. Is just weird. But on plus side, Granny and Grandpa have overcome their political differences and are reunited in relief at return of moronic dog. Mum said let that be end to it all. I hope she is right.

I wish our dog would take to getting the bus for a day out though. All its antics are not at all conducive to revision. This morning it has:

- got its head stuck in a chair,
- eaten four ludo counters and a VAT receipt,
- boil washed Mum's criminal golf jumper.

Latter was possibly act of genius though. It has worked out how to switch on washing machine so it can enjoy endless vibration. Said this to Mum but she says until it can work out the right temperature setting for wool acrylic mix it is banned from operating heavy machinery.

Sunday 15

Father's Day

Oh my God. Have just witnessed horrifying scene. It was

James, attempting to demonstrate he is camp-ready by pooing in the back garden. Ploy has not worked. Mum has reached never-before-seen levels of anger and has banned several things including the partial removal of pants anywhere except fully-enclosed designated toilet areas. Poo has been buried under weeping pear and she is now decontaminating area with patented mix of Dettol and bicarbonate of soda. James has been sent to his room to reflect on the meaning of the word civilization. He claims Mum is missing the point and it just proves he is a man. I said I had not seen Dad pooing in the vicinity of the patio anytime recently. Or ever. Thank God.

On plus side, al fresco poo has completely overshadowed Father's Day so have totally got away with credit crunch present of bag of Fox's Glacier Mints and postcard of Nick Faldo.

. . . .

Monday 16

The house is still in shock at poo incident. Even dog is giving James wide berth. Though do not know why as its displays on the pooing front are hardly civilized. Have pointed out to Mum that revision is suffering due to trauma and that she may need to be lenient when it comes to results time. She said she is not issuing any poo-related amnesties and that if I fail it will be down to my own lackadaisical attitude rather than

James's bottom. Am back in room with annotated *Macbeth*.

. . . .

Tuesday 17

James is jubilant. It is because Mum has agreed to his school trip after all. I said she should not be swayed by his Neanderthal attempts to weaken her resolve with pooing exhibitions. She says it was not the pooing exhibition, it was the letter home that said if he stayed behind he would have to spend four days being supervised by Mrs Bunnet (64, deaf, moves at pace of compromised tortoise). Mum said last year she forgot entire class on school outing to police station and went home to watch *Diagnosis Murder* and eat flapjack. (Though on plus side, Keanu now knows what it is like to spend several hours in cell.) Mum said is also last hurrah for him and Mad Harry as the appeal is due in two weeks and then they will be separated for ever. Pointed out that they will still live less than half a mile apart and can see each other at weekends. But Mum said he will be moving in higher circles once he is installed at St Gregory's Girls, and Mad Harry will get left behind with the rest of the John Major intake, with any luck. I fear she may have overestimated the appeals process and underestimated the staying power of Beastly Boys.

. . . .

Wednesday 18

Yet again I am reminded why drama was wise choice over economics. While I will be spending morning discussing excellent and non-taxing issues like Mrs Macbeth and her mentalism, Scarlet will be struggling with utterly taxing problem of tax. Ha.

4 p.m.

Although have had interesting thought which is that, while I may be having more fun, exam-wise, all the economics geeks are having fun money-wise, i.e. the credit crunch does not seem to be affecting their ability to purchase Warhammer crap. Scarlet says it is down to money management skills. Think it also possibly down to their illegal betting ring. They have made £73.50 so far this term on *a*) how old is Mrs Brain (54, not 103, as guessed by Kyle O'Grady), *b*) how many sheep pellets can human consume before being sick (276, as tested by Mark Lambert), and *c*) who will get the mouldy apple in nut dispensing machine? (Was Mr Knox in end. Was act of mercy though to put apple out of misery. It had started dripping on the dried apricots.)

Thursday 19

Hurrah, exams are over. Though am not at all sure excelled self in English. Was not due to inferior brain power. Was distracting activity in exam hall, i.e. presence of Kylies, Fat and Thin, tutting and sighing and consuming Haribo Tangfastics. Do not think am at all in agreement with written tests for BTEC hair and beauty. It is not at all accurate measure of their wet cut skills. Plus they cannot sit still for more than twenty minutes at time. Thank God the bricklayers just get corralled into their cage and timed on their concreting. Mark Lambert is still claiming he is going to transfer to BTEC nursery nursing as soon as Mr Wilmott's teen pregnancy haven, i.e. crèche i.e. former pig pen, is open. I said he could be waiting a long time. But apparently Mr Wilmott has had genius idea to extend skills and beat credit crunch by getting BTEC bricklaying to design and construct it. Mark is fully expecting it to be ready in six weeks. He is mental. Even if it does stay up for more than five minutes, will take years to remove odour of Gloucester Old Spot.

Friday 20

Today was officially the end of school for Upper Sixth and has been marked by annual ceremonious emptying of sacred talismans (i.e. crap) from lockers to make way for next year's wave of saggy sofa wannabes. There was much weeping over Blu-Tacked Green Day posters and gel pens. And this is just tip of iceberg of nostalgia fest because they will all be back for prom in three weeks. Plus there is the last day of school silly string, false fire

247

alarms, and sheep in places that sheep are not meant to be ritual to endure. Even I was caught up in wave of emotion sweeping over saggy sofa when Duncan Evans put vintage Busted on CD player. Scarlet says I am clinging to rose-tinted view of past like mad World War Two vets who wish Blitz was still on, and it is in fact not sad at all, but day to be embracing future, i.e. chance to lord it over likes of Tamsin Bacon once Scarlet is appointed head girl. I said it was not at all in the bag that she is going to get the job but she says it is a no-brainer. The only other potential prize-winner is Emily Reeve, who has a one year old and cracked nipples holding her back.

Scarlet agrees that head boy is impossible to call though. The maths geeks have no people skills, Reuben Tull is walking advert for rehab, and Sad Ed has no mojo, flabby upper arms, and potential to kill self halfway through term. I said Jack is hard act to follow as is charming, charismatic, and connectable, e.g. brokered Middle East saggy sofa peace deal, proving credentials as future anti-war foreign secretary. Plus he has good arms and mojo. Scarlet said, 'Are you feeling all right, Riley?' Came to senses and said was just caught up in another wave of emotion due to school caretaker Lou polyfilla-ing up hole where Trevor hit head in attempt to avoid getting anti-vampire staked by Mark Lambert last Hallowe'en. Do not want Scarlet thinking want to seize her brother. But it is true about Jack setting high standard. I saw him on the way out, carrying his locker spoils to the non-sick-smelling car of the people. Is historic day, politics-wise. Like when excellently-coiffed Tony Blair left office to make way for Vosene-compromised Gordon Brown.

. . . .

Saturday 21

3 p.m.

There is no way either Sad Ed or Reuben Tull are going to be head boy. Went to see them at lunchtime and they were trying to outwit Pay and Display machine. But, on plus side, have been invited to post-exams party tonight at acropolis (i.e. giant fake Parthenon in country park, and general haunt of tedious stoners). Reuben says everyone is going to be there. I said who is everyone. He said him, Max Calloway in Year Eleven who once saw Jesus's head in his microwave (beardy religious one, not toddler uncle, and under influence of prescription painkillers, not general mentalness like Granny Clegg), and possibly Dean 'the dwarf' Denley, if his hay fever has calmed down and he hasn't passed out on Piriton. Am going. There is nothing else to do except watch James and Mad Harry doing synchronized dancing to Sugababes or listen to Mum and Dad argue about water hazards. Will ask Scarlet to come. And maybe Jack. He does not smoke but is pro-legalization of cannabis (mainly to avoid Suzy or Bob getting criminal record).

12 midnight

Have just got back from party. Was excellent. Max, Sad Ed, Jack, and Scarlet came (pollen count too high for dwarf to vacate concrete-based areas) and Reuben made us all lie on our backs and look at the stars through the roof of the acropolis and think about space and universe and life on other planets. It was best philosophy lesson ever. Am thinking of writing to Mr Knox to demand he adds a practical element to AS level. Although possibly will require protective clothing as bat pooed on Max Calloway's forehead at one point. He said was gift from gods. It was not. Anyway, then Reuben felt inspired to commune with beasts of nature and went to pester cows with Max, Scarlet, and Sad Ed, so was just there next to Jack. And stopped thinking about space and started thinking about life on earth instead and how much weirder it is. And then it just came out. I said, 'I'll miss you, when you go.' But luckily think Jack still mesmerized by space thoughts because he just said, 'What?' So asked if he had decided between Cambridge or Hull yet. He said, 'Depends.' I said, 'On what, your grades?' He said, 'No. On how far away I need to be.' But before could ask what he meant, the cows stampeded (obviously they not in agreement with Reuben about being mystical minotaurs willing to convey him to ABC Barbeque for cheesy chips) so we had to run before they fatally trampled us, which, as James frequently points out, is cause of 0.05 per cent of deaths in UK every year.

Anyway. Is bit depressing as is utterly clear Jack is moving on and wants to leave Saffron Walden as soon as possible. We are not at all on same wavelength any more. I have missed my seizing chance. Sad Ed also very quiet on way home. Maybe he is having internal wranglings over his missing mojo. Or most likely he drank too much of Reuben's 'magic' cider and was having paranoid thoughts about the cows again.

. . . .

Sunday 22

10 a.m.

Oh my God. Sad Ed has just rung with astonishing news. It is his mojo. It has finally returned. He is coming over after *Hollyoaks* omnibus to reveal details. Oooh. Maybe mojo was stirred by Reuben or Max Calloway and he is homosexualist after all! That would explain everything—the lack of interest in Melody, the love of Morrissey, the encyclopaedic knowledge of *Gossip Girl*. Hurrah! Have finally got gay best friend. Was worried would have to procure one at university and that supply might not meet demand as everyone will want one by then.

2 p.m.

News is even more shocking than anticipated. On

downside have not acquired gay best friend. BUT it turns out that Sad Ed's mojo was stirred by none other than other best friend Scarlet! Apparently she was so overcome by fear at Reuben astride marauding cow that she threw herself into his flabby upper arms for comfort. I asked if there was snogging. He said no, but the contact caused massive pant area upheaval. Asked how she did not notice, or is mojo in fact very small. He said is not in fact very small, but that he pretended needed a wee and then hid behind bush and thought about Aled Jones very hard. He has demanded advice. I said I was in no position to give out advice as my mojo has also been stirred by a member of Stone family, i.e. Jack. Sad Ed said that was hardly news. I said was utterly news as had confessed it to no one except him. He said it is blindingly obvious to everyone except, apparently, me. And possibly Jack. And, thank God, Scarlet, who is too busy being stirred by weedy bat boy to see what is going on under nose.

So Sad Ed happy at return of mojo but more depressed than ever as cannot use it. He says it is like being given a limited edition twelve inch of 'Sheila take a Bow' and being told cannot play it under any circumstances. Oh God, our mojos are stirred by people who are wrong wrong wrong. We are doomed to life in a Brontë novel.

3 p.m.
Or are we? Maybe we are just fighting the truth. Maybe

252

our mojos are more attuned than our brains and we are actually right for each other. Will ask Sad Ed tomorrow. Will not disturb him again now as he says he needs to test mojo out to full extent of capabilities and have worrying suspicion what that might involve.

Monday 23

Have talked to Sad Ed about theory and suggested it might be good idea to seize day after all. Sad Ed says he not really seizing type but said he does not actually need to be dynamic, he just needs to be honest. Have suggested that he corners Scarlet in conducive atmosphere of free love and abandonment, i.e. Glastonbury! He pointed out that he did not get tickets after all as he was too depressed by fake wedding and thought presence of Cohen (Leonard, not Seth) might send him over edge. Said thought that was what he wanted. He said if he going to die in untimely fashion, he is not doing it in field of 100,000 sweaty campers waving glowsticks and drinking Fosters. It is undignified. Plus police would probably miss point and declare it accidental death by misadvanture instead of tragic cry-for-help suicide. Said 'whatever' and there are still tickets left due to crapness of *a*) weather, and *b*) line up, so to pull himself together. He is going to ask Scarlet tomorrow. On the condition that I am also honest with Jack about my stirrings. Have agreed. Have nothing to lose.

5 p.m.
Except possibly pride, reputation, and happiness.

. . . .

Tuesday 24
Scarlet has refused to go to Glastonbury. She says any time off school at this point could seriously compromise her battle to be head girl. I said *au contraire*, her absence would only remind us all what we were missing, and common room will descend into anarchy, and then, when she returns, she can restore harmony and win hearts and minds of Mrs Leech and Mr Wilmott. She says she will think about it.

5 p.m.
Scarlet has thought about it and is still refusing to go to Glastonbury. She says she is suspicious as to *a*) Sad Ed's unprecedented proactiveness, and *b*) my motives and that maybe Sad Ed is my henchman and is whisking her away because I am hoping to be crowned head girl and will actually undermine her and spread vicious rumours about her political capabilities. Said I would rather chew tinfoil than try to keep the Um Bongo and Yazoo cushions free from cross-contamination, and that Sad Ed is just keen to mingle with other depressive music obsessives at the John Peel stage. She is thinking about it again.

Did not tell her about Sad Ed's mojo. She needs to realize how much she loves being with him first. Shock of revelation now could actually kill her.

. . . .

Wednesday 25

Hurrah. Scarlet has agreed to go to Glastonbury with Sad Ed. There are several caveats though:

1. They do not purchase civilian tickets but use Suzy and Bob's VIP ones. That way they can poo in comfort, and in proximity to superior celebrity bottoms.
2. Sad Ed sleeps in separate tent pod, does not consume any bean-based produce, and does not attempt to infiltrate Leonard Cohen's trailer and suggest campfire singalong.
3. I whip up ill feeling in common room and initiate riot in time for Scarlet's triumphant return. Possibly involving injury to Trevor that requires Scarlet's nursing skills.

We have agreed to all of them. Although Sad Ed is hoping Scarlet will not be lovingly tending Trevor's wounded wings, as will be too overwhelmed with love for Sad Ed after weekend. Asked how he was going to persuade Scarlet to seize the day and hop pods. He said he is hoping time spent together will be like epiphany and she will realize she cannot spend another minute apart from him. Did not say anything as did not want to dishearten him so asked how he is going to persuade Mrs Thomas to let him go in first place, as she is still convinced he is going to get engaged every time he leaves house. He says he is going to tell her he is staying at mine. Which, he says, is better than prison in Mrs Thomas's eyes. It is true. Mum's regime makes HMP Pentonville look lax.

Thursday 26

Hurrah. The potentially happy couple have left for Somerset. Bob is dropping them at railway station in sick-smelling Volvo. He and Suzy are not going this year due to potential for eel-helmet man pills to compromise adoption chances. Plus he says he is backed up at maternity clinic due to refusal of Saffron Walden to embrace new drop-in anti-sex condom clinic. He says he cannot understand why. Did not mention persistent presence of Marjory and digital camera outside door.

Signs on Sad Ed and Scarlet front not too promising as yet. Mostly due to Sad Ed's outfit of choice, i.e. enormous David Bowie T-shirt, combats, and waterproof hat. Which I know for fact is not at all mojo arousing for Scarlet. She is much more moved by bat capes and tight vegetarian leather trousers. In fact ideal man is Noel from *Mighty Boosh*, whereas Sad Ed more like fat Nabu or the gorilla. Plus they have already had three arguments over Sad Ed's food supplies, i.e. a twenty-four pack of Nik Naks, which Scarlet says is too bulky and will cause tent-pollution issues. But it is early days. And am confident that heady atmosphere of late nights, starry skies, and groundbreaking music, or if that fails, excess of hot cider, will break down tent pod divide between Sad Ed and Scarlet, and they will be united in pro-mojo love.

11 p.m.
Have just got text from Scarlet. It says TENT FALLEN DOWN. AND SAD ED FORGOTTEN SLEEPING BAG. IS MORON.
Think this is actually good news though. In their attempts to find shelter, they will be forced to share each other's body warmth and will be utterly aroused. Hurrah.

Friday 27
Have tried and failed to whip up anarchy in common room. Everyone is too demob-happy to argue about pot noodle residue in the leaky microwave. Plus half the BTECers are on field trip to Ridgeon's Building Supplies to identify tools. Will try again on Monday when new Lower Sixth invade for induction. That is bound to get backs up. Besides, do not want to peak too early.

3 p.m.
Have had phone call from Sad Ed. Asked how things were going tent-wise. He said not brilliantly and he

spent most of last night huddled under shelter of giant Nik Nak bag. So on plus side, he has been proven right in insisting on bringing crisps. Asked where Scarlet spent night. He said he is not sure but she came back this morning to 'freshen up' and said she might see him at Kings of Leon later. I said she has probably just gone to Green Fields to be at one with Mother Earth. Sad Ed said he not so sure and possibly being at one with dirty looking VIP musician who was lurking outside tent while Scarlet changed her knickers. Asked where he was during pant change. He said inside tent. I said that was excellent news, mojo-wise. But he says it just proves she thinks of him as emasculated, despite his massive mojo, and to her he will always be one of the girls. He is too depressed to watch bands now and is going to sit inside the tent, or failing that, the Nik Nak bag, and read Sartre. He is hopeless.

5 p.m.
Have had phone call from Mrs Sad Ed worried that Sad Ed has left his trusty bedtime companion Frobisher the toy rabbit at home. Said he cannot come to phone as was helping Mum prepare nutritious Welsh cakes (i.e. pro-Aled) and that I have lent him Smithers the monkey to make up for missing Frobisher. Am brilliant liar. Which is why struggle with honesty thing. Is wasting talent.

Saturday 28
11 a.m.

No news from Glastonbury as yet. Which am taking as good sign, i.e. that Scarlet has noticed that Sad Ed has functioning man penis and is overcome with feelings and they are at this very minute sharing smelly sleeping/Nik Nak bag of love.

Wish they were here though. Am utterly bored. James and Mad Harry are practising camping in the garden. Though thankfully, are concentrating on tent construction skills, not pooing ones. Maybe Sad Ed should have had session. They have put tent up five times now and have got it down to three minutes forty-three seconds, with only a partial collapse of front awning. Will go into town for wander. Possibly in vicinity of Waitrose. Just in case Jack is doing the shopping again.

3 p.m.

Did not bump into Jack at Waitrose. He is obviously too busy plotting his great escape to Hull. Or Cambridge. Did, however, bump into Reuben Tull, literally, who was busy trying to herd all trolleys in absence of Sad Ed. Trolleys seemed to be also plotting escape as several broke loose and ploughed into back of Mr Wilmott's Vauxhall. He said they are trickier than cows. Offered to help (and thus prove my ability as potential employee) but he said it is against Health and Safety regulations to allow amateurs behind the wheels. Plus my aura might

'bring them down'. Pointed out that *a*) trolleys not alive or affected by auras, *b*) since when has he been blessed with second sight, and *c*) even if he is, he needs glasses as am completely happy. He said, 'Whatever you're telling yourself, Riley. But I see it differently. You need to follow your dream, Rach. Stop holding yourself back.' Said, 'Whatever,' and went to buy doughnut instead. He is obviously doing way too many illicit things if he thinks that trolleys are alive. Or that I am unhappy.

5 p.m.
Oh. Have had awful thought. Maybe all drugs have opened up new levels of perception and Reuben can see things beyond wit of human understanding. Because am, in fact, unhappy. Am racked with potential loss of Jack. And at my failure to seize day with him. Reuben is right (except about trolleys being alive; that is just mentalism) I must follow my dream. I must tell Jack how I feel. Yes, am inspired. Will do it tomorrow. Once have planned speech. And wardobe.

8 p.m.
And watched *Casualty*.

11 p.m.
Have called Ed to tell him about trolley-related revelation. He said Reuben is always seeing things. Some come true, e.g. Les Dennis will make a comeback; and some do

not, e.g. monkeys will rise up and conquer world with superior opposable thumbs and prehensile tails. But that he hopes mine is fulfilled. Asked if he had been fulfilled yet. He said not unless you count eating all twenty-four packets of Nik Naks and sleeping through Neil Diamond. Scarlet is still MIA. Though on plus side eel-helmet man arrested last night, so wherever she is, she is not in herbal-pill-induced coma.

• •

Sunday 29

1 p.m.

Is D-Day Jack-wise. Have spent hour doing 'barely there' make-up, as recommended by Grandpa Riley from this month's *New Woman*. Though is utterly tricky and would be lot quicker to do 'definitely there' claggy mascara and lipgloss. But Grandpa says men go for natural look and my hard work now will pay dividends later. He is utterly pro Jack thing. It is because he had unrequited love for relative of best friend for years and regrets never acting on impulse. Asked who it was. He said it was Bert Holmes's gran. He is weird. Anyway, am taking plunge now. Just hope he is in. And that Bob and Suzy are not. Do not want their gigantic mojos overshadowing me and Jack.

Feel sick. Is because in just few hours could be in arms of true love. Or possibly blackberry pie that ate for lunch.

5 p.m.

Am not in arms of anyone. Am hopeless seizing day chicken. This is what said (ish):

JACK: What are you doing here? Scarlet's at Glasters.

ME: Er. I know. I just . . . er . . . wondered if you'd heard from her. If she'd . . . um . . . said anything about . . . er. . . her and . . . er . . . Sad Ed.

JACK: No. Why? What's going on?

ME: Um. Nothing.

JACK: Riley, you are crap liar. You are totally red in face. Oh no. That is just blusher.

ME: Is not blusher as am wearing imperceptible make-up. Is actual blush. Sad Ed has found mojo. Mojo is in love with Scarlet.

JACK: Shit.

ME: Yes.

JACK: Shit.

ME: Yes.

JACK: ——

ME: Do not say 'shit' or we stuck on endless loop.

JACK: OK.

ME: Why shit? Do you think he's wrong for her?

JACK: Er. No. Not necessarily. And, anyway, does it matter?

ME: So you don't think it matters if someone is wrong for you?

JACK: No. Not if you love them.

262

ME: Really?

JACK: No . . . Are we still talking about Sad Ed here. Or is this about someone else, Rach?

ME: No. Er. Still Sad Ed.

JACK: You really need to do something about your blushing.

ME: Am not blushing. Is blusher. Was misadvised make-up-wise . . .

JACK: So, Riley, any more Frankensteins on the horizon? Exams are over. You can experiment again.

ME: Frankenstein was creator, not monster. As well you should know. And, like, bog off. I've given that up. That's not what I really want.

JACK: So what do you really want, Rach?

ME: . . .

And I could have said it then. It was begging to be said. Like it was hovering in the air above us in neon letters shouting, 'YOU, JACK, I WANT YOU!' But I didn't say it. Because what if I don't have second sight like Reuben? What if I'm just seeing living trolleys all the time and not any truth? Or what if the truth hurts?

So I just said 'I can't tell you.' Which I know is a cop out. But at least was honest. And he just said, 'Right.' And then I said, 'Got to go.' And he said, 'You know where I am.' And I said, 'Do I?' Because thought he was speaking metaphorically. But turns out not as he said,

263

'Er . . . am here, Riley.' Said 'Oh.' And left. Actually. Not metaphorically.

Got home to find Mum celebrating golfing victory. She beat Dad by record twelve shots. So at least one Riley female is fulfilling her dreams.

. . . .

Monday 30
9 a.m.
Yet another day of living utter lie, i.e. that am in love with Jack Stone but am too chicken to admit it. Being honest is not at all as easy as it sounds. It is utterly fraught with rejection potential. At least he is not in school this week so can sit mournfully on saggy sofa without arousing suspicion. Will claim am just traumatized by death of CD player (irreparable after someone tried to 'play' a strawberry Pop Tart).

4 p.m.
Oh God. Have just remembered was supposed to initiate riot at school. But the thing is, even with new intake trying to stake claim on Um Bongo cushion, the common room is place of relative peace. Fat Kylie is doing good business giving minigoths purple highlights and lack of CD player means there is no argument over Take That versus T-Rex. Actually think Scarlet could be root cause of all discord. It does not matter though. She will not care. She will be happy with her higher prize, i.e. true love

with Sad Ed. Though have heard nothing for two days now. But think is good sign. They were probably too busy consummating relationship under canopy of canvas. Or stars, if tent has fallen down again.

6 p.m.
They were not consummating relationship under anything. In fact were not even under same canopy at all. Sad Ed says he has not seen Scarlet since Saturday morning, when she made brief appearance to commandeer her smelly sleeping bag. Asked how Sad Ed had managed to keep warm. He said he had sheltered under cocoon of Nik Nak wrappers and polystyrene noodle dishes. Said he was pathetic and had utterly missed once-in-lifetime chance to reveal true feelings. He said, 'What, so you told Jack, then?' Said no. Was not right moment. Sad Ed said am more pathetic as at least Jack in same room. Asked where Scarlet was now. Sad Ed says he does not know. She is probably on a tour bus somewhere having sex with an Arctic Monkey. He is even more depressed than ever.

8 p.m.
Scarlet is not on a tour bus having sex with an Arctic Monkey. She is at home in vile mood. It turns out that she spent entire weekend trying to find Sad Ed but that tent had weirdly disappeared so she assumed he had gone home. (Asked Sad Ed about this and he said is true, he

was sick of tent pegs falling out every time drunken liggers and C-listers tripped over them, so he just tied the tent on to a Winnebago instead. Asked whose. He said some ginger girl with weird accent. Said Kate Nash? He said possibly. Asked Scarlet about Arctic Monkey man. She said it turns out he is not an Arctic Monkey at all. He is not even in band. He is charlatan, i.e. substandard roadie (and not even for Verve but for Neil Diamond) who tried to lure her into sexually compromising position in portaloo with pair of maracas. She said she ended up sleeping on floor of caravan in Lost Vagueness with transsexual called Kitty Sometimes and her only comforting thought was that I was busy at home paving the way for her head girl glory. I said 'Yes.' Do not want to pee on her already soggy bonfire by telling her that Middle East has lasting and secure peace and that Fat Kylie might turn out to be Madeleine Albright after all.

Tuesday 1

Common room is back to full-scale war. And is all Scarlet's fault. She has been refusing to talk to Sad Ed all day and instead has been hurling macadamias at him across nylon carpet. Mark Lambert got caught in crossfire and then full-scale nut riot ensued. On plus side ceasefire is forgotten so Scarlet is none the wiser about my failure to initiate conflict. Plus Sad Ed says the angrier she is, the more he loves her. So he is in unrequited love heaven. Nut fights are not the same without Jack though. His precision with yoghurt-coated cranberries is unsurpassed.

At least James has been despatched on his camping trip so house will be place of quiet contemplation etc. for four days. Mum has issued him with list of no less than twenty-four instructions including:

1. Do not drink from anything other than tamper-proof bottles of Evian.
2. Do not eat wild fungi, suspicious berries, or pork that has not been heated to 77°C for at least ten minutes.
3. Do not attempt to become forest dwelling hermit or Hobbit of any variety.

James is not best pleased. He says there are times when real men have to rip up the rule book and use their wits and whatever is lying about to survive. Mum says if he even thinks of trying to rip up the rule book or build huts using bits of twig and bin liners she will be up the B172 in the Fiesta faster than he can say Bear Grylls. She has instructed him to phone home every evening and has lent him Dad's mobile for this purpose. James says Scott of the Antarctic did not have a mobile phone so it is not a proper man-challenge. Mum says Scott died and if he doesn't ring she will be up the B172 in the Fiesta etc., etc. I pointed out that Mum was taking a risk and that James could use the phone to call premium rate quiz lines, far-flung relatives, or sex workers. Mum said James is not like me, and knows the value of money. This is true. He makes Scrooge look generous. Plus relatives limited to Cornwall, which, contrary to popular belief, is in same country.

. . . .

Wednesday 2

4 p.m.

Went round Sad Ed's after school. We are both still in unrequited love misery. I said it was more depressing than missing mojo misery. But Sad Ed said nothing is worse than unresponsive pants. In fact he seems quite revived. He says it is because unrequited love is like air or water to a true poet and he is utterly inspired, music-wise. He has already written a song. It is called 'Ballad of the Scarlet Woman' and involves not a lot of rhyming and way too many adjectives. Plus tune is totally lifted from Nick Cave. But said was excellent as did not want to ruin his rare moment of happiness. Maybe he is right though and unrequited love good for literary types. Look at Britney. Her best work was when she was pining over Justin. Sad Ed's ballad just rubbish because he is compromised talent-wise. Will write poem immediately, inspired by Jack situation.

6 p.m.

Is harder than thought. Have got possible title, i.e. 'Stone in Love With You', which is totally appropriate. Even if is stolen from Stylistics. But trouble is every time I try to think of Jack for inspiration just get too depressed at potential loss to write. Plus disturbed by phone call from James to report back from Camp Moron. Asked him how things were going, whittling-wise. He said whittling is for amateurs and so far they have risked their lives crossing a ravine on nothing but nylon rope and adrenalin. Asked how deep was ravine. He said several feet. Said hardly life threatening. He said *au contraire*, Maggot fell off and got bitten by a rattlesnake and might be dead within hours. Said rattlesnakes do not live in Epping Forest. He said might have been slow-worm. Said slow-worms do not bite. He said might have actually just licked him then. Or looked at him funny. But was still terrifying and manly. Then Mum commandeered phone to check he is eating properly. He said he has had apple a day, as dictated by Rule 5, and had a poo, inside latrine tent (Rule 17). Mum said what about Mad Harry's Wagon Wheels. James said he had resisted temptation. He is lying. There is no way

anyone can resist the clever mallow-biscuit combination. Even though guaranteed to feel sick immediately afterwards. Then he said he had to go as they were about to build a giant campfire and sing songs around it. Mum said to wear protective clothing and stay outside a one-metre radius of flames. James said they are not actually going to set fire to campfire as is environmentally unfriendly plus against Health and Safety. Mum put phone down satisfied. Think she is warming to Nige's accident-aware attitude.

8 p.m.
Still struggling with Jack poem. Have got opening line. Which is most important, as any novelist or tragic poet will tell you. Is:
I'm stone in love with you
Which is admittedly just repeat of title. But reinforces message, I think.

10 p.m.
Have given up on Jack poem. Clearly am so in love have been rendered speechless.

10.15 p.m.
Or am just rubbish poet.

10.30 p.m.
No, that is not it. Still have prize (macramé owl) won in Year Two for poem about Terry Wogan featuring brilliant

line where managed to rhyme toupe with hooray). Am excellent poet. Just that brain too compromised by confusing feelings.

. . . .

Thursday 3

9 a.m.
Sad Ed has begged me to test Scarlet waters, i.e. see if he stands chance with her. Have agreed. Though think answer at moment will be no as she has not uttered more than 'knob off' to him all week.

3 p.m.
Asked Scarlet if she was thinking of forgiving Sad Ed at any point. She said she has more important things on her mind than the idiocy of the bingo-winged one, i.e. her maiden speech as head girl. Said still got week to go before announcement. Plus Sad Ed has worked hard to eliminate the sag on upper arms. She said is hard to tell under cavernous T-shirt.

So this has good and bad elements, i.e. she is not at all annoyed about his tent-moving antics any more. But physically, he is possibly repulsive. Will only tell him first bit. And lend him Mum's fitball for extra arm exercise.

6 p.m.
James has phoned in his final camp report. Today Archie Knox (son of hairy librarian and philosophy teacher, also

273

hairy) got bitten by a beaver, or possibly a guinea pig, and he and Mumtaz swam across shark-infested pond to win bet. Said *a*) what did he win, *b*) Mum forbade any 'wild swimming' in Rule 22, and *c*) did not think he and Mumtaz were friends any more. He said, *a*) £1.30 and a packet of fruit pastilles, *b*) she specifically stated 'rivers or lakes', and *c*) he is hoping they will be more than that after tonight's farewell disco. God, even James is luckier in love than me. And he wears an anorak and can sing the books of the Bible off by heart. There is no justice in world.

. . . .

Friday 4

Sad Ed has a black eye. Asked if he had riled Scarlet again and got brained with a rogue brazil, but he says it is fitball injury. He was trying to do press-ups, and ball burst and he hit head on coffee table. He said I should send ball back as is possibly faulty. Have checked small print. It has weight limit. Think Sad Ed's hefty girth may have voided guarantee.

Also James is back from camp. But something is afoot. He is not at all jubilant at having fulfilled man challenge. Mum tried to despatch him into immediate bath, as smell quite overpowering, but he said he cannot even muster the energy to wash and anyway what is the point. Mum said, 'To avoid chafing, and fungal infection, as well you know.'

But James said, 'Not of soap. Of life.' He has shut himself in bedroom with dog and can clearly hear sound of Elvish being spoken (by James, dog still unable to communicate in any form).

6 p.m.
James has refused to come down for his chicken goujons. He says what is point of food. Mum was about to go into growth/energy answer but I said he is probably just tired from all healthy fresh air and will take him nutritious bed-based supper, e.g. Marmite on toast. Mum has agreed. But says he had better be up and fully washed for Shreddies in the morning as she is not having any malingering under her roof. It was bad enough when Grandpa Riley was here. I said would pass on message. And will do. Once have gleaned information from him about cause of malingering using my brilliant sympathetic 'I totally feel your pain' interview technique, as practised by Phil Schofield. I predict it is Mumtaz-related.

8 p.m.
James has confessed all. Would make excellent tabloid journalist. (Although he did not fall for 'feel your pain' line and had to offer him Graham Norton's autograph (as faked by Mark Lambert) instead.) As predicted it was Mumtaz-related. But is on gigantic Jeremy Kyle scale of rejection, i.e. not only did Mumtaz turn down his advances, but she has spurned him for another, i.e. Mad

Harry. James said it was utter tragedy. Especially when he had to watch them slow dance to 'In the Gloaming' in front of the latrine tent (he was peeping through flap at time, trying to fulfil Mum's strict poo instructions). I said it is hard when love is over before it even began. James says it is not just love. It is career. Said what career. He said Beastly Boys. He said he cannot possibly be expected to go on world tours with his love rival.

He is right. It is tragic. In an eleven-year-old deluded pop star kind of way, i.e not at all. Whereas me and Jack is on *Tess of D'Urbervilles* scale.

. . . .

Saturday 5

The pop world has been shattered by devastating news. Beastly Boys have definitely split up. Plus James also has black eye. But is not fitball-related. He went round Mad Harry's this morning to give him one last chance, and said he had to choose between Mumtaz and stardom. Harry chose Mumtaz. James says he is throwing away his dreams for a cheap kiss. Harry said Mumtaz is his dream, and she is not cheap, she does not even eat own brand baked beans. And then he hit James with a stormtrooper. James said black eye is a badge of his commitment to higher art and he wears it with pride. Mum said it is a sign of being common and has sent him to his room with a tube of concealer.

On plus side, bumped into interesting person in town,

i.e former meat mincer, future rock star, and ex-boyfriend Justin Statham. Was in Waitrose car park with Reuben and Sad Ed when saw his unmistakable blond hair wafting in sunlight. Was like halo of an angel. Possibly. Anyway, he came over and said the Braintree lot (i.e. rock foundation, art foundation, and other made-up courses) are having a farewell party up at the acropolis next Friday and we are totally invited. Said will be at prom but might come over after. He said, 'Nice one, Ray.' Which he has never called me before, despite me spending several months trying to instigate it! Then he ambled off like Archangel Gabriel in Nirvana T-shirt towards the tinned fish aisle.

But not everyone so happy at encounter. Reuben said, 'I don't like his vibes, man.' I said, 'You think trolleys are sentient beings, so what would you know.' Sad Ed said, 'Don't even think about it, Rach.' I said I am not. My interest in Justin is utterly non-mojo-related and attendance at party would be purely platonic nostalgia sort of thing. And it would. I am so over Justin. My heart is Jack's.

9 p.m.
Although Jack possibly doesn't want it. And Justin does owe me a snog.

Sunday 6
No, am definitely not going to snog Justin. Jack called today to check I am going to prom. Though was not

actually asking me to be date to prom. Which think he should have made clearer at start, i.e. I said, 'I would love to go.' He said, 'Er . . . I'm in the band so I'm going to be sound checking. I can't pick you up or anything. Sorry. I was just wondering if you were going already.' Said I had considered it (was backtracking and playing hard to get, which is hard to do at same time). He said, 'Good. I've got something I want to show you.'

Hurrah. It is my portrait.

7 p.m.
At least think it is. Could feasibly be mojo.

7.30 p.m.
No, Jack is not like that. Is either portrait, or he has finally conquered the Jon Bonham twenty-minute drum solo thing.

7.45 p.m.
Though is shame about mojo.

. . . .

Monday 7
9 a.m.
There has been another body blow to James. He has lost his appeal for a place at St Gregory's Girls. The letter arrived this morning. James says is final nail in coffin of his hopeless life and begged Mum to let him stay off school as he cannot bear to see Harry basking in

happiness when he is so unbasky. Mum told him to belt up and take the dog for a wee. Said she was being oddly calm in face of rejection. She says school is making mistake, as his SATs results will show. Then they will come crawling back to her begging to send James to their hallowed halls. Said hope this is case. Although halls at St Gregory's Girls not that hallowed. They let Thin Kylie in for a month until she refused to wear regulation pants, sexually provoked the caretaker, and threatened Sister Ignatia with a gel pen.

5 p.m.
Like lightning, or rather, unlike lightning, tragedy has struck Riley household twice in one day. Although is actually Cleggs that has hit so technically is only once. But repercussions have made way to 24 Summerdale Road, so think it counts. Anyway, point is, the Belleview/Pasty Manor Bruce amnesty is over. Granny has finally thrown Grandpa out for his persistent racist/sexist/idiotic tendencies. Dad said he was amazed it had taken this long, but Mum commandeered phone and demanded to know what was straw that broke camel's back. Apparently it is Trelawney's Army, aka Grandpa, Denzil, and Pig Gibbons. They have been arrested for trying to overturn seat of power, i.e. Julia Goldsworthy MP (Lib Dem, Falmouth and Camborne). Mum asked if they have been charged but Granny said no because their weapons were water pistol and cake spatula. Police have

suggested psychiatric care instead. Mum said that is good suggestion and he should remain at home during assessment. But Granny says she cannot harbour a criminal any longer and he is staying at Denzil's. Mum said, 'Until he comes to his senses?' Dad said he wouldn't hold his breath on that one. But apparently that is not it anyway. Granny said her mind is made up and she is determined to stick to her guns (or spatulas), even if it means being a single mum struggling on benefits. Mum pointed out that her children were middle-aged and financially independent. But Granny said Auntie Joyless borrowed a fiver off her last week for a box of fish fingers and a loaf of Nimble and anyway it is symbolic. Mum said she is not worried. Granny will get bored, or will need someone to prise the lid off the Fray Bentos, and Grandpa will be back on the broken Parker Knoll by the end of the week.

. . . .

Tuesday 8

Grandpa Clegg has rung. He is not full of remorse, as predicted by Mum. Instead, was to moan about conditions at Denzil's. He is sleeping on a chair in the kitchen, and ate jar of beetroot for dinner last night. Mum told him to swallow pride (instead of pickles) and say sorry to Granny and then he can move back. But Grandpa says the only way he is moving back to Pasty Manor is if Granny moves out. That will never happen. Granny is like Hammerite. Immovable.

. . . .

Wednesday 9

There has been movement in St Slaughter situation. It is Grandpa. He says he cannot be expected to cope with conditions at Denzil's any more (the floor is so sticky he actually got stranded last night and had to be heaved to safety by Pig). Instead he is back on the broken Parker Knoll with the *Daily Mail* and a cup of Ovaltine. BUT it is not with permission of Granny, is in breach of her demands and she is going mental with rage. Grandpa says he is man of Pasty Manor and, if Granny does not like it, then she can leave. But Granny says she is steadfast in her determination to remain at Herbert House and has God and Hilary on her side. James suggested that offspring should decide who can stay, like in custody battle. And in absence of resident minors, it should be Bruce. Mum said there is no way she is leaving fate of her parents to that moron. He has gone missing five times since his testicles were removed plus he drinks Harpic. She says instead, Granny and Grandpa are going to have to find a way to live with each other's foibles. Like she and Dad have. Dad said that was unfair as he has never brandished a kitchen implement at an MP, or Hammerited his face. But Mum raised the ugly spectre of the morris dancing hoo-ha so Dad went off to strim the lawn before his ego could be battered any further.

Thank God it is head girl announcement tomorrow to take mind off idiotic family. Also because Scarlet is becoming unbearable in her zeal to follow in Jack's

footsteps and lead the masses. Or the common room at least. So far this week she has initiated a hockey field sheep-poo pick, a common room carpet shampoo (carpet now frightening royal blue colour, causing eye damage threat to stoners, who need to wear sunglasses at all times) and a wipe down of leaky microwave. Plus she has tried to woo Mrs Leech's vote by giving her some Nigella recipe Florentines. This could backfire though. Not because Mrs Leech is not open to bribery (she is) but she has simpler biscuit tastes, i.e. Malted Milks and Jammie Dodgers. She thinks Florentines are too bitty. On plus side, campaign has brought Sad Ed and Scarlet closer. He has undergone an utter transformation and is her willing slave in all matters. It is amazing. Normally he barely heaves his mass off Um Bongo cushion unless it is to use toilet facility (and even then he has been known to withhold wee for up to an hour to avoid effort). But now his mojo is revived he cannot jump to her assistance fast enough. And as bonus is losing weight! Arms of T-shirts are no longer threat to circulation.

* * *

Thursday 10

A political travesty has occurred. Scarlet has not been appointed head girl. Unbelievably, it is Thin Kylie! Mr Wilmott said he has decided to go for Northern Ireland style power sharing, i.e. one BTECer and one A leveller.

Kylie must be Martin McGuinness, i.e. possibly evil, definitely controversial, but weirdly respected amongst her peers (i.e the Criminals and Retards). BUT, in another shock move, Ian Paisley is Sad Ed (i.e. grumpy and fat). Mr Wilmott says he has shown a new side recently, i.e. involving himself in all recent common room changes. Yes, plus he is always giving Mrs Leech his gypsy creams. Scarlet is outraged. She says he only got the job thanks to her efforts. But that she has been passed over for the less controversial candidate, and it is like Tony and Gordon at Granita all over again. But, in cunning diplomatic manoeuvre, I said in fact was excellent, as Sad Ed is clue-less and will rely on her for all guidance. So she can still do what she wants, and take glory when things are good and blame it on stooge when goes badly. She will be pup-petmaster, pulling strings, and he will be mere mari-onette. She is now excited by idea and is going to use him to introduce her controversial compulsory vegetarian footwear next term.

Sad Ed was not too happy about it either as he does not embrace responsibility of any kind. But said, *a*) he gets to spend more time with Scarlet, and *b*) there are bis-cuit privileges, i.e. he gets key to Mrs Leech's store cup-board, home of the Jaffa Cake. Hurrah. Am like Alastair Campbell, greasing the wheels of power, or whatever it was that he did.

Walked home with Martin McGuinness, aka Thin Kylie, in spirit of cross-party co-operation. Asked what

her first act as head girl would be. She said she is going to do Mark Lambert in the language lab tomorrow night. Said that was more information than was looking for.

. . . .

Friday 11

5 p.m.

Hurrah. Is prom in less than two hours. And official anointment of Thin Kylie and Sad Ed as lords of the saggy sofa, i.e. head boy and girl. Plus is Jack Stone Five farewell gig. And official unveiling of portrait of me, Rachel Riley, muse and general artistic type person. Am wearing best woman dress. Was going to wear Jack's Led Zeppelin T-shirt and cat-hair-covered socks, so that am instantly recognizable as subject of painting, but dog has chewed several sections of T-shirt so it just reads 'Le Z', which think will overexcite BTECers. Think aura of muse will shine through anyway.

Also, have made momentous decision. Am going to tell Jack tonight that am actually, in fact, in love with him. Prom is utterly a seizing day sort of moment. Just need to find courage this time. Will maybe have little drink of Mum's cooking sherry. James says is not proper alcohol drink for men. Is for ladies. Like Listerine Softmint. Plus has been open for month so probably lost most of potency.

284

6 p.m.
Sherry definitely lost potency. Have drunk half of bottle and do not feel any different.

Oooh. Is door. Will be Sad Ed and Scarlet in limousine, i.e. sick-smelling Volvo. Hurrah. Tonight am just run-of-mill Essex sixth former, with a poor record on snogging. But tomorrow will wake up as famous muse, in arms of renegade artist, drum genius, and lover, Jack.

* *

Saturday 12

9 a.m.
Feel sick. And am not sure where am. Will shut eyes and try again in hour.

10 a.m.
Oh God still do not know where am. Perhaps am in bedroom of Jack. Except walls not black. Are magnolia. Will shut eyes again and try to remember.

10.30 a.m.
Is definitely not Jack's room. Oh God. Maybe is Justin's room.

10.45 a.m.
Oh. Is my room. Was just upside down. James has just come in with patented hangover cure breakfast of Marmitey eggs on toast. Said in fact do not have hangover. As

285

was not drunk. James said if was not drunk, then why did wake him up at two in morning singing 'Back for Good'. Do not remember that. But think maybe was little bit drunk. Asked where Mum was. James said she is at driving range, practising her chip shot, but that I can expect full punishment on her return later.

11.30 a.m.
Oh God. Have remembered stuff. Is not good. Is not at all as planned. Is coming back in flashes, e.g:

- Tripping over Dean Denley during coronation and impaling head on Thin Kylie's tiara;
- Reuben Tull giving me 'something for headache';
- me going to look at Jack portrait and it not being beautiful Pre-Raphaelite thing but hideous wonky woman;
- me telling Reuben Tull he prescient genius and was going to seize day and follow dream;
- me staggering to acropolis and seizing day by flinging self on Justin;
- me and Justin going back to his house and taking some, possibly all, clothes off;
- Justin saying, hang on minute, Riley, am having whitey, think need to be sick;
- me coming home and finishing off Jack poem.

Oooh. Maybe have written work of genius in state of trauma. Where is poem? Oh, is here under pants. Says:

Ten Things I Hate About You. Oooh. Is like in film. Am Julia Stiles repressed but weirdly attractive type.

1. You are shite at drums even dwarf thinks so;
2. Justin has much better nipples;
3. You are complete knob;
4. Can't think of any more but is enough anyway.

Oh. Maybe not like in film. Is not very good really at all. Am not weirdly attractive. Just weird.

Oh God. Is all mess.

1. Jack does not love me but sees me as ugly witch woman and only good for painting in freak show kind of way;
2. Have only narrowly avoided having sex with Mr Small Nipples because he so repulsed by naked self that he actually sick;
3. I have subconscious nipple issues;
4. Am completely pants at poetry of any kind.

Only plus side is that at least did not humiliate self and tell Jack I love him.

12 noon
Oh God. Have just remembered something else. Need to check phone.

12.15 p.m.
Oh, is bad. Think may have told Jack love him after all.

According to phone, drunk dialled him at 10 p.m., i.e. on way to acropolis. Do not remember talking to him though. Maybe he not there so hung up.

12.30 p.m.
No. Do remember shouting into phone. Must have left message. Is not good at all. Oh. Is doorbell. Is probably Sad Ed. Thank God. Need friendly face in time of trauma.

12.35 p.m.
Oh God. Is not Sad Ed. Is Jack! James has conveyed message that he is on John Lewis sofa and is demanding talks. Have told James to tell him am dead. Or at least have leprosy.

12.40 p.m.
James says Jack says it is important and he needs to see me. Plus has large parcel. Asked what shape parcel. He said rectangular, inch thick. Possibly jigsaw of historic building, or large board game like Pictionary or Buckeroo. Have said to bring parcel up. But leave Jack downstairs if at all possible.

12.45 p.m.
Parcel is not jigsaw of Buckingham Palace. Or Buckeroo. It is portrait. Of me. But is not same one as last night, i.e. this one is not wonky. Is pretty. Beautiful even. Think

may need to talk to Jack after all. Oh, can hear steps again. Is James. Will send him down to tell Jack to come back tomorrow when do not look like witch. Or smell of Justin.

3 p.m.
Was not James. Was Jack. And he is still here. And think am possibly going to burst with day seizing and honesty issues. But need to write this down now as is historic. And want to remember for the rest of life!

So Jack came in. He said, 'You look peaky, Riley.' Said, 'Yes, have possibly leprosy.' He said, 'No, you do not.' Said, 'No do not. Is true,' (i.e being honest). He said, 'What do you think then?' I said, 'Of what? Third world debt? The Barnett formula?' i.e. was witty even in face of supreme humiliation. He said, 'No, Rach. The picture.' I said is very nice. Is just shame he did not think to put that one in exhibition last night. He said, 'Are you still drunk?' Said, 'No do not think so.' He said, 'Is same one.' Said, 'Where is giant nose and eyes like Miss Beadle (bulgy, like Joey in *Friends* or rabbit with myxomatosis).' Jack said is possible sight was affected by mushrooms. Said did not have mushrooms for tea. Had ham omelette. He said not Waitrose ones, Reuben Tull ones that I ingested at gig. Said thought was aspirin. In herbally liquid form. Jack said was not. Was mild hallucinogen. Said, 'Shit.' He said, 'Yes.' Said am not getting in that endless cycle again. He said, 'Good.' Said, 'So am not hideous ugly freak then.'

He said, 'No. Can't believe you would think that's how I saw you.' Said was how saw self sometimes. He said am blind. Or mad. Said very possibly. Then was pause for long time like in films where you can hear clock ticking etc. but could not hear clock, only James singing 'Bleeding Love'. Then Jack said, 'So was it true what you said on phone last night.' I said, 'Maybe.' He said, 'Well either it was or wasn't.' I said, 'I understand semantics of possibility. Just that do not remember what actually said.' He said, 'Was something like, "You are total bastard, Jack Stone, and cannot believe thought liked you in pants-based way. Hope penis falls off. Oh shit, who put drain there?"' Said, 'Yes is true. Look still have bruise.' Jack said, 'Not bloody drain, Rach. The liking bit.'

And could have said no was all drunken/mushroom-based lie. Except that did not want to. Wanted to tell truth. So said, 'Yes, thought—no, think—am in like with you. So is all true. Oh. Except bit about penis falling off. That not nice. And you being bastard. You are not bastard.' He said, 'Really?' Said, 'No. You are like the coolest person I've ever met and you don't even have to try.' He said, 'I try really hard actually.' Then I said, 'So does sun shine out of ass?' And he said, 'Yes sun definitely shines out of ass.' And then was about to do more brilliant and relevant *Juno* quoting but could not. Because mouth was too busy. Being kissed!

And was utterly best mojo-moving kiss of life. Even had twinkly sounds and head spinning. Although that could be after-effects of mushrooms. Anyway, it doesn't matter. Because I love Jack. And think he loves me. And is all because we have seized day and been utterly honest.

Well, mostly. Have not told him about almost doing it with Justin. But only because there is no point. Is so over. Jack is only one I care about.

Plus he will never find out. Is secret that will take to grave.

Or possibly reveal in biopic, with Summer out of *The OC* playing me.

No. As knowing my luck would probably end up with bloaty one out of *EastEnders* anyway. Will keep secret. Jack will never know he was second in snogging queue again. And now am going to do more. Snogging I mean. Before Mum gets back and grounds me for ever.

Is funny how things turn out. Maybe luck is about to change after all. And from now on will have utterly brilliant life. Just like in books.

Is about time, after all.

Joanna Nadin was born in Northampton and moved to Saffron Walden in Essex when she was three. She did well at school (being a terrible swot) and then went to Hull University to study Drama. Three years of pretending to be a toaster and pretending to like Fellini films put her off the theatre for life. She moved to London to study for an MA in Political Communications and after a few years as an autocue girl and a radio newsreader got a job with the Labour Party as a campaigns writer and Special Adviser. She now lives in Bath with her daughter and is a freelance government speech writer and TV scriptwriter. She has written five books for younger readers, several of which have been shortlisted for awards. *Back to Life* is her fifth book for Oxford University Press.

Liked

back to life?

Then visit

www.rachel-riley.com

for more about Rachel and her friends, competitions and games.

Plus check out the author blog, have your say, and join up to our email bulletin for regular updates.

Have you read Rachel's first diary yet?

I need more **tragedy** in my life.

In other words, it is earth-shatteringly **NORMAL**.

It's time for my **so-called life** to be brought up to speed. Starting now.

Rachel's diary continues in . . .

My quest to find **THE ONE** starts right now!

I need to learn to **SNOG** properly – and fast.

Or maybe I should just give up on **boys** altogether . . .

Rachel's back in . . .

Am ready for year of utter **LOVE!**

But what if he wants me to do it?
After all, it is the Meaning of Life.

Thank goodness I have definitely
found **love of my life** and am not
hung up on Jack any more. **Not** at all . . .

Catch up with Rachel in . . .

Am racked by **torture** and **loss!**

Have made plan to deal with **post-break-up trauma.**

It will be utter **Simple Life.**
Am starting now.